FORTY

A STEEL BONES MOTORCYCLE CLUB ROMANCE

CATE C. WELLS

Cover art and design by Clarise Tan of CT Cover Creations.
Edited by Nevada Martinez.
Proofreading by Raw Book Editing at www.rawbookediting.com.

Special thanks to Jean McConnell of The Word Forager, Sarah, and Erin D.

Thanks for reading! Like what you read? Please do me a solid and leave a review.

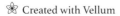 Created with Vellum

1

NEVAEH

I'm going to die from my own stupidity.

Breathless, I slam the bathroom door shut and drop to the cold tile, bracing my bare feet against the vanity and pressing my back to the wood.

"Get out here, you bitch!" Carlo bangs so hard my spine rattles.

"Screw you!" I scream before my brain sputters to life, and I shove my fist in my mouth. What am I doing? Don't bait the man. Sweet Lord, Nevaeh. *Think.*

This isn't a normal fight; this isn't Carlo getting pissed and letting off steam. He popped me in the eye. Yeah, he was talking with his hands, emphasizing how much he thinks I suck, and it was an accident, but he's not sorry. I don't think the blow even registered. He kept on screaming.

There's a hot, wet trickle dripping down my cheek. I swipe my face with the back of my hand and bite back a whimper. Oh, yeah. That stings. Did he split my eyebrow? I half stand to check my face in the mirror before I remember. Rampaging boyfriend. Blockading the door. Royally screwed. I'm back.

And somehow, I've backed myself into a corner. How do I get out of here? There's a small window over the toilet, but my ass wouldn't fit, even if I could even get it that high. I'm too short to reach, and too thick to squeeze through.

And we're on the tenth floor.

Goddamn my glitchy brain.

Bang. Bang. "Get out of my bathroom!"

"*Just back off.* I'll go." Laundry hamper. Bottle of hand soap. Electric razor. There's nothing in here I can use as a weapon. Maybe I could pull the towel rack off the wall?

Carlo's voice booms through the vent, loud as day. "Damn fucking right, you'll go. I'm done with your shit! You can't even do one little thing right, can you? All you had to do was keep your mouth shut and smile. How hard is that? Isn't that literally your job?"

Literally, my job is hostess at L'Alba, the club owned by Carlo's boss. Guess I can kiss that gig goodbye after tonight. If I can talk my way out of this bathroom.

Thud! The door strains, lower than before. He's kicking it now. Good thing it's solid wood. There's only a twist lock, so that's not keeping him out, but if I stay wedged here, and my thigh muscles don't give out, he's not coming in. I'm safe.

I snort a laugh.

Shit, I'm not safe. I haven't been in years. My entire post-pubescent life has been a series of misadventures, dumb luck, narrow escapes, and poor choices—like this asshole.

"What are you doing in there? You touch my shit, so help me, Nevaeh!"

What *am* I doing in here? Ack. *Brain.* Function! How do I get out of this? You catch more flies with honey, right?

"I'm sorry, Carlo. Okay?" I aim for contrite. I nail exasperated.

"For what? Making me look like a bitch in front of my

associates? Or running off at the mouth and making your-self look like a dumb whore? What are you sorry for this time, Nevaeh?"

My fists curl, and I bite the insides of my cheeks. I am *not* going to say that he didn't need any help from me looking like a bitch. And I am *not* going to say his mother's a dumb whore. I've met her a few times.

She's always in the kitchen. She keeps her head down and makes herself busy, but she's a nice lady. She raised an asshole, but I'm dating him, so who's the dumb one?

"Just back away from the door, and I'll leave." I try harder to keep my voice even and apologetic, but I'm a crappy actress. I do sound terrified and pissed, but mostly I still sound like I'm talking down to a piece of shit.

"You telling me what to do? Fuck you!" *Bang. Bang.* "I'm done with you. You're a fuckin' mess. Your place is a mess. Your life is a mess. In eight months, how many times have I fronted you rent money? Five? Six? You're thirty years old!"

Twenty-nine. I'm twenty-nine.

"I paid you back!" I shout through the door.

"You're a leech, Nevaeh. That's what you are. You thinking you're gonna get your hand in Dominic Renelli's pocket now? He don't want my sloppy seconds."

Oh, for heaven's sake. I only reached across the guy for some calamari, and a glob of marinara landed on his crotch. Dominic Renelli's terrifying; I was nervous. I dove into his lap with my napkin and started rubbing before I realized what I was doing. Everyone knows that's my M.O. Renelli made a joke about it, and I played along. It was *nothing*.

But this is what always happens. I think I'm making better choices, and it ends like this. Carlo Fiore was supposed to be the smart bet. Yeah, he's "connected," but he's just a money guy. An accountant. I mean, he went to Penn State. How dangerous can he be?

A drop of blood dribbles into the corner of my eye; the socket throbs. I bend forward, tear off some toilet paper, and dab. I didn't even see Carlo's arm coming. One second, I was spouting off as we walked into the apartment. The next, I'm flying backwards over the arm of the couch. If I didn't have a brother I'd sparred with constantly growing up, I'd have been down for the count. I can take a punch, though.

Bang. "What are you doing in there?"

"Staging a comeback," I mutter under my breath. From the thumps and the swaying of the door, I guess he hears me.

"Always with the mouth!"

"Just let me out of the bathroom. You won't see me anymore. I get it. I screwed up. We're over."

Matter of fact, we were over the minute we left the restaurant. He'd dug his fingers into my upper arm, his other hand clutching the stupid messenger bag he totes everywhere like he's got the nuclear codes. Then he called me a stupid whore, and I was done.

I let him bring me back here because I wanted my stuff. That was another mistake. I'm going to die over a ratty old Steel Bones MC T-shirt and a bottle of expensive shampoo for curly hair.

It's weird how calm and focused I am right now even though my body is going crazy. My heart's racing; blood is whooshing in my ears. I'm fidgety, like always, but I have to keep my legs braced, and there's nothing to fiddle with.

My mind is totally clear, though. It's *wild*. I have ADHD —got a prescription I don't fill and everything—so I'm never this present and in the moment. Except when I smoke up.

Or sometimes during sex. Not with Carlo. Or anyone, really, except Forty Nowicki back in the day.

What am I doing? Focus.

I'd like to say I don't usually find myself in these sorts of predicaments, but it's kind of my thing. I pet the dog that bites. I think I can make it—the yellow light, the staff meeting, the rent—but I fall a skosh short. I go out with a mafioso, and it turns out he makes his points with his hands.

People call me free-spirited. The truth is I'm eternally out of control.

Living in my head feels like running as fast as you can downhill. You know when you hit that point where you can't stop, you can't even turn if you want to without tumbling ass over teakettle? That's my normal.

Before Carlo and the bathroom standoff, there was Nick and the long walk on the shoulder of I-97. Paulie and the night in jail. Aaron and the cat fight video. I could blame the ADHD for the sensation-seeking, the risk-taking. And sure, blame the diagnosis for the string of jobs and the speeding tickets.

But the men? That's me grabbing for a handhold as I fall to my doom. And just like with Carlo, all my relationships blow up in my face. Usually not with a blow *to* the face, but I'm quite familiar with the get-your-shit-and-go. No one wants to be a handhold. And the guys that don't mind... they're not stable either.

I press my ear to the door. Carlo's gotten quiet. Maybe he's cooled off.

"Carlo?"

Nothing. I wait a minute, and then I rise to my feet with caution. I catch a glimpse of myself in the mirror. Damn. I've sweated so much I've got Cher "If I Could Turn Back Time" hair, and there's blood splatter on the drapey neckline of my gold cocktail dress.

"Carlo?" Still no answer. Maybe he left.

Where did I leave my jacket? If I make a run for it, I'll need it. It's forty degrees out. Did I hang it up? I'm sure I didn't. I probably threw it on the recliner. Or on the floor?

"I'm coming out, okay? I'll get my shit and go." I ease away from the door, duck into the shower, and grab my shampoo and conditioner. My crazy, beautiful curls are a legacy from my Jewish grandma on my dad's side. Hair products aren't cheap.

I've got a bottle in each hand when there's a thud, a crack, and then the door flies open so hard it immediately swings shut again. I scream and scream at the top of my lungs, grabbing shit and hurling. Air freshener. A shaving brush.

Carlo muscles in, ducking the projectiles, and grabs me by the arm.

"Shut up!" He drags me into the living room, and I buck and flail, knocking over a lamp. He's heading toward the front door. He's going to throw me out. That's good. That's what I want.

Stop it, Nevaeh. Cooperate. Let him drag you out.

Oh, but I can't. I'm pure adrenaline, one hundred percent reaction. My arms and legs have their own mind, and it's not giving up. I kick and flop and scratch and bite. I'm *not* going down easy. I fall silent, past words, all body, all fight. The sound of grunts and panting and the slap of flesh-on-flesh fill the apartment. We're almost to the door.

Open it. Please. Open it. Throw me out.

Then, inches from the foyer, my stupid, flailing fist connects with Carlo's cheek, and his head jerks back. My brain doesn't even have time to register the hit before I'm dangling in the air, slammed against the wall, Carlo's hand tightening around my neck. I dig my nails into his forearms, and I pull, but I can't breathe, and I've got no leverage. Blood is trickling into my eye, blinding me.

How did this happen?

I want to take it back, take it *all* back. I'll go quietly this time. Keep my mouth shut at dinner. Turn Carlo down when he sidled up to me on a dance floor eight months ago.

"I'm going to put your body in the trunk of your shitty car and drive it into the river," Carlo spits as he leans his weight forward, bearing down on my chest.

Black spots float across my field of vision. I jerk my knee up, but there's no room between us. I scrape my nails down his arm, clawing, but my fingers slip down the fabric of his suit jacket. He tightens his grip.

My lungs burn. I want to go home. Please. I'll fix everything. I'll change. I'll make it right.

I want to go back. I didn't mean for any of this to happen.

There's a loud pounding on the door, mixing with the roar of blood in my ears.

"This is Greg and Don from 10C. We've called the police. Whatever's going on in there needs to stop. The police are going to be here any minute."

Carlo's head jerks as if he's waking up, and he drops me. I collapse to the floor. Tears spring to my eyes, and I gulp down a wheezing breath. My throat burns. Everything's bright and blurry.

"Open up!" a very serious, very official-sounding voice orders.

Oh, thank the Lord. Greg and Don! They invited me over once when we ran into each other at the trash chute and got to chatting. Carlo had been running late. We shared a bottle of Glenfiddich and Greg showed me his memorabilia from when he competed in the Tour de France back in the early nineties.

Greg and Don don't like Carlo, so that was the only time we hung out in person, but we follow each other on social media, and Don and I play *Words with Friends*.

"Nevaeh? Are you okay? What's going on in there?" That's Don. He speaks like a cross between an evening newscaster and a Kennedy. I try to answer, but all that comes out is a croak.

"You goddamn bitch," Carlo hisses, and he runs a hand through his black hair. He's still wearing his gray suit jacket, but the buttons have come undone. There's blood splatter on his white dress shirt.

I used to think he was handsome with his sharp cheek bones and his perfectly even teeth. I can't believe I didn't see it before. His face looks like a skull.

He pinches my chin and squeezes. "When I come back, you're gone. Every trace of you is *gone*. Capisce?"

I try to nod, but he won't loosen his grip.

He spits in my face, hot splatter hitting my cheek, and he digs his nails into my jaw one last time. Then he flings open the front door and strides off. A man shouts, and then Greg and Don are crowding in, two silver foxes fresh from the gym, and they gape at the mess.

"Oh my God!" Greg rushes forward, helping me up, guiding me to the sofa. "Don, we need to really call the cops."

"No." I croak, hardly loud enough to be heard. I hack, clearing my throat, and it hurts so bad. "No cops."

"Of course, we'll call the cops. You're bleeding." Don digs in his pocket for his phone, and panic breaks through my shock. If he makes that call, I'm dead for sure.

"Don, listen," I pant, voice raspy and thin. Don's a

lawyer. He's not a trial lawyer, but he knows this town. He'll understand what I'm about to say. "Carlo and I were at dinner tonight. With Dominic Renelli. *No cops.*"

Don freezes, exhales a low sigh, and after a pause, he nods. Greg looks confused, but he'll follow Don's lead. "Okay. No cops, then. You'd better get out of here."

"Not a problem." I slide on the shoes I'd kicked off by the door and grab the yoga pants and T-shirts I keep in the dresser drawer Carlo finally gave me a month ago. I retrieve my coat, shampoo, and conditioner from the floor. There's no way I'm going to be able to carry all this. I dig through some kitchen drawers, looking for a plastic bag, and I come up empty.

Shit. I need to bail. If Carlo comes back, he could hurt Don and Greg. Greg's still recovering from knee replacement. I should just run. Screw the shampoo. What am I doing digging in the cupboard?

And then my eye catches on Carlo's precious messenger bag, sitting on the kitchen island.

You know what?

Screw him.

He can buy himself a new man purse. I dump all his papers on the counter, jam my stuff in, and buckle it closed.

"I thank you, gentlemen. Sorry to have interrupted your evening." I do a stupid bow-salute thingy. My brain's still woozy and reeling. Even though I have this awesome super-power where I can pretend horrible shit isn't actually happening while I'm in the moment, I'm past it. I'm shaking so hard that it's a miracle my high heels don't snap.

Don and Greg hover in the doorway, whispering to each other, matching expressions of horror and pity on their faces. "You're going to go to the hospital, right? Get that looked at?"

"Absolutely," I lie. From their expressions, they know it. "I'll message you. Let you know I'm okay. I think I might leave town for a while. Visit family."

"That's a good idea." Don takes my hand and squeezes, pinning me with his kind, crinkly eyes. "I think you're in over your head here, kiddo."

"Story of my life." I give him a peck on the cheek, and then I wink and strut out, swinging Carlo's messenger bag over my shoulder. I throw Don and Greg a jaunty wave over my shoulder as I head down the stairs. Got to make it look good.

Ten floors in heels is a pain in the ass, but I'm not getting stuck in an elevator with my newest psycho ex if he decides to come back. Especially since I'm liberating his precious messenger bag.

I keep a carefree smile plastered on my face all the way down ten flights, even though there's no one to see me. If I'm smiling, I'm good.

I didn't just almost die.

This is only another crazy misadventure, one more story to tell at the bar. The time I played with a mobster's dick by accident and nearly ended up feeding the fishes. I can spin this. It's spinning right now, whirling in my brain, a tornado tearing loose all kinds of carefully propped up lies.

I'm happy.

I'm normal.

I'm okay.

On the fifth-floor landing, I puke, my raw throat aching and burning. I'm still shaking, but I have to keep moving, so I'm lurching. As I sprint down the sidewalk toward the subway, people stare, and it's such a familiar feeling.

Look at that hot mess. Party girl. Wasted. *Rough night, eh, baby?*

To get to my walk-up from Carlo's condo, it's a half-hour subway ride, and I have to change trains downtown. Then it's a four-block walk. That's how long it takes for the adrenaline to wear off and the real shakes to come on in earnest, so hard my teeth chatter.

I barely get past the threshold of my efficiency before I bolt the deadlock and collapse against the wall. I tuck my knees to my chest and wind my arms tight around my legs. I try to hold myself together, exert enough pressure to stop the shakes, but my grip isn't nearly tight enough. I have thin arms. I always have. I've got a thick ass and thighs, and spindly arms and tiny feet. Like someone stuck toothpicks in a pear.

I'm not designed for fighting. How come I keep ending up like this?

I sniff back the snot, and look around my tenth—twelfth?—apartment in the last decade. From down here on the floor, I can't ignore the mess. Dirty black dress pants in a heap, underwear still stuck in the legs. A stack of mail that got knocked off the kitchen island and kicked halfway under a throw rug.

Is that my fancy water bottle under the sofa? I thought I lost it at work. Last week, I gave up on finding it and bought a new one. Well, that's fifty-four bucks down the drain.

It looks like someone came by and tossed the place, but it's always like this. I'll straighten up, and then an hour later —anarchy.

The floodgates burst, and tears stream down my face, trickling down my neck. I sob, and it echoes.

Oh lord. I could have died. Carlo could have killed me, dumped me in the river, and who would notice except maybe Carolyn from work? She'd be pissed that I didn't show up for my shift to relieve her. And then they'd probably call Mom in Florida, but she's been done with me for years, so it'd be up to my little brother Lou to clean this place out. Sweet Lou. It'd break his heart.

I almost died.

My stomach lurches, and I gag and wretch, but nothing comes out. And that hurts, too.

I want Forty.

And that's *stupid*—the most stupid thing my broken brain can conjure up.

Whenever I get scared or lost, I want the asshole who left me a hundred years ago. And the wanting isn't a small feeling, not like sentimentality or nostalgia or wishful thinking. It's an overwhelming longing, so strong I can actually smell the Lava soap the Nowicki boys always used.

Forty was this redneck in my English class freshman year of high school. He was older, built like an action hero, closemouthed, and scary as hell. Even though he was only a sophomore, he ran with the Steel Bones MC. Somehow, I wrapped him around my little finger. He worshipped the ground I walked on. We were inseparable for three years, and then he decided he needed to go make a man of himself in the Army.

Until the day he left for Fort Jackson, I didn't think he'd really go. Like I said, I have a superhuman ability to pretend that terrible things aren't happening.

I begged him to stay. My home situation wasn't good. I couldn't talk about it, but I tried so hard to convince him not to go. I fucked him like a mad woman, so often, in so many dirty ways, I gave myself a urinary tract infection. But he left anyway. I reacted badly, acted out, and he dumped me over the phone from basic training. I had it coming.

Our friends, the entire Steel Bones Motorcycle Club, turned their backs on me. Harper Ruth and Annie Holt, the

MC princesses, jumped me in the Finnegan's Ice Cream Parlor parking lot. Beat my ass and told me I was dead. I dropped out, went to New York. When that went south, I bopped from Miami to Boulder, and then here to Pyle. One G.E.D., ten years, and a hundred poor choices later, here I am.

A weeping, bloody ball on a dirty linoleum floor, wondering what exactly is making it so sticky.

Did I spill some pop? Sigh.

Forty Nowicki was a rite of passage, the kind of heartbreak everyone goes through with their first love, but somehow my soupy grey matter doesn't get that it's long over and probably wasn't as intense and earth-shattering as I thought it was at the time.

But I still dream about him. Not all the time. Only when I'm stressed or I fall asleep drunk.

And at some point in every relationship, usually when I'm trudging along a highway in the pouring rain or stuck in a bathroom with a maniac beating down the door, I have the same epiphany.

Aaron, the guy who baited me and his ex into fighting? And then videotaped it and posted it on a porn site? He had a softail bike like Forty.

Paulie, the guy who picked me up for a date in a stolen Lexus, landing me in City Jail until it got sorted out? He was gruff, a man of few words. Like Forty.

And Nick, the guy who kicked me out of his truck on the side of the highway after two years together? He had Forty's exact build. Height, weight, haircut. Everything. And I didn't see it.

Not 'til it was over.

And oh shit. Big reveal. Thinking about it now? Carlo has that "lethal violence simmering just under the surface" that Forty had. Ugh. I couldn't have picked a guy who likes professional wrestling and monster trucks? Forty was into those, too.

I stretch my legs and wipe my nose with the back of my hand. Carlo's messenger bag is plopped next to me on the floor. It was stupid to take it. Hopefully, he was attached to the papers that I dumped on his counter and not the bag itself. It's real leather, I think, but it's not custom or anything. Too late now. I'm not taking it back.

I sigh, shoulders slumping. So, what do I do now?

I obviously can't go back to the job at L'Alba. Rent is due in two weeks. Without a paycheck, I'm gonna be at least three hundred short. The landlord isn't cutting me any more slack.

Anyway, I've got way bigger problems than rent. Everyone knows the Renelli organization doesn't leave loose ends. And isn't that what I am now? I must have fingerprint bruises around my neck. My face is busted up. That's physical evidence. If I was suicidal enough to go to the cops, they'd press charges. They'd have Dominic Renelli's money man in lock up. For a prosecutor, that's leverage.

Renelli would never let a nobody like me walk around holding that kind of leverage.

At the very least, I'm due for a warning visit from some goons. And I don't want to see how sideways that could go with my mouth.

It's depressing. I've been in this city for five years. I know everyone. But push comes to shove? I'm a nobody with no one to call. No place to go.

It's my fault. I keep it light, never get too close. I friend people, but I'm not *friends* with people, you know?

I wish it was different. Once upon a time I had real friends, crazy people that rolled with my crazy. Well, I thought I did. Then Forty dropped me, and my "friends" turned on me in zero seconds flat. That kind of loyalty? It's admirable in a way. Hurts like a bitch to be on the flip side, but you can't help but respect it.

I sigh, kick off my shoes, and wriggle my toes. What am I doing on the floor? I need to pack.

I can't stay here, and there's only one person in the world who loves me enough to let me crash, no questions asked. My baby brother Lou. We have different fathers, and we're nothing alike, but he still thinks I'm cool. He's the only decent person in the family. Gentle. Oblivious.

Lou still tags along with Steel Bones, all these years later. I brought him around the clubhouse when Forty and I were together, and when I left town, he never stopped showing up. The brothers never iced him out like they did me.

When we talk, Lou keeps me posted about the MC. My girl Shirl, the only one who didn't drop me completely, lost her husband Twitch to cancer. Ernestine put Grinder out. Forty's coming home on a medical discharge. Scrap's getting early release. I told Lou I didn't need the updates, but he doesn't stop sharing. Like I said. Oblivious.

If I go home, I'll see Forty. He's been back three years or so now, and Petty's Mill is too small to avoid anyone for long.

A thrum begins in my belly, shooting bubbly tingles of anticipation to my nerve endings. Some of the tension seeps away. Ah. Sensation. Better than any drug.

Maybe I don't want to avoid Forty. Maybe I have some things I want to say.

There's an exhaustion competing with this new adrenaline surge. Butterflies are going crazy in my belly, while my arms and legs feel like weights dragging me down. This always happens when I think about going home. There's a large part of me that would rather walk through fire than confront the past.

But damn, I need a bolthole right now. A place to feel safe, even if it's an illusion. To feel like I did for that golden moment in my life when Forty Nowicki wouldn't leave my side, and no one could touch me.

I want to turn this shitshow that is my life around. Start again. Figure it out this time and get it right.

I sigh one last time, long and loud, and I haul myself to my feet. I've got a lot to do. I need to bail before Dominic Renelli hears about this. I need that man to understand that I am in no way, shape, or form a threat to him or his organization.

And now that the idea's firm in my mind, I'm more and more excited to see what's still back there in Petty's Mill. Is there anything left to salvage?

Could I go back and do it right this time.

'Cause every day's another chance to get it right.

Isn't it?

2

FORTY

The woman is a definite maybe. She's tall, and she works in an office. It's our third date. I'm still not exactly sure what she does, but "the system" goes down a lot, and it's always Mike's fault.

It's unclear what Mike is doing to the system, but she's convinced he's the problem. I asked her if she wanted me to rough him up. She laughed. So, I laughed, too. Guess that's a no.

I took her to Broyce's tonight. It's a great place. Started out fifty years ago out as this dark dining room. Then they built on the bar, the buffet, the party room, the outside patio. None of it level. You got to step up to the bar, step down to the buffet. Best steaks in the county, though. She ordered the surf and turf.

She's probably planning on putting out. She got her eyebrows done. The skin above her eyes is red under her makeup. Bet she got her pussy waxed, too.

I check in with my dick. See if that thought gets a rise. Negative.

I force myself to unclench my teeth, try not to let the

stress fuck with my face. Women already find me intimidating. *People* find me intimidating. When I'm with civilians,
especially women I might want to fuck, I have to be mindful.
Harper Ruth calls my normal expression "Terminator with
its skin off."

There's a kind of woman who's into that, but that's not
what I'm looking for. I want a good woman. Loyal, decent,
with good common sense. A woman who can hang with the
club. Be a good mother. Low maintenance. Hard working. I
don't see why it's such a tall order. Been looking a few years
now, but no luck.

"What are you thinking about?" The woman, Amelia,
leans over and rests her hand on my forearm. Her pupils are
glassy. She's on her second Chardonnay. I'll have to switch
her to water. If we're going to fuck, she needs to be sober.

I ask her one of my go-to questions. "Do you like the
wine?"

That sets her off about the winery she toured on vaca-
tion last year, and how she thinks this year she'll go to Cabo,
or she might go to Punta Cana. If Mike can figure out how to
work the system without her.

Amelia is talkative. That doesn't bother me. I like
listening to women talk. It's something different.

My mother got sick of dealing with my dad's shit when I
was eight. After she skipped town, Dad basically let the club
raise me. When I enlisted, I was infantry, and I went to
Ranger school before there were any women. Except for
those three years with Nevaeh in my ear 24-7, I haven't spent
much time around women. I like how they talk. Like I said,
it's different.

I feel my jaw clench, so I crack it and try to refocus on
Amelia. She's saying something about getting a free hotel by
sitting through a timeshare presentation.

That's sounds like a bad idea.

"Have you been to Mexico?" Amelia leans over the table, rolling her shoulders to squish her tits together. She doesn't have much up top, but that's all right. She checks all the boxes, physically. Tall. Straight hair. Athletic, sturdy, and thick physique.

"Not yet. The only places I've been overseas were with the service."

Her eyes warm with pity. We haven't had the conversation yet. She hasn't pried, which I appreciate, but she's seen the burns. On our second date, we screwed around in my truck when I dropped her off. She unbuttoned my shirt. The scars don't cover much except my arm and side, but they're nasty. She didn't mention them at the time. I figured it would come up tonight.

"Where did you serve?"

"I deployed a few times to Afghanistan. I was injured in Germany. My Black Hawk made a hard landing." I don't make her ask for the details. Everyone wants to know. Curiosity is natural.

"There was a fire. I was pinned by some shrapnel. Took a little while to get free." The phantom scent of burning flesh fills my nose. I breathe through it. It's not real.

"Oh, my God." Amelia grabs for my hand. I'm still holding my steak knife. I don't know what to do. She's holding my hand. I'm holding the knife. I freeze. "You could have been killed."

True. I wish she would let go of my hand so I can put the knife down.

"Did everyone make it?"

"We lost two men."

"Oh, I'm so sorry. Were they friends?"

I shake my head. I'd met them that morning. They were

my ride to Stuttgart. I can't even remember their faces. The pictures I have in my head of Specialist Daniel Gates and Staff Sergeant Alvaro Ortiz are from their memorial services. I can remember their screams, but I don't know what their voices sounded like.

"Are you okay?" Amelia drops my hand and inches back in her chair. I guess my face has gone Terminator, and I've still got the steak knife in a really tight grip. I carefully place it on my plate, blade facing in.

"Yeah. Sorry."

"Not at all." Her eyes get shiny. "You've been through so much. I can't even imagine."

I swallow a few times until I don't feel like puking. It's survivor's guilt. The doc at the VA talks about it a lot. He served in Nam. Oddly enough, he was in the same unit as Twitch, a brother who came up with my granddad. Doc's a good guy. He makes valid points, but it doesn't help anything. I still have nightmares.

While I've been stuck in my head, Amelia's gotten her courage back. Her hand's wandering now. She's reached under the table, and she's squeezing my thigh.

"You don't have to talk about it if it's too much."

I didn't plan to, but I'm happy she's willing to leave it be.

"You related to anyone in the service?" That's another one of my go to's. Everyone in this town knows someone who served. Petty's Mill is as small-town America as you can get, and until Steel Bones turned legit and got into construction, there were shit-all jobs to be had when the blast furnace shut down. Lots of people enlisted to get out.

"My cousin's in the Army reserves, and my granddad was in the Navy."

I expect her to tell me all about it. That's why it's one of my questions; it keeps people talking with minimal effort on my part. Amelia must be done with the heavy shit, though, 'cause she's sliding that hand up my thigh and leaning so close her tits brush my forearm.

"I don't know what's sexier," she purrs real low. "A soldier who served or an outlaw biker." Then her hand creeps up to rest high on my thigh. Blood rushes down, and I get a semi. Nice to know the plumbing ain't totally broke. "It's like I'm with the good guy *and* the bad guy."

The way she says "bad" tells me everything I need to know. She's ready to go, and she's not the one. Amelia, the systems analyst, wants a walk on the wild side. It isn't a total let down; I can work with that. But that's not why I shaved, put on a button-up shirt, and left my cut at home.

When I got my medical discharge, I decided I was gonna get myself a wife and family. The whole reason I joined up out of high school? It wasn't 'cause I'm some kind of patriot. No more than the next man. I enlisted 'cause I needed a job that would let me support Nevaeh Ellis.

I was gonna buy her a big house, fuck half a dozen babies into her, and raise our kids better than hand-to-mouth, the way I came up. I was a dumb fuck who barely graduated, and the Army had done well by my Pops.

Then Nevaeh ground that dream into dirt, and I became a sniper instead. I have good aim. Always have.

I did well in the Rangers. When shit went south three years back, I'd just been tapped to go to Fort Benning as an instructor. But I'm home now, that life's all done, and there's no reason I can't have what I planned on in the first place.

I already bought the house up in Gracy's Corner. Don't stay there much. Clubhouse is more convenient. The house has all the amenities, though. Big fenced yard. Energy Star appliances. Finished basement.

All I need is the woman and kids.

I have preferences, but no real requirements except loyalty and good sense. Someone who'd be a good mother, who'll stick around when the going gets tough. I don't think Amelia's it. I'm not saying that a woman lookin' for some strange is *unappreciated*, but she isn't wife material in my mind.

She clears her throat and raises her eyebrows. Oh, yeah. Guess she's waiting for me to say something.

"Steel Bones isn't an outlaw MC. We're in construction."

"That *is* what they say." She digs in, really kneads my junk. "Pounding wood, right?"

Well, this is taking a turn. What with the kind of women I've been dating, work, and all the shit that goes with being VP of Steel Bones, I don't fuck much. I steer clear of club pussy. Not my type.

It could be good to let off some steam, though. I'm down with Plan B.

But Amelia's gotta know what kind of man I am. I snatch that wandering hand, and before she can react, I've got it tucked between her own thighs and pressed into the seam of her jeans right over her clit. She kind of moans and pants at the same time, and her eyes glaze over.

My gaze scans the restaurant. We're in a corner booth, and the joint is dimly lit.

"We done here?" I ask. "Should I get the bill?"

She's swallowing hard, about to say yes, when my phone goes off. It's Heavy's ring tone. Damn. Bad timing.

"I need to take this."

I stand, drop my napkin on the table, and head for the hall by the men's room. My dick's tenting my cargo pants, but it's not obscene. Besides, it's not like there's kids in the place this late. The crowd starts getting rough about nine o'clock, and it's nearly ten.

Heavy knows I'm here with a woman, so he wouldn't call unless it was urgent. There have been some incidents lately with the Rebel Raiders. We've been handling it as it comes, but Heavy and I both have the feeling we're on the precipice. We don't deal with this beef decisively and soon, it's gonna be all out war. That's not good news for our legitimate businesses.

When I'm back by an alcove where the pay phone used to be, I swipe to answer. "Speak."

Raucous clubhouse noise spills from the speaker, shouts, music, laughter. A woman is shrieking, really going off. They're startin' early tonight.

Heavy's voice booms over the noise. "Did you know Nevaeh Ellis is at the clubhouse tonight?"

In an instant, my dick isn't kinda stiff, it's rock hard. Then, immediately, my free hand balls into a fist and pure rage, mindless and raw, whips through me out of nowhere, a ghost from the past with teeth and claws. I rock back on my heels, and it takes me a second to straighten, square my shoulders, pull it together. I can't calm my heart down, though. It's beating to break my ribs.

She's back.

"No," I finally manage. "I was not aware."

"Did you even know she was back in town?" Heavy asks. There's hollering in the background. Quick-talking. A woman screeches. A fight's brewing.

"No." My teeth are clenched so tight, it's all I can say.

"Danielle, Cheyenne, and Annie are about to beat her ass. Should I let them?"

An old impulse from when I was young and stupid flashes to life in my chest. Nobody touches Nevaeh but me. *Mine.*

Such a joke.

"What's she doing there?" I ask.

Nevaeh Ellis isn't welcome. Not at the clubhouse. Not in Petty's Mill. I deployed, and she fucked half the guys in town. She even tried to fuck Heavy. She couldn't wait six months. She was riding another guy's dick before I got off the bus at basic training. More than likely, she was spreading her legs the whole time she was with me.

"She says Fay-Lee invited her."

"What does Fay-Lee say?"

"Couldn't tell you. Dizzy saw who she brought with her and dragged her straight upstairs. He's probably bustin' her ass for instigating."

Dizzy and his old lady have their own way of doing things. Dizzy rules Fay-Lee with a firm hand, and Fay-Lee runs wild to bait him into it. She likes the rough stuff. She only gets really salty when he's gone too long on club business. Fay-Lee's a handful. I ain't surprised she's fallen in with Nevaeh somehow.

"Forty? Danielle's got Nevaeh by the hair. You want me to intervene? Last call. I ain't losing an eye over your ex."

A picture flashes in my head. Nevaeh's hair, those crazy, springy curls bouncing while she rides my cock, her fingers furiously rubbing her clit, eyes screwed closed. My dick throbs, and a cold ache sears my chest.

How long after she hopped off me before she hopped on someone else? Bile scores in my throat. Why? She doesn't mean anything to me now. Hasn't for years.

"Get her. Send her home. Tell her not to come back."

"Ladies! Drop that bitch." Heavy's booming bass cuts through the racket, and then the call disconnects.

I'm left standing by the men's room, hard as hell, heart racing, my whole body alive and hungry for the first time in years. I roll my shoulder, and the constant pain from the pins holding my arm together barely even registers.

Goddamn. Nevaeh Ellis.

I don't ever let myself think about her, but I can't forget anything, either, and the memories are burrs, thorns. Pebbles in my boots.

We had ninth grade English together. She was fourteen, mouthy, too big for her britches. I was a year ahead, on my second go at earning the credit. She pissed off this asshole from the lacrosse team. He kicked her chair out from under her. I beat his ass. She wouldn't leave me alone after that.

She sat next to me, scooting her chair close enough so she could rest her leg against mine. She'd run up to me as soon as she got off the bus in the morning, careening to a stop, hands bracing against my chest, mid-sentence since she'd start babbling at me before she got anywhere close to where I could hear her, totally unconcerned that she'd elbowed her way through a bunch of delinquents to get to me.

She was everywhere I turned, and then I couldn't leave her alone, either. I brought her around the clubhouse. Everyone loved her. Shirlene practically adopted her. Nevaeh never did like going home.

I waited until she was sixteen to pop her cherry. She was at me to do it for months beforehand, always grinding on me, sucking my fingers, trying to get me to lose my shit. To date, the hardest thing I've ever done is waiting two years to fuck Nevaeh Ellis. I was gonna marry that girl. I told her I loved her. Bought her a ring. Not a diamond; I couldn't afford that. This was way before Heavy went to college and came back with the plan that turned everything around.

The ring was a pearl. The band was too big, and the gold was too thin to resize. She wore it on a chain around her neck, and it'd roll between her tits when we fucked. When she'd get antsy—and she was always antsy—she'd click-clack the pearl between her front teeth. I nearly came in my pants from watching her tongue roll that pearl.

She was perfect, and I was a dumb redneck with zero prospects. I joined up so I could make a life for us. She had a year left of school. I had it all figured out. All she had to do was sit tight, and I'd be able to buy her a house and a car. Whatever she wanted.

Instead, almost the minute I got to basic, I got emails that she's out fucking around on me. I'd call her, and all she'd do is cry and tell me to come home. Like I had a choice. Then, one night, she came on to Heavy. She didn't deny it. I dumped her. And all she said?

"You're not coming home, are you?"

Heavy said she left town the next day, and as far as we know, she hasn't been back since.

My blood's burning as I shove my phone in my pocket and duck into the men's room. I run some cold water, splash it on my face. That all happened a lifetime ago. We were kids. What some seventeen-year-old chick with issues did back in high school shouldn't throw me for a loop.

Back then, I decided she did me a favor. After all, my mom was the same type: weak when it mattered. When the mill went under, Dad was out of work for years. He was Steel Bones, and he made ends meet by doing what he had to do, but it was feast or famine, depending on how the jobs panned out. He was on the road a lot. My mom couldn't handle the lean times, so she left. Haven't seen her since.

I don't let myself think about her, either.

Now that the shock of hearing Nevaeh's name is wearing off, my body's chilling out. My dick's hanging loose, and my muscles feel normal again. Stiff, tight across the shoulders, ready. The right amount of tension.

I've got an attractive woman, well fed and ready to fuck, and damn—I no longer have the slightest bit of interest in taking her home.

My teeth grit. What the fuck is Nevaeh Ellis doing coming around the clubhouse now?

She never had any sense. No loyalty and no common sense.

You always had to make things crystal clear to her. Speak loudly, be direct, and repeat yourself.

I should ride out to Lou's place; she's probably staying there. Lou's her half-brother, a decent guy, although he's rides a Suzuki. He hangs around the club, comes to parties. He never brings his sister up, so we're cool.

He better not have anything to do with this. I like the guy, but he won't be welcome anymore if he brought her around.

Yeah, driving out to Lou's is a good idea. I'll paint her a picture so there's no room for confusion. When she came on to Heavy, she tried to drive a wedge between me and my brother. Steel Bones is a brotherhood. She's not coming back from that. Not in ten years. Not in a hundred.

Even though it doesn't need it, I slick down my hair with my wet hands, and I head back to Amelia. She's ordered herself another glass of wine since I've been gone, and she's posing, legs crossed, back arched. She's hot. Nice proportions. Shiny hair.

"Emergency?" She smiles. She has very white teeth.

"No. Nuisance."

She smiles wider. There's a bright pink lipstick smudge on her front tooth. "So we have time for dessert?"

"Yeah. Sure."

I sit in Broyce's another hour regretting that "sure." I don't like sweets. Amelia seems to have forgotten she was feeling me up, and now she's really into a story about a time her car broke down. It keeps going, and the whole time, my brain flashes through still shots of Nevaeh—shit I haven't let myself remember in years.

Nevaeh's chin dimpling when she tried to keep from crying that time she wanted to try anal. Her thighs hot around my obliques in the freezing water of Lake Patonquin. Her giggles tickling my ear in the back of the dollar movie theater.

My face flushes, feverish, and so I make myself remember the rest. My muscles swell with rage. Pictures of her twerking on some guy's jock. Another guy's arm around her shoulder, his hand in her hair. Heavy describing the mole right below her right nipple. I force myself to drag in a deep breath.

It's insane to get upset about shit that went down when I was eighteen. Still, while Amelia goes on about roadside service and estimates, my brain's projecting the world's most fucked up slideshow.

Over and over, the instant I wrestle the rage under control, my dick gets hard enough to pound a nail. Again, nothing I've felt in years. My balls ache under the table as my fingers drum the table and my knee jiggles.

I want to stroke soft skin, sink my cock into hot pussy, but I don't want this put-together woman with the matching leather boots and purse. She's confident. Driven. Calm, cool, and collected. She's a ten.

I don't want her.

I want to touch a wild woman who'll wriggle and buck and lose her dignity. I want a short woman with a fat ass— all meaty and jiggly—who'll climb me, ride me, let me do whatever I want. A slut who'll *beg me* to do whatever I want. That's what Nevaeh was like right before I left. Starving. Insatiable.

I was eighteen. I didn't have the first idea of what to do with that kind of enthusiasm. I do now. Much good that does.

Besides. Who knows what's happened with her? She was always so hyper, so crazy. If you didn't feed her, she'd forget to eat, and even though her ass wouldn't shrink an inch, her ribs would show. She'd get knots in her hair, in the back, and she wouldn't notice. And she always had skinned knees or scabs from whatever stupid stunt she'd tried that ended badly.

That look doesn't age well. A skinny, twenty-nine-year-old woman with knotted hair and scabs? That's a drug addict.

Hell, what do I know? Maybe she's done fine for herself. Calmed down, got married. Maybe she has a kid or two, and she's going through a divorce, back in town to take a stroll down memory lane. My chest tightens. Now why does that possibility somehow bother me more than her ending up a mess? It shouldn't. Only an asshole wishes people ill.

Amelia's launching into the sequel to her broken-down car story. I can't take it anymore. I wave for the check, and she blinks in surprise.

"Well! Time flies, I guess, right?" She licks her lips, a question in her eye. I guess it hasn't escaped her that my mind is elsewhere. Shit.

"I'll drop you off at home." I grab her hand and squeeze. Friendly. Noncommittal.

Her face falls for a second, but she's not the type to stay down. By the time I open my truck door for her, she's telling me about a dog she used to have who shed too much. Not sure how we got there from the car with the bad clutch, but I'd be hard pressed to keep up my end of a conversation at this point, so I'm happy to listen.

When we get to her place, I open the door for her, and she kisses me as I help her down from the cab. Tastes like wax. She rubs the lipstick off with her thumb.

"Am I going to see you again?" Amelia smiles.

I like her. She's not pushy; she's confident. She reminds me of Deb, Pig Iron's old lady. Deb does the books and keeps the clubhouse running. She wants things to be her way, and she's tough enough to make it happen.

That's the kind of woman who makes a good wife and mother. Maybe I judged Amelia too hastily. Kind of fucked up to rule out a woman 'cause she wants your jock, anyway.

"I'll call you." I smile back.

Amelia hops down and moves in for a hug. She nestles her head against my chest. I give her a quick squeeze and a pat, and then I step back.

"I'll watch until you're inside."

She pauses and cocks her head, taking my measure. Then she smiles and winks. "I'll see you around."

I nod.

I wait until the lights come on inside before I hop back in the truck. Without thinking, I head for Lou Ellis' place on Barrow Road, death metal blaring, adrenaline rising in my veins, dick throbbing in my jeans.

I'm going to tell Nevaeh not to show her face in my club again.

I'm going to stake this thing in the heart.

I straighten my collar and crack my neck.

My boot is lead on the gas.

THE LIGHTS ARE STILL on when I get to the Ellis place, an old rancher out towards the river. I pull off onto the front lawn, and it's like no time has passed. I haven't been out this way since I came home. There's been no reason. Barrow Road is a country lane that leads to nothing but shotgun shacks and flood plain.

As I slam the truck door, I can almost hear Nevaeh's mom primly ordering me to stop tearin' up the grass. Even in the dark with no porch light, it's obvious no one much cares about the lawn these days. I heard that when Nevaeh's stepdad passed, Mrs. Ellis moved to Florida, leaving Lou the house. Looks like he takes care of it about as well as any guy in his twenties who installs cable and plays bass in a jam band.

There are two overturned buckets by the front step with cigarette butts scattered around, a few empties on the step itself. Mrs. Ellis' kissing Dutch couple is knocked over, and at some point, someone mowed around it, so the little boy and girl are lying flat in an island of tall weeds.

Lou's work van, his bike, and a beat-up red Hyundai take up the short driveway. Must be Nevaeh's ride. Back left tire is low.

Clearly, they're home, and my truck's not subtle. I'm surprised no one's come out yet.

I hop up on the running board, reach through the open window, and lay on the horn. Mrs. Ellis used to hate when I did that. She'd hassle Nevaeh, tell her only sluts go running when a man honks. Nevaeh'd cry about it, but it was always easy to distract her. She was the kind of girl who wanted to be happy.

I told her I'd walk up to the door—it was the right thing to do, even I knew that—but she didn't want me anywhere near her folks. Guess they didn't approve of me.

Still no movement in the house. I lean on the horn again, and I keep the pressure on until I see the curtains flutter. Then the porch light flickers on, the door flies open, and there she is. Every muscle in my body goes as hard as stone.

I round the truck, stalk forward, my legs drawn to her, my brain struggling keeping up. Nevaeh Ellis. She's here. In real life.

She's the same. But more.

The force of her standing there sends a sizzle of electricity down every nerve, priming me like the sound of gunfire.

She's framed by the doorway, backlit, her mess of curls still the biggest thing about her. No matter that round ass and those thick thighs, she's so damn small. Short and compact. She's got her hands on her hips, and damn, but they're even curvier than I remember.

"Lay off the horn, asshole!"

I already have. I'm nearly on her; she's almost in my arms. I need to see her face, plunge my hands in that wild hair, shake her and make her cry and take her mouth until she whimpers with need. I'm furious, horny, and crushed, sickened by the weight of time passed. It's been too long.

Then when I get four, five feet away, her chin loses the arrogant tilt. She crosses her arms, hugging herself. Glances over her shoulder into the house. Is she scared? Nevaeh Ellis? No way.

Still, I stop. I'm a few steps away from the porch, and I can make out every inch of her now. She's wearing a white long-sleeved sweatshirt with a rainbow across the chest. It's cropped, revealing the gentle swell of her belly. She's got on a pair of white boy shorts, so tight I can see the cleft of her pussy lips.

I stand, shoulders back and level with my chest, heels together, arms at my side. I realize as I'm doing it that I'm standing at attention, presenting myself to her, and blood rushes to my cock. I'm as ready as I've ever been. It takes everything in me to be still while she fidgets, gnawing her bottom lip, scratching her heel with the toe of the opposite foot.

Then her big, brown eyes dip below my belt. She snorts, the fear or whatever it was gone. "At least someone in this town is happy to see me." Her gaze slides to my truck. "Where's your bike?"

My face burns, but damn if my cock doesn't press harder against my zipper. "Where are your pants?"

She rolls her eyes. "Same place you left your manners, I suppose." She wrinkles her nose. "No *Hi, Nevaeh? How are you? Long time, no see*?"

"Hello, Nevaeh."

I'm close enough to see her shiver when I say her name. Goosebumps pucker her belly and legs. It's early spring, and it's cold out here. Where's her jacket? Where are her *shoes*? She's in her socks. White with pom poms on the heels. They've got to be filthy on the bottoms.

She ducks her head, suddenly shy, and her hair shifts. I see a bruise above her eye. It doesn't look fresh, but it's hard to tell with the shadows. I steel myself as a wave of aggression rolls over me.

I jerk my chin toward the shiner. "Danielle fix your face?"

"Which one's Danielle? The one with the hair or the one with the eyebrows."

"The eyebrows." I can't act like I don't know what she means. Danielle paints those suckers on. They make an impression. Cheyenne must be the one with the hair. It's always some color or another.

"Nah. That one's all mouth."

"What were you doing at the clubhouse?"

"Looking for you."

"We have no business."

"I wanted to talk."

"I've got nothing to say to you."

She winces like she's hurt. Fuck. My abs tense, and my fingertips twitch, like they want to grab the words back.

She swallows, and her gaze dips before rising again. "You look different." Her voice is shy.

She doesn't look different at all. Except for the tiniest laugh lines at the corner of her eyes and twenty or so extra pounds, most packed on her ass and thighs, she's the same. Messy. Squirmy. Beautiful.

"You're taller than I remember." She offers me a half-smile, a quirked corner of her mouth. My breath catches in my lungs.

I am taller. I left for basic before that last growth spurt. I got on a plane, and she got under every asshole she could the minute the wheels took off from the runway. Several helpful sweetbutts sent me blurry pics. Nevaeh sitting in some loser's lap. Nevaeh grinding on a Rebel Raider at a bonfire. The stale, familiar rage rocks me in my boots.

What am I doing here? I was having a nice dinner with a nice woman, and I dropped her off early to drive out to the boondocks and waste time on a crazy bitch who couldn't stay faithful for a *week*. I'm a fool. I need to say my piece and get gone.

But all the words I want to say would shame me as a man. No matter what a woman shows herself to be, it isn't right to call her names to her face.

"Well? You gonna stand there and hate fuck me with your eyes all night long?" She raises her eyebrows. She's got nerve. Always did.

"You gonna stand there and act all innocent?"

"Not all night, no." She taps her foot. My pulse skyrockets.

"Why did show up at the clubhouse? You know you're not welcome. What's your game, Nevaeh?"

"No game."

I bark a bitter laugh. "It was *always* a game with you."

She snorts, but her eyes drop to the ground. "I guess it could have seemed that way."

"It was that way. How long after I left before you were spreading your legs for any random asshole? Did you even wait until I left?"

She wrings her hands and rocks on her feet. She was always fidgeting like that. I attributed it to nervous energy, but from where I stand now? It looks a hell of a lot like guilt.

"I never cheated on you."

"Bullshit."

"I know what it looked like."

"I got pictures of you crawling on men from here to Pyle. You snuck into Heavy's room topless and asked him to fuck you."

She opens her mouth to protest, but I guess she thinks better of it. Instead, she draws in a deep breath, and instead of hanging her head again, she comes at me with those huge, brown eyes.

"Yeah. I did do that."

I wait. Crickets chirp. Leaves whisper in the huge maple beside the house. What am I even waiting for? An apology? An explanation? As if anything she said—then or now—would change anything. She's disloyal. Selfish. Nuts.

Her throat bobs as she swallows, and she shifts. It's like she's waiting, too. What for? What's her game now?

"You seriously want me to believe you never cheated? If you didn't, it wasn't for lack of trying."

Fuck. Why do I still care about this at all? It happened a lifetime ago. I've been around the world since Nevaeh Ellis. Stared death in the face. Came out the other side, scarred and fucked up, sure, but alive.

And some girl screwing around on me back in the day has got me this twisted? Why am I not at my house in Gracy's Corner right now, balls deep in Amanda or Amelia or whatever her name is?

Nevaeh chews on the inside of her cheek, and stares at her feet. "I wanted you to get jealous and come home. Or, like, confront me. I was desperate. I wasn't thinking straight." She glances up, and her eyes are shining.

The tears piss me off. "That's childish as hell."

"I *was* a child!" Her voice breaks, and there's pain in it. Something inside me lurches for her, and I barely stop myself from loping up the steps and folding her in my arms.

That hurt in her voice? It's fake as hell. She's not innocent. She never was. She's a liar.

I'm about to tell her so and bail, but she keeps going.

"You know, I'm still mad, too."

She scrubs angrily at her eyes, dashing away those tears.

"I hate you, too, so you can just fuck off with your wounded, wronged man routine. You said you'd always be there for me? Well, you weren't, and I know that's the way the world works, and you're a hero or whatever, but you can just go fuck yourself, Forty Nowicki. And fuck your fancy ass truck and *fuck* you coming here with lipstick on your collar. You look like a detergent commercial."

I glance down. Oh. There's a hot pink smear on the shoulder of my shirt.

Nevaeh spins on her heels and flings the screen door open. I start forward—to do what, I don't know—but she suddenly changes her mind and whirls back around. Her shoulders are heaving, her entire body wired. Then she sucks down a deep breath, like she's steadying herself, and she exhales slowly.

"I'm sorry. That's not what I planned on saying. I was going to apologize for what I did back then. It was immature, and it was selfish and messed up, and I knew it was stupid and wrong at the time, when I was doing it, but...I was...I had my reasons, okay? And they weren't good reasons, but I was young, and I know that's no excuse. But still. I'm sorry. That's what I meant to say."

She pauses for air, and then she waits, fingers plucking nervously at the hem of her sweatshirt.

I don't know what to say. My brain's on overload, glitching with the desire to grab her, shake her or throw her into the truck, tear those white panties to the side and fuck her raw, or curse her until she cries. My mind's a wreck, like I'm eighteen again, and I know nothing.

I can't act, can't find words to say, so all I do is stare.

God, I've missed the shape of her. The way her tits slope to a peak. She's clearly not wearing a bra under the crop top. I manage to drag my gaze away, and then my eyes are instantly drawn to the swell of her hips and the crease where her thighs press together. Those twenty pounds found the right places. She's all sex. All bounce, all curves.

And she'll pass it around to anyone and lie about it to your face.

"Aren't you gonna say something?" Her voice is small. Meek. She's not meek.

"How many?" I shouldn't care. I should turn around, get back in my truck, and let the past be the past.

"What?"

"How many other guys did you fuck when we were together?"

"I told you. None. I never did. I was...I don't know how to say it. I was trying to make you jealous. I had this idea in my head that you could come back if you really wanted to. I mean, I knew better. I'm not stupid. But..." Her brow furrows, and she presses her fingers to her temple. "It was magical thinking, I guess."

"No, you weren't stupid, Nevaeh. You understood the deal. You leave basic, you're A.W.O.L. Everyone knows that."

"I never wanted you to go."

"It was for us."

She shakes her head, in denial or disapproval, I don't know. The stale rage rises in me again. Same old argument. Meaningless now.

"What was I gonna do here?" I ask. "Pump gas? Drywall?"

"You would have been there for me. And yeah, pump gas. You too good to pump gas?" Her face is flushing red. I remember the look. She's holding on to her temper by a thread. "I'm not saying what I did made sense. I was young, and I was confused by a lot of shit."

"Confused? Is that what you call it? That's all you got to say in your defense?"

She balls her fists. "I'm not gonna stand here on the porch and spill my guts to you."

"No. You were gonna spill your guts at my clubhouse, in front of all my people. You always did have to put on a show, didn't you?"

Her brown eyes spark. "It always took a show to get through to you, didn't it?"

"You could have *talked* to me." I'm shouting. Fuck. I don't shout.

"You *left*. And then you rang me up one Sunday, called me trash, and told me we're done. And then you blocked me. How was I gonna talk to you?" Her voice cracks; her eyes darken. She's remembering. I was in a rage. It lasted months. Years. I can't really recall exactly what I said.

There's no reason for the pit in my stomach, though. No matter what words I used, I meant them. She tried to come on to my brother. What did she expect?

"You flashed Heavy your tits and asked him to fuck you."

"Yeah. Not one of my finer moments." She sniffs. Is she really crying? "I should've given up way before then. Packed my stuff and blown town with a little dignity left, you know? But I was such a stupid little kid. I guess I thought you'd get so pissed, you'd demand that I tell you what's going on." She snorts.

"What was going on?" I can hardly follow her; she's making no sense.

She blinks and glances over her shoulder like she hears a noise behind her. Must be Lou.

"It doesn't matter now. We were kids. I'm sorry for how I acted. That's all I wanted to say. If it makes you feel better, I lost all my friends, and it wasn't easy, starting over in a new city."

I feel unsteady, as if my feet aren't on firm ground. "Why now? Why come around now?"

"Better late than never?"

I scrub the back of my neck in frustration. "Can you just be straight with me? For once?"

She draws in a shaky breath. "I guess I'm trying to put some things right."

"Why?"

"Does there have to be a reason?"

And there it is. The reason this isn't gonna end with peace between us. She *can't* be straight. People like her never change. Answer a question with a question. It's all a game. And maybe her crazy was hot as shit when I was a teenager, but I'm a grown man now, and this kind of bullshit is just sad.

I don't care if she's working the ninth step, or she's on some kind of journey to find herself. It doesn't matter that my dick's harder than it's been in years, and I haven't thought about the pain in my arm once the entire time we've been talking. I don't need this in my life.

"I tell you what, Nevaeh. It doesn't matter. You've said your piece. Now stay away from the clubhouse. Stay away from me and my brothers. We're done now. For good."

She takes a half step back. I guess she thought this conversation was going a different direction. Maybe for a second, before I remembered the complete havoc she wrought on my life, it was.

But fool me twice, shame on me, right?

She opens her mouth, as if she's gonna argue. But then she sighs instead. She lifts a shoulder and flashes a weak smile. "Okay, Forty. It was good to see you."

And then turns on her heels and disappears into the house, the screen door swinging shut behind her. My gut drops and for a second, my body mindlessly lurches forward, demanding that I take her back.

She's gone too quick.

I'm left standing on the front walk, my brain spinning.

This is what I wanted, right? I don't need to relive my

worst choices. I was given a second chance when they pulled me from the wreckage of that chopper, and I'm not using that gift to take a walk down some misguided memory lane. I'm gonna go home, call Amelia, tell her I had a good time. Ask her out again. Move on.

I force my feet to move toward my truck, drag my body into the driver's seat.

I did what I came to do. Nevaeh's not going to cause a problem again.

I'm satisfied.

And it feels like shit.

3

NEVAEH

"Swing and a miss?" Lou's lounging on the sofa with a longneck, watching some show where celebrities dress in mascot costumes and sing karaoke songs.

"Were you listening the whole time?"

"Just during commercials."

"You mean my love life is less interesting than a dude dressed up like a papaya singing 'Sweet Caroline?'"

"It's a mango. And yes."

I flop down next to Lou, burrow into him, get him good with my elbow as I tousle his hair. He jerks his head away.

"Quit it, Backwards."

That's Lou's little nickname for me. 'Cause Nevaeh is "heaven" backwards. Get it? He thinks he's funny.

I give his flawlessly-styled naturally-blond hair one last tousle, not even the teeniest bit totally jealous, and then I rest my head on his shoulder.

"Doesn't he ever talk about me? Not ever?"

Lou groans. "I told you. Forty doesn't talk to me. I don't really hang with him. I go to the clubhouse for Bucky. You know that."

My brother has had an unrequited crush on Bucky Turvey since middle school. The first time I brought Lou around the clubhouse—he was maybe thirteen at the time —he was a goner. It's pretty much hopeless, not because Bucky's ever shown interest in the ladies, but because he's a raging asshole.

"When are you going to get over that loser?"

"About the same time you get over Forty Nowicki, apparently."

"He looked like I ran over him with a Mack truck when I came back inside."

He was miserable when he told me to fuck off. That's the only thing keeping me from moping right now. As soon as I saw him, a wave of memory rushed to the surface, toothachingly sweet and painful, so powerful I swear my feelings made a whomp, whomp whooshing in my ears.

I was on the edge of bursting into tears and telling him I love him when I saw that lipstick on his shirt. Good thing, or I would have completely humiliated myself.

Which reminds me. "You never told me Forty's dating someone."

"He dates a lot of someones."

"So he's a man whore?" My skin crawls. The Forty I knew wasn't that kind of guy.

"Not exactly. He's not into club pussy. He goes out with the put-out-on-the-third-date kind of women. So, you know, mathematically, he's probably getting a third of the ass of the other brothers."

"Mathematically?"

Lou shrugs. "I can do math."

Lou sucked at school as much as I did. He doesn't have attention issues like me, but he had a lot on his mind. Academics weren't a priority. Making it to senior year without getting outed was kind of more important. Petty's Mill High wasn't exactly a drum circle when we were kids. More like a trial by fire.

Lou sighs and shoots me a side-eye. "You shouldn't fuck with him if you're not serious."

"I'm serious."

I am. Until I saw him in person, it was all kind of theoretical, me bungling along with a half-assed plan like usual. I saw a chick in a Steel Bones cut at the coffee shop and struck up a conversation. She turned out to be Dizzy's old lady, Fay-Lee.

When I left town, Dizzy was still with his first wife, but Lou hadn't bothered to keep me updated on that drama. Even though I hadn't heard of Fay-Lee, she'd heard of me. She asked me if I really was a cheating whore who fucked around on Forty Nowicki while he was serving his country. I asked her if she's really a nosy bitch who desperately needs a sandwich and a flea bath.

She cracked up. I paid for her cappuccino.

We hung out for hours. Around closing time, we didn't feel like calling it a night, so she invited me to the clubhouse. I went.

Hilarity and a cat fight ensued. It felt so normal. Ill-advised and crazy fun until it went south. Monkey business as usual.

And then Forty showed up. I didn't know how strong the need would be to run to him, to leap into his arms and climb up him until I could burrow my nose in the crook of his neck to see if he still smells like leather and motor oil and Lava soap. All the best smells in the world.

Real. Solid. Safe.

The only reason I didn't throw myself at him is because he's scary now. His expression is dead cold. He's taller and wider than any man I currently know, and he obviously works out. A lot. As soon as I saw him, I couldn't help sucking in my little paunch, even though I think it's adorable, and I wouldn't turn it into abs even if I could.

I was dressed like a kid, and Forty was all business, as if he'd come from church, one of the cool ones with a guitarist who plays acoustic Christian rock. He was wearing a white button-down shirt and crisp cargo pants, no rips, no sign of wear.

He's got a flattop, he's clean-shaven, and his boots were polished to a shine. If I didn't know better, I'd wonder if he's Steel Bones anymore.

He's definitely a grown man. And the way he looked at me...he thinks I'm trash. Which is understandable. But it still makes me mad.

He couldn't look away, though. There is that. And he couldn't hide that raging hard-on.

Lou digs his elbow into my ribs until I scooch over and give him some room. I oblige.

He's been cool about me coming home. He even cleared his weights out of the spare room. I told him moving back into my old bedroom upstairs would make me feel like too much of a failure.

I know he's nervous that I'll screw things up for him somehow. He's not exactly out of the closet. He's not exactly living a life where that's a real choice. It's true—I do have a big mouth and no filter, but I'd die before I hurt my little brother.

"You tryin' to get him back?"

"I don't know. Maybe?"

"So, what's your plan?" Lou asks. "If you're thinking you can come with me to the clubhouse, no way."

I playfully slap him across the back of the head. "You

little ingrate. The only reason you have an open invitation with Steel Bones is 'cause I dragged you along with me back in the day."

"That was a long time ago. The club's different now. They're serious business."

"And I'm not?"

"You got a job yet?"

"It's only been two weeks."

"You put in any applications?"

I've filled out about a dozen online, but I'm waiting for my face to heal up before I click submit. I'm not about to bring that up though. Lou lost it when I showed up in the middle with of the night with my face busted and everything I own in my car. He wanted to go kick someone's ass, and he wouldn't let it go until I threatened to drive back to Pyle.

"I'm polishing up my resume."

"Steel Bones owns this county. Did you know that?"

"Maybe I should see if they've got openings."

He shakes his head. "It's not like when we were kids, and they were some redneck motorcycle gang. They're big time now. They've got the construction business, the Autowerks, the strip club. They've bought up a lot of the waterfront downtown. Made some development deals."

"And?"

"And if the club's VP wants you gone, no one's gonna hire you."

"Forty's the VP?"

"Yeah. He's Heavy's right hand."

I shrug. "Forty doesn't want me gone."

"Sure sounded like he did."

Yeah, it did. A twinge twists my heart and makes my belly ache.

When I first fled town, I was so furious and lost and terrified that—to be honest—I hoped he was hurting half as bad as I was. And then he never reached out, and life kept moving. By the time I grew up enough to realize I'd acted like an immature asshole, it'd been water under the bridge for years.

I'm a slow learner, but I'm like that dopey blue fish in the movie. Just keep swimming. Keep 'er moving.

Tonight, when Forty came so close, the porchlight shining on his face, his entire body stiff and indestructible and hostile, I was scared for a second. Then I saw his eyes.

He's got secret-decoder brown eyes. Always has. Everything shows if you know the code. Lust. Anger. Hurt. I have no idea if I put the bad shit there. Probably not. He's been places since high school. He got injured overseas, so badly he got a medical discharge. How much damage could I have done him at seventeen years old?

Still, seeing that hurt made me feel like garbage. I feel that way a lot, and usually, I indulge it a second, and I shake it off.

But you know? I'm kind of sick of always waiting for that "I'm crap" feeling to come back. How do you get rid of it, though, if age and wisdom and distance don't help?

Ugh. I can't sit still on a couch anymore.

I hop to my feet. "I'm gonna see what's in the fridge. You want anything?"

"I'm good." Lou's already lost in his show again. For how complicated his life can get, he's a simple guy. All he wants is a cold beer, dumb TV, and someone else to clean the house. That's my job in exchange for crashing here rent-free.

I head for the kitchen, but in the hall, the stairs catch my eye. I don't go up there except to clean.

I need to keep moving. Put a load in the dishwasher.

Take out the trash. Shove the garbage feeling deep, deep down, distract myself with something shiny.

I pause with my hand on the bannister knob. My palm's sweaty.

There are a hundred things I could be doing. Places I could be. But here I am, back here in Petty's Mill. In this house. At the bottom of these stairs.

I made the choices, took the exit off the interstate to come here. I could have run anywhere. But I drove myself here.

My stomach turns, and a sour sweat breaks out behind my knees and under my boobs. I should go back to Lou, watch TV, get blitzed on cheap domestics.

Shit, no, I should get in my car and keep going, head south and see how far I can go before I run out of gas money. I could get to the Carolinas, Florida maybe. Spring comes earlier there. I could sleep in my car until I find a job.

I might have this far, but I don't have to walk up these stairs. But I do. I traipse down the hall to the bedroom at the end. My bare feet pad soundlessly from tread-to-tread, slow step-by-step along the carpet.

I can keep carrying the past, widening my arms as it gains weight year after year, keep moving fast enough that the load never becomes quite unbearable.

Or I could open this door.

While my brain's been churning, I passed Lou's room and the master suite, and I arrived at my old room at the end of the hall. My heart is thudding against my ribs.

I haven't gone in this room since I've been home.

If Lou noticed, he didn't say anything. There's a lot we don't put into words with each other. A lot we leave in the dark. Denial ain't just a river in Egypt; it's a way of life with the Ellis family.

I stand outside the flimsy door without a lock, cracking my knuckles, finger by finger. I pick at the remnants of a sticker at eye level. The torso of a unicorn and half a sparkly rainbow.

I'm not good at standing in one place, so I twist the knob, and ease the door open.

A whiff of stale vanilla hits me first, and my stomach churns. That was my signature scent back in the day. I had the body wash, the lotion, the essential oil.

I flick the switch, but nothing happens. The overhead bulb's burned out. I can see by the hall light, though, that nothing much has been touched. I cross to the nightstand and turn on the lamp.

Nausea washes through me. I brace myself against a sudden weakness in my legs and a seizing in my chest.

Yeah. Nothing's changed.

Half-empty perfume bottles, an earring tree, and a basket of hair styling supplies are crowded on my dresser. A drawer is open, the arm of a sweater hanging over the side. My collection of solar-powered dancing figurines is still lined up along the windowsills. Hula girls. Flowers. They're motionless in the dark. Someone made my bed.

They made my bed, but they didn't shut that drawer.

Another wave of queasiness turns my legs to jelly, and I sink to the floor, cross-legged. The carpet's pristine. When I left, I didn't bother to straighten up, let alone vacuum. I threw what I could into the bags I could find, and I ran.

Someone picked up my dirty clothes and books and the random crap I left on the floor. Then, they vacuumed and left everything else the way it was.

A biology textbook and *Beowulf* are stacked on my desk. Guess I owe Petty's Mill High School a fine. There's a coffee mug. A tin can filled with Sharpie markers. But no desk chair.

I broke the chair over my stepfather's back the last time he snuck into my bedroom in the middle of the night. Lou was sleeping over at a friend's house. My mom had polished off a bottle of Merlot and passed out on the sofa.

It was a Saturday night, and I was at home. Forty was gone. He'd dumped me, and I was *persona non grata* at the Steel Bones clubhouse. The few girlfriends I had outside of the club were busy, probably bored with me crying over my own stupid mistakes.

I knew he'd come. He was an opportunist.

I'd kept my clothes on, and I'd piled a whole bunch of shit in front of my door. Not the dresser or desk. Nothing that could wake my mother. 'Cause the absolute worst thing would be if someone saw, right?

But I heaped up enough so that there'd be an obstacle. Advance warning if I happened to fall asleep.

A full laundry basket. The trash can. A pile of shoes.

After I left for Pyle, someone tucked the trash can back under the desk. Someone emptied the laundry basket. I took the shoes with me when I left.

He'd muscled right through my sad little blockade. He said he wanted to talk. He was worried about me.

Here's the thing that people don't understand. Hell, it's the thing that *I* didn't understand until I was twenty-five or twenty-six. When these things happen, you have a choice.

People who don't understand say *I'd never let that happen to me! I'd fight. I'd tell someone. I'd scream. I'd kick him in the balls!*

But the choice isn't between telling and not telling. Fighting or not fighting. It's between making it real or keeping it a bad dream.

If I made it real, I'd lose another father. Like when I was six, and my real dad disappeared, and I had nightmares for months about being chased by a monster while all the people around me turned to wax statues. My mom would be broken again like she was before she met Ed Ellis. She'd hide in bed all day, chain smoke, and she wouldn't take her blood pressure meds or go to the grocery store.

If I made it real, Lou would lose his father, too. Just like me.

And I was *tough*. I handled it when my dad left. I kept Mom alive. Hid the bottles. Flushed pills. But Lou's not me; he doesn't have my dumb resilience. If I told, what would happen to Lou, my brave brother fighting so hard to be okay with himself and the world? If I told, would Lou love me anymore?

And I would *never* tell Forty. Not if you tortured me. He'd look at me different. He'd be disgusted. He'd want to love me, but he wouldn't be able to anymore.

I know I'm hard to love. Teachers barely tolerated me. Other kids got irritated with me right quick. I could never keep a best friend more than a week or so. Forty, Lou, and my mom. They were it.

And what was it really? A few minutes every so often. A few grunts. Hands I could ignore. A mess on my sheets I could wash the next day. I could stare at a wall while he did it. Hold my breath. It never lasted that long.

I'm a tough girl, right?

One night, my mom caught Ed coming out of my room. She started looking at me funny. She drank more, and all she had to say to me was clean your room. Unload the dishwasher. Don't you think it's time you got an afterschool job? See? No one can love you if they know. It's too gross.

I was down to Forty and Lou.

Then Forty left for basic. Then the look in Ed Ellis' eye changed.

The walls were closing in, and Lou was all I had left. Make it real or keep it a bad dream. You get to make the choice over and over again. Every morning when you wake up.

In the guidance counselor's office while she's checking a box and meeting with you about your four-year plan. On the bus ride home from school when Miss Amy asks you if something's wrong. At the dinner table when your stepdad tells you that you can do better than the grease monkey you're dating.

A thousand choices a day, a choice every second you're alone with nothing to distract yourself. Your mind rolls on a loop, and every time you decide to eat it, the choices pile up in your belly like rocks.

And here's the worst of it. The reason I never said a thing. If I made it real, then it really happened. To me. And somehow, I'd have to live with that, and at sixteen, I didn't know how. So I decided it was a bad dream.

And when Ed Ellis looked around, saw I had no one left, and he tried to make it *really* real? I beat him with a chair, and I got out of this house, this town.

I did come back for his funeral. He passed from pancreatic cancer. He went quickly. Mom begged me to come see him. He was asking for me. I refused, and she's never talked to me since.

I'd half-thought maybe I'd see Forty at the funeral, but he'd been gone a few years at that point. He'd never come back from the Army.

I was sitting in a corner of the funeral parlor, playing on my phone, when I felt a hand on my shoulder. It was Shirlene Robard, this old lady from the Steel Bones MC who kind of adopted me for a while. She's a hardcore, old-school biker chick. She came to the viewing in a faded *Appetite for Destruction* T-shirt, skintight black jeans, and snakeskin cowgirl boots.

Back when I was with Forty, I'd help her out around the clubhouse. Ran errands and such. She was a nurse, so she was always fussing over the older guys. We'd been tight, and when I left town, she still called me every so often. I'd entertain her with stories about the big city. She'd reminisce about Twitch and bitch about how the old dudes wouldn't take care of themselves.

Shirlene paid her respects to Lou and my mom, and then we'd stepped outside—mostly to avoid my mom's disapproving stares—and she slipped me a half pint of whiskey. We passed the bottle, taking baby sips, and she listened while I told someone for the first time why I wasn't sorry Ed Ellis was dead.

She listened for what felt like hours. Then she'd patted my knee and said, "Too bad we can't kill him. You're a tough cookie, Nevaeh."

You know what? I was.

I shake myself, stretch my legs. I should drop by Shirlene's place. See if she needs anything. She's retired now. Even though she keeps herself crazy busy, she might need help with her lawn or something. She's a proud woman. Not likely to speak up if she could use a hand.

Yeah, that's what I'll do tomorrow. I wrinkle my nose. It's gloomy as shit in here. I pop up to my feet.

My heart's raw, and everything's wrong. For almost ten years, a drawer's been open with a sweater hanging out. A chair is missing. Forty Nowicki has pink lipstick on his collar, and he still hates me.

I'm living off my little brother, maybe hiding out from

the mob, and—to be one hundred percent honest—I'm not really sure where my pants are or why I'm hanging out in my underwear.

But I'm breathing a little easier.

There's nothing in this room I haven't carried with me in my memory.

I don't need to run.

I can stand on my own two feet. I can walk out of this room. Shut the door. I left before, and I was young and broke and friendless. I couldn't help but take this room with me.

But I'm older now. Maybe this is just a room.

Maybe I'm not what I learned I was here.

Maybe I'm strong.

Maybe I have been all this time.

4

NEVAEH

I sleep really well for the first time in forever. When I wake up, I spackle on the concealer and head over to Shirlene's. It's early, around noon. She's already on her trike, strapping on her helmet.

When she sees me, the corner of her lip quirks up, just barely. She's so happy to see me.

"Well, look what the cat dragged in." She tugs on a glove. I give her a little salute.

"Is that new?"

She's got herself a fancy touring trike in teal, complete with a trunk and everything.

"Yup. Had myself a midlife crisis. Bought a bike." Shirlene pats the passenger seat behind her. "Hop on."

"You got a spare helmet?"

"Your head's hard enough. And I'm not planning on laying her down. It's got three wheels." Shirlene revs the engine. I shrug, grin, and climb onto the seat behind her.

Shirlene pulls off cautiously, gets herself up to an audacious fifty miles per hour, and I lean back against the backrest and lift my arms into the wind. The sun is warm on my face, and the sky is a perfect robin's egg blue.

"Where are we going?" I shout as she turns down toward the river.

"Makin' the rounds."

I don't know what that means, but I'm up for anything. I'm already bored out of my mind at the house, and I really need to let my face heal up more before I go job hunting. I spackled on concealer this morning, but it didn't do much.

Shirlene takes it down to twenty-five as she enters a rundown neighborhood and turns into a cul-de-sac that ends at the river. There's a boxy building that looks like it's been broken into apartments, and across a parking lot, there's a rancher right on the water with a very fancy two-story addition. A pier juts out into the slow moving Luckahannock, and at the end, there's a grizzled old man in a wheelchair.

"Boots!" I swing off the trike and go running. I haven't seen Boots in years. He always used to smoke me up back in the day and tell me stories about following the Dead.

He's fishing. Well, he's holding a pole, but he has a beer in the other hand, and by the way he startles as I go pounding down the wood slats, he was dozing.

"Boots!"

He grins, and this guy has the best smile. It's goofy as hell, teeth missing, but as innocent and joyful as a baby. He doesn't look any older than he was when I left town, but he was old as shit then.

"Wild child!"

I'm not sure if he remembers me. He knew my name back in the day, but he always called me wild child.

"What are you doing?" I plop down next to him, slide off

my white sneakers, and dangle my feet over the side, dipping my toes in the river. It's deliciously freezing.

"Drinking for fish. Fishing for beer." He wrinkles his weathered forehead. "I don't know, baby. I was lost in my dreams."

"Good dreams?"

"Oh, yeah. Always. Help yourself." He bumps a red cooler with a wheel. "And hand me another while you're at it."

I grab myself a cold one and crack one open for him.

There's a heron swooping in for a landing, and a gentle breeze rustling the trees. I close my eyes and tilt my head back to soak in the sun.

"You been gone awhile, haven't you?" Boots hands me his pole. I lift it high enough to see he still has a worm on the hook. I give it another cast, but I'm rusty. It doesn't go far.

"Yup. Ten years."

"You married with kids now? All boring?"

I laugh. "Nope."

"I got myself a grandkid."

"Oh, yeah? Charge gave you a grandbaby?"

"Yup. His name's Jimmy. He's got a good head on his shoulders."

"That's a good thing to have."

"I don't know. You and me done okay without one, yeah?" He snorts and nudges my arm with a wheel.

"It does seem so." I smile, enjoying the prickle of my skin warming, listening to the soft lap of waves against the river-bank. Far away, a screen door slams. I wonder what Shirlene is doing in the house. I should go see if she needs help, but it's so peaceful here.

"That's what's wrong with this new generation. They

can't live in the moment. They always got plans and shit."

"Plans are for suckers."

"Amen, sister." Boots holds out his beer. I bump my can to his. We both chug. He beats me, but not by much. "You get it."

"Hasn't gotten me anywhere." I smile ruefully and tug on the line. No bites yet.

"Got you back here. 'Bout time. Forty's asshole is clenched so tight he's turning his shits to diamonds."

I snort. I'd kind of been thinking that Boots had no idea who I was. "I don't know. I saw him last night. He gave me a lot of shit. No diamonds."

Boots cackles. "You keep at him, girl. Boy's not totally lost it yet. Not like Heavy."

"Heavy's lost it?"

"Yeah. It's a sad thing." Boots shakes his head, but his eyes twinkle. "He talks all the time about 'the performance gap' and 'untapped markets.' He don't make no sense no more."

"If Forty's that far gone, I think I'll leave him alone."

"Nah. You keep at him, girl. Give him what he needs, he'll come around."

"What is it that he needs?"

"You know, girl. You got that free spirit. You tell me."

I turn and look up at Boots. His long, gray hair is tied back in a lank ponytail, and he's wearing his cut over a motheaten undershirt. His jeans are safety pinned at the knees. His lazy smile reaches ear-to-ear.

"Crazy love?"

"Sweet, crazy love," he agrees. "Remind him why the Lord made us."

"I don't know, Boots. I might be fresh out of sweet, crazy love."

"Bullshit, girl. You can grow it yourself."

"Like weed?"

"Like weed." He chuckles, and then he hoots, pointing past me. "Bite! Bite! Pull up!"

I yank, but the fish is too quick for me. I lose the worm. "Damn it."

"Cast again, girl. While the sun shines and you got bait, you got as many more chances as you'll take."

I do, and I get another nibble or two while Boots and I polish off two more beers a piece, but I don't catch anything. He tells me all about Charge's old lady, Kayla, and her son Jimmy. They live with him, but Jimmy's at camp, and Kayla's taking classes at Shady Gap State, studying social work.

Apparently, Shirlene doesn't have to come over and look after him anymore, but Shirlene says Kayla has enough on her plate, and she doesn't mind helping.

Boots thinks Shirlene's carrying a torch for him. I doubt it, but the world is wonderful and strange.

After two hours or so, she hollers for me, helmet in hand.

"Want me to roll you back to the house?"

"How many beers I got left?"

"Two."

"Nah. Leave me here. Hand me back that pole. You're a terrible fisherman, wild child."

"They always slip away."

"'Cause your heart ain't in it. When you're all in, your hand's more firm on the rod."

"Well, the fish were lucky today, then."

"Lucky fish," Boots chuckles and tilts his cheek for a kiss. I drop one, and he slaps my ass for good measure. "Tell Shirlene I love her."

"Will do."

I grab our empties, crack another cold one and put it in the cup holder attached to Boots' wheelchair, and I skip back to where Shirlene's sitting on the trike, gloves, helmet, and sunglasses on.

"Ready for our next stop?"

"Yup." I've got nothing else going on.

We head into town, stopping at the pharmacy to pick up a prescription, and then we visit Ray Bayliss, a real old timer. He was a founding member of the MC. He's at least eighty-five, maybe older, and he's a hoarder. After Shirlene makes him take his meds and lay down for a spell, she and I tackle a corner of his living room.

You can see that Shirlene's been at this awhile. There's a rental dumpster in the side yard that's mostly full. She says Ray won't let anyone else in the house, but she rolled the dice with me, since I'm pretty, and "he's old and crazy as a shithouse rat, but he's still a man."

After Ray's, Shirlene buys me a sandwich at Duck's diner. While we're waiting for our BLTs, she hands me thirty bucks' cash, and asks me if I'm up for more tomorrow.

"Like a job?"

"Like a job."

"How many old guys are you taking care of?"

"I don't know. A dozen or so. Not all guys. Some old ladies, too. And I keep an eye on Hobs so Aunt Carol gets a respite."

"He's no better?"

"Not much."

Hobs is Heavy and Harper's younger brother. When he was in high school, a Rebel Raider took a baseball bat to his skull. Traumatic brain injury. He was another victim of the war between Steel Bones and the Raiders. Poor kid. Senseless.

"Yeah. I'll help you tomorrow."

"Wear grungy clothes. While I've got you, we're gonna go back to Ray's. Attack that kitchen."

"Holy Lord."

"He can't help you. Only bleach and an N95 mask can." Shirlene sneaks an arm across the table and pats my hand. "You hangin' in there?"

"I'm a tough cookie." I crunch on my pickle.

"You in trouble?"

"I'm always in trouble."

"You need a gun? I got one in my purse."

"Shit, Shirlene. Lower your voice." I glance around the diner, but it's mostly empty at this point in the afternoon.

"Relax, city girl. This is still a concealed carry state."

"I don't need a gun." Probably. Maybe. "But I'll take the job."

"All right. But if you change your mind, ask. End of the day, a woman has to rely on herself."

She digs back into her rice pudding, ignoring me, and I take the opportunity to soak her in. Unlike Boots, she looks older. Her silver hair doesn't have the shine it used to, and she has age spots on her cheeks. Her elbows seem like the bones are wearing through the skin.

She's still a tough broad, but there's a carefulness to her movements that's new.

Who's been making sure that Shirlene takes care of herself?

"I'll do the driving tomorrow, okay?"

Shirlene narrows her eyes. "You got a problem with my driving?"

"Not at all. I love a leisurely drive in the country with Grandma."

She flips me the bird and then waves the waitress over to

wrap up her leftover sandwich. She makes sure to do five miles over the speed limit all the way back to her house.

She makes me take half a frozen banana bread home to Lou. I have to admit, I'm feeling kind of lonely as I head for Barrow Road. The day was nearly perfect. It's easy being with people from the club. It sucks so hard most of them dropped me like a hot potato. I'm taking the long way home, rocking out to outlaw country, feeling sorry for myself, when I get a call from Fay-Lee.

"Girl! Up for round two?"

A second ago, before she called, I'd been planning on drowning my sorrows in salt and vinegar potato chips, so round two sounds pretty good. I love Fay-Lee. She's bean-pole skinny with the thickest hick accent I've ever heard and the devil in her eyes. She speaks to me on a deep, deep level.

"Hell, yes," I say, no hesitation. "What do you have in mind?"

"Last night did not go quite as planned."

"Are you okay? You didn't get in trouble for bringing me around the clubhouse, did you?"

I don't think that was what was going on, but Dizzy sure did yank her up as soon as he saw us waltz in. I know him from back in the day, and he was never violent. More of a downtrodden, sad dad type than a wife beater. It sure looked like he was gonna wail on her ass, though.

"Just a little. And just the kind of trouble I like. No worries."

"Is this a kink thing?"

"Oh, yeah."

"Cool." I don't judge. Variety is the spice of life.

"So what happened after I left?" she asks.

"You mean after your man threw you over his shoulder and started tanning your hide?"

She snickers. "You saw that, did you?"

"Everyone saw that."

"Wouldn't be the first time. So, quit stalling. Did Forty see you? Were there fireworks?"

"He wasn't there. Three chicks jumped me, and then Heavy broke it up and kicked me out."

"Well, that sucks."

"Yeah. But Forty came by my place later."

She squeals. "Fireworks?"

"He honked his horn a lot. And told me to stay away."

"But in a hot, smoldering, filled-with-longing kind of way?"

A picture flashes in my mind—Forty standing on the front walk, ramrod straight, shoulders squared and chest raised, his eyes eating me up. Devouring me. My pussy spasms.

"Yeah. Pretty much."

Fay-Lee screeches so loud I snatch the phone from my ear. "This is gonna be *epic*. I'm gonna pull off the greatest shenanigans Steel Bones has ever seen. Harper Ruth thinks she's the puppet master. She ain't nothin'!"

I disagree. Besides being a lawyer, Harper Ruth is a perfect ten and a next-level evil bitch. She was off at college when I was with Forty, but whenever she came back on break, she'd sow chaos and gnaw on the bones of unsuspecting sweetbutts. She's legend.

"What are you even talking about?" If Harper's involved, I'm out.

"Okay. Let me back up. You know Crista Holt, right?"

Of course. Crista is Shirlene's niece and the daughter of Pig Iron, the club treasurer, and Deb, the woman who actually manages the money. Crista's younger than me by a few years. Her older sister Annie was one of the reasons I left town. Annie's not afraid to go for your eyes, and she wears inch-long acrylics.

Anyway, not long after I skipped out, Crista was attacked by the Rebel Raiders MC. Retaliation for something. What they did to Crista...it was brutal. Lou told me about it, and he was shaken up. Crista almost died.

"Sure. What about her?"

"We're taking her dancing tonight. To Sawdust on the Floor." Sawdust is a honkytonk with five-dollar pitchers of beer and an extremely lax carding policy. Every Petty's Mill high schooler's first drink at a bar is at Sawdust, whether you're into country music or not.

"Okay. And how does this count as shenanigans?"

"Because Crista *never* goes out. Scrap Allenbach is gonna hear about it, he'll show up, and boom! Fireworks!"

Scrap is the one who killed the Rebel Raider who attacked Crista. He recently finished his sentence. According to Lou, it's been awkward. It was supposed to be this romantic reunion, but Crista wasn't having it.

"Okay. I'm down. But this does not seem like Harper Ruth-caliber shenanigans."

Back in the day, during the first wave of clubhouse renovations, Harper finagled it so the brothers demolished a wall at the exact moment Creech was getting a blowjob from Pam, Cue's grandmother. The logistics alone boggle the mind.

"Keep up, Nevaeh. Scrap is gonna show up with his boys. No one'll want to miss this show. Forty'll be there, and he'll see you, and boom! More fireworks!"

"Won't Dizzy get pissed at you?"

"Yup, and boom! Orgasms!"

There are a lot of ways this could end in disaster.

"You're in, right?" she asks.

"Oh, yeah."

I haven't been in a bar brawl in a few years. And I haven't been country line dancing since I was seventeen and polishing off five-dollar pitchers at Sawdust.

A few hours later, I've learned a few things. First, Crista's dog Frances is ah-flippin'-dorable. He's a blood-hound with ears like an elephant. I want to snack on him at midnight.

Second, Crista's in a bad way. She's even twitchier than I am, always looking over her shoulder. I can identify. I'm fairly sure Carlo and the Renellis are in my rearview—if they were seriously looking, with their resources, they would have found me by now—but I've still been waking up in a cold sweat. I kind of wish I didn't get a new number when I left town. As it is, I don't know if they're looking for me or not.

I deleted my social media, the whole shebang. I know they can find me if they want to, but I wanted to send a message that I'm gone, and I've got no intention of being a problem.

And the final thing I've learned in the past hour or so? When push comes to shove, after all this time? I haven't learned a thing.

It's all Forty's fault. An hour ago, he strolled in with some of the brothers—Heavy, Dizzy, Creech, Wall, Scrap, and a couple prospects—and now, I've gone stupid.

He's sitting at a table, his back to the wall, surveying the room and ignoring me. I'm dancing, and yeah, I put a little more shake in my booty than strictly necessary, but I'm playing it cool.

And then Scrap convinces Crista to dance. It's so damn cute. She doesn't know how to move her feet, and he's way more confident than he should be. He's smiling just for her, and her lips are finally curling up, the first hint she's having fun I've seen all night.

I feel a little glow in my chest, and my feet really find the rhythm—point-cross, rock-back, heel-dig—as the man in a black shirt and silver bolo tie calls out the steps from a low stage along the far wall.

I'm sweating, my breath's coming quick, and all my limbs are loose. I get that dancing high. Life is good.

Maybe Forty and I aren't meant to be civil, but it's a small town, and maybe there's room for us all. I can put down roots. I can make friends.

Fay-Lee's nowhere to be seen. Dizzy hauled her off as soon as he spotted her. She'll be back, though. We're gonna have a great time, and everyone'll get over themselves, and she'll be my bestie.

Maybe this thing with Shirlene will pan out. Become a full-time gig.

With the fiddle singing, the boots stomping, and the hoots and yelps, everything seems bright and happy and possible. My body's buzzing just from Forty being in the same room. Also, the beers.

My hair's sticking to my damp forehead, so I shake it out and accidentally make eye contact with a man dancing near me. I grin 'cause it's ridiculous. It must have looked like a stripper hair flip.

The guy's about my age, built, with a red beard and freckles. He grins back and dips his head, cowboy-style. This is fun. I hope they play Garth Brooks next. Do they take requests? I scoot and stomp, and then I make the mistake of glancing at the table where Steel Bones are sitting.

Shit.

Shivers shoot down my spine like someone dumped a bucket of ice water over my head.

There are at least seven huge-ass bikers glaring daggers at me as if they're seconds from flipping the table and throwing me out on my ass. Heavy, Nickel, Creech, all of them except Forty who's purposefully staring over at the bar. People have cleared out of the tables nearest them, and everyone in the vicinity is shooting them wary looks.

Ah, crap. Back in the day, Steel Bones wasn't down with attacking women. But like Lou says, a lot has changed. My heart kicks into gear, and adrenaline shoots through my veins. Fight or flight. This isn't for show. These aren't the hard faces the guys put on with their cuts and wallet chains. There's hate in their eyes. Banked violence. Scorn.

I should make sure Crista's okay and bail. She seems all right now that Scrap's here. Fay-Lee drove, but I bet there's someone hanging around out front who I know somehow. Petty's Mill is a small town. Already tonight I've seen my old bus driver and a handful of people I went to school with. Someone will give me a ride, and if not, I can call Lou. Shit. Petty's Mill is way bigger than it used to be. Maybe the town has ride share by now.

While my brain's spinning like a top and my feet are going nowhere, Steel Bones is shifting in their seats, all menace and hostility. Creech is spitting something in Heavy's ear, animated, the gauges in his ears flapping as he gesticulates toward me. Heavy narrows his eyes. People start cutting *me* wary glances.

Yeah, now would be a good time to get gone.

Forty's still staring at a wall so his face is in profile. His jaw's clenched so hard the muscles in his neck have popped out. He's not wearing business casual tonight. He's got on a black T-shirt under his cut. His biceps are straining against cotton, his hands rest motionless on the table. It's weird how someone can *sit* at attention. He's doing it though.

My belly swooshes. It's part justifiable fear, part extremely ill-advised excitement. I want him to look at me. I want to mess up his perfect control.

He sits there, ignoring me, surrounded by people who have his back without question. Hard as stone. Like when he blocked my number. *Nevaeh, we're done.* Click. The end.

He's staring at the top shelf liquor now. In case I was unclear about whether I'm worth noticing. I'm not.

Dick.

You know what? I wonder if he's really not watching.

I wonder what he'd do if one of his brothers comes after me. Bet he'll look at me then.

The gentleman in the bolo tie calls out, "Now shake your booty."

Yes, sir. Perfect timing. I can do that. I amp it up to ten, make it pop.

The redheaded guy hollers, "Shake it, don't break it, sister." Unlike the folks at the tables, he doesn't seem to notice there's a motorcycle gang fixin' to murder me.

I laugh as loud as I can, and I'm not even faking 'cause the line was funny in a cheesy way, and truth be told, I'm really tipsy and a lot high on life. There's another ominous shifting from the Steel Bones table, but I don't care. A tic has shown up in Forty's temple. Bingo. My man has great peripheral vision.

My man? Where did that come from?

Doesn't matter. The genie is out of the bottle. My heart's racing, and there's tingles dancing across my skin. Men and women are swirling and colors are bright and blurry. Finally, the world's moving at my speed, and I can surf the music and laughter and danger like a wave. I shimmy my shoulders, and throw my head back.

Oh, yeah. I'm about to make some bad decisions.

"What's your name?" Red Beard asks, easing over to me, smiling wide and flirty.

"Nevaeh." Toe, heel, step left, step right, grapevine. I'm singing along to the song. Where did I learn the words?

I let my body go. It feels so good.

I've been nothing but well-behaved. All I do is clean the house, and until the beers I had with Fay-Lee when we first rolled up tonight—and those few with Boots, and a couple with Lou—I haven't been drinking.

I don't want the fun to end. It's not too much to ask.

Forty wants to pretend I don't exist? Let his boys menace me from across the room? Whatever. I'm gonna shake my ass just for him, and when they come for me, I'm not gonna go quietly.

I can take 'em. I can take the whole world.

Heavy and Nickel and the rest of them are all about loyalty? Bullshit. Back in high school, they watched me spiral, and except for Shirlene, no one said shit. No one asked me what the hell I was doing. They ran straight to Forty and told him to kick me to the curb.

I own my fuck ups, I do, but maybe it's okay to be a little mad, too. A little spiteful.

I catch Red Beard's eye and swing my hips, really swoop and jiggle. His smile's eating up his face now. He rakes his eyes down my front, licking his lips in appreciation.

I dressed to impress tonight, dark blue painted-on jeans, a drapey top with spaghetti straps in emerald green, and brown cowgirl boots with fringe. No bra and a thong so I've got no panty lines.

Damn straight he should be smiling. I'm a snack.

I'd feel bad about leading him on if he didn't seem so cocksure. It's not gonna crush this guy when I cut things off after a dance or two. I'm kind of hoping for a slow dance when the guitars and twang fades, and to my utter surprise, a fat beat drops instead.

A holler rises to the rafters and people flood the dance floor. Holy shit. We're doing this? In Petty's Mill? All right. Let's wobble.

The caller sets down his mic and takes a swig from a water bottle. Everyone knows the steps to this one apparently. We all fall in line as a dude growls at us from the speakers to back it up and drop it down.

I back it *all* the way up, and drop it *all* the way down.

Damn. I've done this dance at weddings, but never surrounded by boomers and rednecks in big silver belt buckles and cowboy hats.

I'm having so much fun, legit fun for the first time in I don't know how long. I kind of forget about Forty and Steel Bones, and I get lost in my body, the burn in my thighs, the scuff and tap of my boots. Crista's beside me dancing, too, watching my feet, and it feels great, being the one who knows what to do.

Her cheeks are pink, and she's lost that jumpy vibe. She seems younger somehow. She's really pretty when she's relaxed.

"You doin' all right?" I ask.

She nods.

"Having a good time?"

She shrugs and smiles softly. Score! I got Crista Holt to smile.

I go back to shaking my ass in dramatic, mind-boggling fashion, and then the song is over and the music slows.

"Now grab your girls, fellas," the man in the bolo tie says.

I turn to check on Crista, but Scrap is there. Red Beard ambles over and holds out his hand. I take it. Why not? He pulls me a little closer than I want, but I love this song, and we're in the middle of a dance floor. I focus on the feet of a lady nearby. I'm not really familiar with the two-step, and the caller isn't helping on this one either.

"Just follow my lead, sweetheart," Red Beard purrs into my ear, and when he steps forward, his thigh slides between my legs. What? Gross.

I kind of hop backwards, but he's wound his arm around my back like a vise, and he's lunging forward. This is not what I want.

I scan the dance floor for Crista or Fay-Lee to give her them "rescue me" look, but I swivel my head too fast, and my hair flies in my face. I'm pushing curls out of my eyes while simultaneously ducking Red Beard's invading leg when I see Scrap leading Crista off the dance floor.

She looks terrified, but she's holding his hand. She catches my eye, and her brow furrows with concern.

Oh, she's being brave. My heart fizzes. I can handle Red Beard. I wave and blow her a kiss.

A new song starts, and I try to ease away, but Red Beard's not taking the hint. He's grappling me closer when an enormous hand clamps down on my shoulder, squeezing hard.

The hand yanks me back as Nickel and Creech appear on either side of Red Beard. They don't need to touch him. Red Beard sure as hell notices them now, and he backs off like his pants are on fire. I catch it all in the nanosecond before Heavy spins me to face him.

"What the fuck are you doing, Nevaeh?"

My back is to Forty now, and I resist the urge to search for him over my shoulder. He's made himself clear. I don't exist. Instead, I tilt my head up and up to glare at a glowering, righteously pissed off Heavy Ruth.

My stomach drops. Shit. This just got real.

Heavy Ruth is a giant. Like a literal giant from a fantasy novel. His hair's longer, blacker, and wilder than mine, and usually, his face is unnaturally calm. Inscrutable behind a thick, black beard. He's the mastermind of Steel Bones. Not in this moment, though. Right now, his mouth is twisted in a snarl, and there's pure disgust in his eyes.

"'A wise woman builds her home, but a foolish woman tears it down with her own hands,'" he quotes.

I see he's still in the habit of reciting Scripture. He used to have us rolling when we smoked up by the bonfire. *Every moving thing that liveth shall be meat for you; even as the green herb have I given you all things.*

"A wise man fucks off and minds his own damn business." As established, when backed into a corner, I don't get smarter. Panic sweat breaks out behind my knees.

"No one's interested in watching you show off. You need to get gone, Nevaeh."

"You're not the boss of me." Seriously? I've got great comebacks tonight. At least my voice doesn't break.

"We can make a scene if that's what you want. I know you crave the attention."

Ouch. That one hits a little close to home.

"You're the one making this an issue. I'm only dancing. This town's big enough for the both of us."

Okay. So now I'm a sheriff about to have a shootout on Main Street?

Heavy drops his voice and steps to me, toe to toe. "This is *my* town, and you're not welcome in it. You can make this easy, or you can make this hard. Please. Make it hard." He smiles, and I swear, his teeth are pointed like a wolf's. My gaze skitters around the room, searching for a friendly face. Fay-Lee. My old school bus driver.

Everyone's backed away and staring. The music's play-

ing, but only the totally jaded old timers are still two-step-
ping. Shit. This is a scene.

And Forty's nowhere to be seen. Guess he left his
brothers to do his dirty work. My heart kind of falls and
splats like a deflated ball.

"What are you gonna do, Heavy? Pick me up and throw
me out in front of half of Petty's Mill? Everybody's gonna be
really impressed at the big, strong man tossing around a
hundred-twenty-pound woman." I haven't weighed one-
twenty since high school, but I'm exaggerating for effect
here.

"Nobody'll say a word. You're nothin', Nevaeh. You're no
one. You should pack up and go back to Pyle. There's no
place here for a woman who'd fuck around on her man
when he's off servin' his country."

There's an audible gasp from a middle-aged couple
pretending not to eavesdrop nearby. Heavy's purposefully
projecting his voice. My scarlet A's getting polished tonight.
Damn.

"Back off, Heavy. Live your life, and let me live mine."

He leans closer, looms over me. I want to curl into a ball,
but I puff my chest and fold my arms. There's no way he's
going to hurt me in a public place. Probably.

"You ain't gonna strut around this town again, fuckin'
with my boy's head. He sacrificed for his country. You get
that at all? He almost died. He's home now. And he's not
gonna have to deal with you, I promise you that. Game's
over, sweetheart."

And then he grabs my upper arm, not too tight that it
hurts, but tight enough that I have no hope of wriggling
loose.

"Time to go home." He frog-marches me toward the
door, my feet tripping to keep up. It happens so quickly, I've

got no time to fight or comply. I'm being herded along toward the back exit like a toddler. The crowd parts to let us through.

Oh, crap. There's always scads of smokers out front. Out back? I'm gonna be all alone. Would Steel Bones hurt me if there are no witnesses? I don't know anymore.

Why do I keep getting myself into these kinds of situations? I have a death wish. That must be it.

As we near the hall to the bathrooms, I start to struggle in earnest, scrabbling against the wood floors, trying to dig in my heels. When that doesn't work, I go limp. Hot damn. My arms are going to pop out of my shoulder sockets. I open my mouth to scream, painfully aware of how futile that's going to be, when a solid figure blocks our path.

"Drop her."

Immediately, I'm dropped flat on my ass. Oh, ouch. My hair bounces, temporarily blinding me, as I scramble back to my feet. I wrangle the curls back and tug my top so it's straight.

It's Forty. Looks like he just came out of the men's room. My heart starts tripping in a whole new beat. He's standing like a soldier again, but his face is black with rage and his eyes are flashing. Oh, I know this look. He's *pissed*.

"I got this." His voice is clipped, pitched way deeper than it was last night. He's furious. At Heavy? At me?

Ice water douses the sliver of relief that had sprung in my chest. This isn't a rescue.

Boots stomp off behind me. Forty glares. The tic in his jaw pulses. Yeah, he's mad at me.

"Uh. Thanks?"

It's like I said the un-magic word. Forty swoops forward, throws me over his shoulder, and strides out the back door. The screen nearly slams into my head, but a hand snakes out and grabs it. A skinny kid with a prospect rocker follows us out to the lot behind the bar.

Forty's rock-solid shoulder grinds into my soft belly with every step he takes, and it's not helping that the world is upside down. I'm gonna puke. Right down the back of Forty's cut. Serves him right.

"Let me down! Asshole!"

The prospect's grinning. He's an asshole, too.

"Wash, watch the door," Forty barks. "Nobody comes out."

"Yes, sir."

"And turn your back."

"Yes, sir!"

Oh, this is not good. I writhe and kick, but all I manage to do is flip myself off his shoulder to go plummeting into the dirt. I yelp as my hip bone slams into the ground hard.

All this man-handling is getting old. My stomach's heaving. My pride's not doing so great either.

"What the hell, Forty?"

"What the hell do *you* think you're doing, Nevaeh?" Forty hauls me to my feet.

The soldier act is gone. He's dropped his emotionless mask, and I'm hypnotized. Little zings light up my chest. There's my man. The one who patiently stood waist-deep in the frigid Luckahannock while I played Tarzan on an old rope swing, catching me or fishing me out of the river every time because I couldn't swim, and I didn't want anyone to know.

Who popped my cherry in a hotel room in Maynard that must have cost him an entire paycheck from Big George's garage.

Who rescued me from Liam Devers in Freshman English.

Anger and hurt and something else, something raw, war in Forty's eyes. He's so handsome. So achingly similar to the boy I loved so damn hard.

"You just won't listen, will you?" Forty growls, his grip tightens on my shoulders, but unlike Heavy, his fingers dig in.

"No," I say. It comes out husky, like a whisper. "I won't."

"How do I make you listen?" It's like he's asking himself, and the sheer bafflement in his voice makes the corner of my lips twitch. He's right. I am a hopeless case.

"I do what I want, Forty. You know that."

"I don't know you at all." The words sting, even though they're true. I lash out on instinct.

"Hard to get to know people when you've got your head so far up your ass."

"Why don't you watch your mouth, Nevaeh?"

"Why don't you make me?" I smirk at him then, the snottiest, brattiest smirk I can manage when my butt's dusty, my hip aches, my spaghetti straps have both fallen down, and his hands are cutting off the circulation to my arms.

For a good five seconds, he's at a loss for words. And then he nods to himself as if he's decided something, and—oh, crap—he's grabbing me again, and he's hauling me over to a rickety picnic table a yard or so from the dumpsters.

"Remember that you asked for it," he says.

Asked for what?

Forty lowers himself to the bench, and he drags me over his knees, knocking me off balance, and then I'm draped there, his knees digging into my stomach, my hair swinging around my face. I can't see anything. His lap's so broad, and I'm so short, my legs are sticking straight out.

Is he going to *spank* me?

"Works for Dizzy," he mutters, and then his hand

wallops my behind. Hard. My teeth snap shut, and I taste copper. I bit my tongue.

"What are you doing?" I buck, and his arm tightens over my shoulder blades like a bar of steel.

"Stay still." He nails me again, this time on the other cheek, and this one hurts more than it surprises me. It reminds me of falling down when you're roller skating, that kind of blunt whack that clears your sinuses.

Am I okay with this? We used to play around with rough stuff when we were together. We didn't have safe words or anything. Didn't know we were supposed to.

I could just say stop. He would. I'm ninety-nine percent sure. But then this would be over. And I don't want that.

Thwack. I sniff back the tears that spring to my eyes. I can't believe this is happening. I jerk, but all I can do is raise my hips and give him a better target as his hand comes down again. I shriek this time.

I kick, but I can only twist so far before he forces me straight again. I'm a doll, and he's Goliath.

"This isn't funny!"

"Isn't meant to be." He lays down three or four more quick ones, and it smarts, really bad, but he doesn't know me. Or he doesn't remember. I *never* know when enough is enough.

His jean-clad leg is eye level, and I yank those pants up and sink my nails into his calves. His leg muscles are as hard as the rest of him, but his skin's no thicker than a normal man's. He grunts, and I gouge my nails deeper. Maybe his skin *is* thicker. I'm getting nowhere.

He fights back with a huge wallop—a jarring impact followed a second later by searing pain—and I'm distracted so much I let go of his leg.

He lays down another thwack, and ouch, ouch, ouch. I

can't take much more. Fay-Lee is into this? Holy hell. Girl-friend is insane.

I scramble for Forty's leg again, but he's wised up and tucked it behind the other so I can't get the pants up again. I flail my arms, but I can't get a shot. My eyes are leaking. I don't want to cry. I don't want to give him the satisfaction.

I chomp down on the side of Forty's thigh, getting a big mouthful of denim. I bear down, but it's like biting a fabric-covered log.

"Stop that." Forty doles out several swats in quick succession on my left cheek, and my ass is throbbing now, burning. Snot's mixing with my tears, and it's hard to breathe, but I'm not giving up.

"Make me!" I angle a leg and manage to nail his arm with my boot heel as he lands a sharp smack.

I shriek and struggle with all my might.

And the weirdest thing happens.

In between the bursts of pain? My body's coming alive, sizzling with energy and adrenaline. Oh, hello sensation. My favorite drug. Waves explode over me, heightening every feeling, blocking everything out except this.

I'm pinned in place, my ass is on fire, and my skin's hot all over. I'm sinking my teeth into impossibly hard flesh, clawing and bucking and flailing, landing a blow here and there, and it hurts so bad, but on the other hand, it's ecstasy.

My brain is perfectly clear. There's only this.

I'm out of control, but I don't need to be in control. For once, I'm not failing at anything. I'm not scared. I'm angry, mindlessly pissed, and every smack keeps me anchored in this moment. The static and chatter and constant zigzagging thoughts are quiet for once.

Forty's talking, but it's background noise.

"You're not going to put a wedge between me and my brothers."

Smack.

"You're not going to stir up shit."

Thwack.

"You're going to do as you're told."

There's a rapid clap on my ass punctuating the do-as-you're-told. I scream, but it's muffled by the denim. God, it feels *good* to scream at the top of my lungs.

"Understood?"

I'm jerking my hips to try and lessen the impact, but his hand is huge, and my ass is huger. Each blow *stings*. Should I say yes? Yes. I should say yes.

If I say yes, he stops.

"Do it harder!" I shout at the top of my lungs. "I love it! More!"

"Not funny, Nevaeh!" He slaps the hell out of my upper thigh, and, ouch, ouch, ouch, that's a hell of a tender spot.

"You're not funny either!" I'm just talking complete shit now. "You're a bully and a jerk and no fun and your friends are bullies, too."

"Yeah? Yeah?"

I'm about dig my hole deeper when he shoves his hand between us, pops the button of my jeans, and drags them down until they get stuck around my knees. I stop kicking.

My chest is heaving, but the rest of me freezes in place.

The night air is cool against my burning ass. I squeeze my cheeks together, wincing with the pain and bracing for a really nasty blow, but instead, a low groan rattles Forty's chest. My breath catches.

Then his palm gently cups my bottom. His hand is cool, too, against my hot skin. I halfheartedly jerk my hips away, but I only end up pressing myself more firmly into his grip, and damn, that smarts! But it's also his hand on my bare ass. Forty's touching me, and a giddiness rises, a physical memory. Recent events notwithstanding, my stupid body vividly remembers that whenever this man touches us, we feel good.

"Your ass is really red," Forty murmurs, his voice raspy and raw. Almost reverent.

"Yeah?" I kick my feet and get nothing but air. Forty ignores me, trailing his fingers over the swell of my ass to my bare thighs. I kick again on principle.

"Be still now."

"Get off me." I wriggle a little, but my heart's not in it. I'm focused on those rough fingers, stroking down the back of one thigh then up again to cup my burning ass. A different kind of heat kindles between my legs. Oh, lord. At some point, my pussy got wet. There's no way he can't tell.

He smooths a rough hand over my aching hip. "You've got a bruise here."

"You dropped me on the ground."

"You did it to yourself. I would have put you down easy."

His fingers wander higher, dancing up my spine. A shiver races ahead of his touch. At some point, I stopped fighting. I'm draped limp across his lap, and is that his cock? Oh, yeah. A hard length presses into my belly. I remember what that feels like. My pussy spasms, and I choke back a moan. With all the snot and tears, it sounds like a sob.

"Are you crying?" In an instant, Forty flips me, cradling me in his arms, pushing my hair away so he can examine my face. His brow is knitted, alarm in his eyes.

"No." I glare at him. He doesn't get to worry about me now, when it's way too late and the damage is done.

He keeps searching my face, somber and intense. He used to do this whenever I tripped or cut myself or fell. I *am* accident prone. He'd poke and prod until he'd reassured himself that I wasn't seriously hurt, and then he'd slap my ass and say, "Rub some dirt in it. You'll be fine."

I guess he decides I'll be okay because he grunts and grabs the hem of his T-shirt, yanking it up to wipe my cheeks. I get an eyeful of perfectly defined abs and the edge of an ugly, puckered scar. That must be the injury that got him discharged from the Army. I squirm. The scar was bad. Really bad. Way worse than his arm.

"What's this then?" he says, holding up his damp shirt. "Always lying, aren't you." Despite his words, he doesn't sound mad anymore.

I'm gonna clap back. I search my brain for a retort, any retort, but his mouth is right there, inches from mine.

"It didn't hurt at all," I grumble. He's got a five o'clock shadow, and there's a thin white line in the divot under his nose. That's an old scar; he had it when we met. He got it when his older brother Bullet split his lip.

"You were squealing like a stuck pig."

"I was being dramatic. I did it all for the attention. Isn't that how you all have me pegged?"

"Isn't that how you are?"

"I don't know, Forty. You know me. Is that how I am?"

We're so close. His scruff tickles my nose. I'm on a ledge. No, I'm hanging from the end of a rope, and I'm waiting, breathless. Is he going to catch me?

He closes his dark brown eyes. Leans forward the slightest bit.

"Don't say you don't know me," I murmur against his soft lips.

And he springs into action, wrapping his strong arms around me, clutching me hard against his chest, his mouth on mine, devouring me. Did I start it? Did he? Who cares? He tastes like I remember, but different, and he's as demanding as he was when we were younger, but there's a new hunger now that I can taste on his tongue as he delves into my mouth.

I wriggle and fight against his embrace. I want to touch. I *have to* touch.

At first, he won't give, but then maybe he realizes I'm not going anywhere and he relaxes his arms. I raise myself up so I'm kneeling on his thighs. My jeans have been pushed to my ankles. He braces me with a sturdy forearm propped under my still-stinging ass, and I know he's got me.

It feels so good. There's nothing but him in the entire world. Goodbye garbage thoughts. Goodbye ever-present anxiety that I'm missing something or forgetting or fucking up or annoying.

There's only Forty. The scent of Lava soap and leather fill my nose. My belly does a funny flippy thing, and moisture drips between my legs. My clit pokes through my pussy lips and throbs, tender and needy.

Forty plunges a hand into my hair and draws my head back. Is he pulling me off of him? My heart drops. I don't want this to be over. But no, he's only holding me in place to kiss down my neck, suckling and nibbling, and oh—he remembers what I like.

My body dissolves in shivers, and he chuckles, which makes me quiver more, delicious zings shooting from the sensitive spots where he nips and nuzzles.

We used to do this for hours back when I was too shy to let him put his hand down my pants. It feels even better than it did then. He's doing it 'cause I like it. My heart warms.

I tilt my head, grab him by the nape of his neck, hold him to me, and then there's a bite and a twinge. Is he giving me a hickey? Oh, hell no. I'm a grown-ass woman, I can't have a—a gush spills from my pussy, dribbling down my inner thigh.

"You like that," he growls, and then he slips his fingers between my legs, gliding them through my juices, stroking up and down, grazing my clit, gathering all this want and need as he circles the hard nub that aches for him.

"Yes," I pant, writhing my hips to force his fingers where I want them, but he's following his own plan, gently sliding a finger into me, and then another, and I rock up and grind down, riding those fingers, while his thumb flicks my clit. He was never this coordinated before.

Who taught him this?

No, no. I shove the thought back, drive it away by focusing on the greedy pleasure coiling in my belly.

"You love it, don't you?"

"Yes!" I throw my head back, chase the pulsating ecstasy, let myself go, free falling, and a wave crests inside me as my pussy walls clench, a release and an aftershock of pure, molten amazingness ripples from my core to the tips of my toes and the top of my head. My body is electrified and wrung out at the same time. I blink my eyes open, dopey and grinning.

"You do this with all those Raiders?" Forty's lip is lifted in a sneer.

Oh.

Ouch.

Forty's face is hard, colder than I've seen it yet. And in his eyes? Raw agony.

Before I can react, he stands, and I go tumbling into the dirt, pants down, arms and legs akimbo like a ragdoll. Shame turns my cheeks as hot as my ass.

Welp. Didn't see that coming. This is a new personal low.

Forty snarls, glares at me as if I stubbornly dropped my own ass on the ground. I give him the finger. As I scramble for my jeans, he scoops me up, plopping me on my feet.

"Shit. I didn't mean to drop you. I stood without thinking."

Then he stares at me a few seconds in consternation, hands gripping my upper arms, holding me in place. Then, he gently swats my sides, brushing the dust off from where I landed. He smooths my hair back, tucking a few curls behind my ear. It's useless. They spring free immediately.

He leans over for my jeans and begins to ease them up.

I bend over, too, almost knocking my forehead into his. "I can do that."

"Let me." He bats my hands away, and he works my pants the rest of the way up, careful when he gets to my tender ass. Then, he buttons the button and zips the zipper.

"I'm sorry." He adjusts my spaghetti straps although they're fine. His fingers skim lightly up my neck and across my cheek, so quickly the touch almost doesn't register.

"So...we good now, or what?" I summon up a doofy smile. It's weak, but I mean it.

His fingers return to a sore spot on my neck. He swipes it with the pad of his thumb. He's gazing intently at what must be a doozy of a hickey, his disgust gone, his mask dropped, a look like grief shining in his eyes. A lump lodges in my throat, and my eyes prickle.

He sighs. "No. Not good. Stay away from me, Nevaeh. We're no good for each other. I end up hurting you. You end up hurting me."

And then he smooths my hair, tucking an errant clump of curls behind my ear, before he stalks back into the bar. I stand there, my heart leaking cold into my chest, staring after him.

The screen door slams, and the prospect comes loping toward me. Oh, great. Just what I need. An audience.

"Forty says take you home," he says, smirking like an idiot.

"Saw that, did you?" I reach in my pocket to make sure I still have my ID and the change from the twenty I used to pay the cover. I don't want to come back here. Ever. I want to go home and hide under the covers and then run as far away as my crappy little Hyundai can take me.

"Nope." The prospect snickers. "Heard it, though. You wanna ride standing on the pegs, I got no problem with that."

Sad patchy-bearded, barely-pubescent, chicken-legged smartass.

"I'm not riding anywhere with you." I take off around the building. I hate this feeling. I hate all of these feelings.

He has to trot to catch up with me. "Forty said."

"Unlike you, Forty doesn't tell me what to do."

"You better."

I stop in my tracks and look the little shit in the eye. "I *never* do what I better. Fuck your ride, fuck you, and when you see him, tell Forty Nowicki I let a hundred men fuck me when we were together."

The little shit has nothing to say to that.

"In the ass."

I take off again. "And I loved it," I throw over my shoulder.

You know what? If I've got a Scarlet A, I'm gonna wear the hell out of it.

∿

I STAY mad for almost six hours.

That's how my brain works. Sleep is an automatic reset. I could feel any sort of way the night before, but in the morning, I'm base model Nevaeh. Ready for action right after coffee.

I figure Forty will drop by. Or call. Or text. Last night was intense. I know what he said, but how is he going to stay away? There's no way he didn't feel that. It was like two pieces sliding together and going clink.

I wait around the house for him all day. Not a peep. He's probably being stubborn.

The next morning, I call Shirlene first thing, and we go out and work on Ray's house. I figure when Forty drops by, it'll serve him right that I'm not there. Lou's home all day. No Forty.

Screw him.

The next day, Shirlene takes me to visit Mona Wall. She has two little ones under two. She brought the newest one home a month ago, and this lady is *sleep deprived*. Crazy happy, and very sweet, but she has a congealed gob of what looks like Velveeta cheese in her hair—in her bangs—and she's run her hand through it several times and not noticed.

We watch Hope and baby Trip while Mona takes a nap. Trip sleeps on Shirlene's stomach while Hope and I play "what is this, what can we stick it in, and what sound does it make when we knock it over."

I know Forty will be there when I get home. Or he'll have left a note. Or called Lou and asked for my number.

Nope. And nope. And nope.

The next day, I take a break from home healthcare. That's what Shirlene calls our rounds. She's talking to me about the classes I need to take to make it all legit. I could do them at the community college, and it would only take a few months.

I like the idea, but on days like today, it's hard to see that far ahead. I can't pull myself together. I fill the tub with scrubbing bubbles, let it set for a few minutes to soak in, and forget about it until after lunch. Pretty much the same thing with the laundry and the dishwasher.

By early evening, I give up. I get my ear buds, I give the tub one more rinse, and then I fill it to the top with the hottest water I can tolerate. I never took baths when I lived here before, but I got addicted after I left town.

I exfoliate with a loofah until I'm bright pink. Then I let my eyes drift shut. My brain flips through memories and thoughts like one of those old slide projectors. Forty spanking my ass red. It was still rosy that night when I checked it in the mirror. No distinct hand prints, but an overall glow. I stared for twenty minutes.

Does this mean I'm kinky? I don't want anyone else to spank me.

I guess I'm kinky for Forty Nowicki?

Why is he staying away? I saw his eyes at the end when he was dusting me off. They *recognized* me. It's so hard to describe. Yesterday at Mona Wall's house, baby Trip was gumming Shirlene's finger when his mama rejoined us from her snooze. Trip looked immediately at Mona, and there was that look in his eyes. *It's you. The one who belongs to me. Hi. You're back.*

Forty had that look when he came over the other night, too. Our mouths were moving, and we were spouting our stupid, angsty bull crap, but I swear I could read his eyes. *Hey. There you are.*

My mom never cared that I was hanging out with Forty. Correction. She *hated* him, and she hated that I was friends with bikers and girls who cussed and wore belly shirts. But she didn't care enough to give me a curfew or anything.

Maybe she thought the less time I was home, the better. In a way, she was right.

I ended up crashing at Shirlene's a lot if Forty was away on a bike run or something. Shirlene, for whatever reason, had a "no boys in the bedroom" rule. Shirlene Robard, who dealt marijuana for medical purposes before it was a thing. Shirlene, who has a half sleeve tattoo of the Army emblem in the middle of a burning American flag. *Shirlene* had a no boys policy. People are complicated.

Anyway, one weekend night I was sleeping over at her place. Forty had been away on a job. Heavy's dad had them doing stupid shit. Running black market cigarettes, stuff like that. I was asleep in the guest room under an old quilt. I'd left the window open 'cause I love the feel of being warm under the covers while the night breeze nips at your nose and the tips of your ears.

I was in the middle of a dream when Forty slipped under the quilt with me, scooping me to his chest, dropping kisses down my neck.

I'd told him no boys allowed. He said he wasn't gonna disrespect Shirlene.

He held me all night long, listening to me deliriously ramble on the edge of sleep, for hours it seemed. We were the only two people on the planet, and he could follow what I was saying no matter how tongue-twisted I got, and whatever happened to make him so wild-eyed and spooked when he crawled into bed, I made disappear. When the sun rose, he'd let himself out the window the way he came.

I haven't thought about that night in forever.

What did happen that scared the shit out of him?

Whatever it was, he never told me. His brothers knew. They were definitely there when it went down.

I guess we weren't the only two people on the planet after all.

The water's turned lukewarm. I pop the drain, and I squeeze the water from my hair, wrapping it in an old Budweiser towel. I use a Cap'n Crunch towel to wrap around my body. Guess Mom didn't leave any linens when she left for Florida.

I wash my face with some witch hazel wipes, and I grab my phone. I've still got my ear buds in, although all music is background noise once my brain starts cranking.

I head for the kitchen to get a bowl of cereal—the power of subconscious suggestion—and when I round the corner into the living room, I freeze in place. Dripping on the carpet.

The entire Steel Bones Motorcycle Club is in our house.

Forty's here. He's in the dining room. Heavy and Pig Iron are with him, staring at something on the table. A map?

Big George is by the sofa. Charge and Nickel are leaning on the wall by the kitchen.

They all look up at me in unison.

I clutch my towel, even though it's tucked tightly around my boobs.

I search Forty's expression for clues as to what's going on, and I watch as he shuts down his face. His eyes go blank. His jaw tightens. He turns away.

Oh. Guess whatever this is, it's not about me.

That's when Lou grabs my elbow and hustles me back down the hall. I pluck out my earbuds.

"Why is Forty here?"

"Club business."

"Why is there club business in our house?"

He shrugs and pulls me into the room I've been crashing in. "Here." He reaches in his wallet and takes out a twenty. "Go into town and get yourself a few drinks. Gimme a call in a few hours. I'll let you know if the coast is clear."

"Why am I leaving my house for Steel Bones' club business?"

"You're not." The vein at Lou's temple tics. "You're leaving *my* house because *I* asked you nicely."

"I can't believe you pulled the *my house* card!"

"You were the one who left. You were the one who cut Mom and Dad off."

And there's another choice. Tell or don't tell. Take the twenty and go get beers or ruin Lou's memory of his dad. I take the bill.

"I need a minute to get dressed."

"Go out the back."

"I'll go out whatever door I want."

Lou waves his hand at me and goes back to whatever drama's going down in our dining room. I take my sweet time pulling on skinny jeans and pink crop top. I tug my hair into a ponytail—the dryer's in the bathroom—and then I leave. Out the back.

Then I creep around the house to the dining room window.

The sun's gone down, and the lights are blazing in the house, so I can see everyone clearly. Nickel looks like he's about to punch a wall. Charge seems to be talking him down. Big George is pacing, yakking on the phone.

Forty, Heavy, and Pig Iron are still leaning over the table, pointing at the map or whatever like generals in an old war movie. Forty and Heavy seem to be disagreeing. They're something to watch.

When I left town, Heavy was an impressive guy, but he

wasn't this oversized character of legend. He used to be kind of nerdy for a redneck. He was so hulking, he was always careful not to bump you. He walked like a waiter holding a full tray.

Now, he's an extra on a Viking series or video game hero with superhuman strength.

Forty's changed, too. In a different way. He's a machine. It's not only how he carries himself, which screams *soldier*. It's not just his ability to shutter his face and dismiss me or go toe-to-toe with a behemoth like Heavy without flinching. It's everything.

There's no fear in this man. Not a second of hesitation. Not like there was with me the night behind Sawdust on the Floor.

I can't imagine this man snuggling anything but a gun.

I do know him. And he's deeply unhappy. Like me.

Whoa. Epiphany.

In the dining room, Pig Irons rolls up the map. I should get out of here before I get busted for spying.

Forty's giving orders. Heavy's getting on his phone. I creep toward my car.

There's no way that man in there is going to swallow his pride and come after me. Not unless he has a reason. Or an excuse.

Whatever's going on in the house, it definitely has to do with the Rebel Raiders.

I eye the hood of my car as a crazy idea pops into my head, and like all my crazy ideas, I know it's going to blow up in my face, but I'm also fully, enthusiastically committed.

If Forty Nowicki won't come for me, I'll come for him.

5

FORTY

"This table is fuckin' ridiculous."

My dad, Eighty, leans back in his leather office chair, hocks, and spits under the twelve-foot, custom granite conference table.

"Show some respect. This is a ten-thousand-dollar table." Pig Iron slaps Dad on the back of the neck and shuffles past him to his customary seat. He sets the three longnecks he's carrying down in a line. Guess church is gonna run long tonight.

"Waste of money," Dad grumbles.

"Cost of doin' business." Pig Iron cracks open beer number one.

"We ain't fuckin' businessmen," Dad snaps.

Dad's never held a job. Never did anything around the house except bitch and make a mess. After Mom left, he didn't even bother to come home much. He crashed at the clubhouse or his girlfriend's. In my opinion, he ain't any fuckin' kind of man at all.

Grinder stomps in and claps my back. "Who's fuckin' businessmen? We fucking businessmen now?"

Boots rolls in a second later, filling the room with the reek of dank weed like the world's funkiest *Little Tree* car-freshener. "I'm five minutes late and someone fucked a businessman?"

"You're not late. It's not eighteen hundred yet." I silence my phone and set it on the table. I don't have any calls or texts. Not that I'm expecting any. Wash already reported back from his daily drive by. Nevaeh's car is in the driveway. She's hasn't left town yet. She'll have to soon. We've put the word out that she doesn't get hired in Petty's Mill.

Shit. This is not what I need to be thinking about.

I roll my shoulder. It's been givin' me trouble the last few days. I must have slept on it wrong.

A second later, Heavy tromps in with Charge in tow, and I crack my knuckles, exhaling the irritation that's been riding me for days. I've been restless in my skin, impatient, not to mention my dick's decided it works just fine again.

God, Nevaeh was so damn soft. Smelled so good. Her neck's still sensitive, and when she cums, she still jerks like she's possessed.

The first time I saw that I was seventeen, and I didn't know shit about women. Nearly called 9-1-1. When I figured out what was going on, I was a kid with a shiny new toy. I lived to make her body convulse like she'd been zapped. Her belly muscles would ripple, and her thighs would twitch.

Perfect. Now I have a full-blown hard on in church. Unacceptable. I can't afford this distraction. Shit's been going down, and this meeting has been a long time coming. My head needs to be in the game, now more than ever. Lives are on the line.

I try a little trick I learned in Ranger school. You draw your awareness to the shit buzzing in your brain, and then you shoot it.

Drunk loser Dad, running his mouth like always? Boom.

The scent of Nevaeh's pussy that's been teasing my memory since Saturday night? Boom.

The racket from the clubhouse's main room, the constant pain in my arm, the nagging feeling that I'm needed somewhere else? Boom, boom, boom.

We might not be businessmen, but it's business time.

As if he reads my mind, Heavy bangs his gavel. Boots carved it for him as a joke, but the joke's on us. Heavy thinks it's funny as shit to wail it against the table, and it's annoying as hell.

"We got a quorum?" Heavy booms.

Club charter requires ten patched-in members in good standing and three officers to pass motions. We got Heavy, Pig Iron, and me for officers. Dad, Gus, and Grinder speak for the old timers. Boots is like, their moral support.

Cue from the strip club and Big George from the Autowerks represent the small businesses. Charge, Nickel, Wall, Dizzy, and my brother Bullet represent the rank and file.

Perched in a seat off in the corner, Harper Ruth scrolls through her phone. She's our permanent exception. Our legal representation. She might be a female, but church doesn't happen without her. She's smarter than Heavy, and she's kept this club from going down in flames many times.

Thankfully, unlike everywhere else, she doesn't peddle her brand of bullshit in church.

"Ayup. All present," Charge says. That'll probably be it from him. He's a good lieutenant. Solid man, loyal as hell, but he's not one for making plans. Especially not since he's become a family man. These days, all he wants to talk about are the renovations he's doing for his new wife. Like I know shit about laying tile.

"No Creech?" Heavy raises a bushy eyebrow.

"Passed out under the bar," Cue offers.

"Scrap?" Heavy asks.

"I got him covering the garage," George says, shifting his gaze to avoid Heavy's eye.

Heavy screws Pig Iron with a knowing look, snagging one of his beers. "Scrap has more than earned his place at this table."

Pig Iron shifts uneasily in his chair. "Let the boy enjoy his freedom a spell before we set him up for violating parole, eh?"

Obviously, Pig Iron arranged it with George to make sure that Scrap missed church.

We all get it. Scrap paid a steep price for protecting this club when he murdered the man who attacked Crista. Ten years upstate is real time. This business heating up with the Rebel Raiders...shit's gonna get serious. We're all gonna have real skin in the game. If Scrap gets busted, he's not seeing daylight again.

Scrap's his own man, though, and he can make his own calls. He proved that many moons ago. I'm about to say so when Boots pipes up from his wheelchair at the foot of the table.

"Ain't how this works." The table at large does a double take. Truth be told, Boots spends most of church snoring. Grinder elbows him when it's time for a vote, and he raises his hand if Grinder does.

"Every man makes his own choice." Boots slaps the table and points his finger at Pig Iron. "That's freedom. What'd I give my legs for if not so every dumbass can do as he damn well pleases?"

"Leg," Charge corrects. "You lost that second one off eatin' too much sugar and shit."

"Point still holds," Boots grumbles, folding his arms. He's said his piece.

Heavy bangs his gavel. "Point seconded?"

"Seconded," Grinder spits around a mouthful of chaw.

"Motion carried." Heavy slams the table.

My dad bitches about Heavy's "college boy shit," says they never took votes and signed paperwork in Slip Ruth's day. I remind him that in Slip's day, the club was stuck hauling black market smokes into New York, providing protection for the Russians' gun operation, and doing wet work for the Renelli's. Dead end shit. High risk, low reward.

"College boy shit" bought the RV that Dad's got parked in his driveway and the weekend trips to Atlantic City. I've only been back a few years, and it's already bought me a big ol' empty house, a Softail Slim, a Jeep, and a Ford 450 Limited.

"We gonna talk Raiders now or what?" Nickel asks, swiping his nose. He's on edge, hardly sitting still. He's like Nevaeh in that way, always in motion. With him, it's aggression. Nevaeh's more like how a bird or a bee goes flower to flower. Busy going nowhere.

Fuck. Where's my head? This is my cue.

I clear my throat. "We need a strategy." All eyes pivot to me.

Heavy and I plotted this out beforehand.

I propose the plan. Cue and Big George will nix it 'cause they're focused on the businesses. Pig Iron, Dizzy, and Nickel will want all-out war 'cause of what the Raiders did to our women. Dad, Bullet, or Grinder will suggest doin' something stupid. Heavy'll act like he's considering everyone's point, and then he'll go with my plan, which is really his plan.

I told him I feel like a damned liar. He said I should feel like a politician. I said same difference.

I take a deep breath and swallow my spit. I'm not much of a public speaker. "Here's the situation. The Raiders vandalized the Patonquin site and The White Van. We went after them, shook the trees, but they'd gone to ground. We torched their clubhouse and Rab Daugherty's tattoo parlor."

"That was a public service. Their clubhouse was a rat-infested shit heap." Cue interjects. Pig Iron raises a beer in agreement.

Growing up, Heavy, Charge, and I used to hunt rats out back of this place by the junk heaps, but I guess we've got a short memory.

"Then the Raiders attacked Fay-Lee and Roosevelt," I continue.

"And Story," Nickel snarls.

The way we hear it, it was more that Story attacked the Raiders, but I'll allow it.

"And Story. For that, they paid in blood." I cross myself. Mom was a good Polish Catholic before she broke bad and took up with Dad. She raised us in the church, and Grandma kept dragging us there after Mom bailed.

"Not all of them paid." Nickel stares me down. "The skinny guy with a tattoo. He's in the wind."

"True. So, that's a good dozen or so men we can't find, and we've burned down all their assets and hidey holes. We're fighting an insurgency."

"I did that once. It sucked." Dizzy leans back and sniffs. He did two tours in Iraq. He was a jarhead. Hard to imagine now with his 80s's rocker 'fro and mountain man beard.

"Knocker Johnson is not going to quit. And he's not smoking his own product like the Daughertys."

"Motherfuckin' blown job." Eighty slaps his palms on

the table. "Been plaguing us for too damn long. I say we call chaos on Knocker Johnson, the Daughertys, and any asshole in a Raiders cut. Put an end to this bullshit once and for all." There it is. The stupid idea.

"Amen," Grinder adds. "Goddamn blown job."

In this club, everything traces back to the blown job. It went down back when we were young. Heavy's dad Slip was president. His mom Linda had just had Hobs, and she was having a hard time. Turned out to be cancer, but we didn't know it then.

Slip was up in the rotation to make a run into New York. Linda asked him to stay home. Stones agreed to take the load. Brought his kid Knocker along for the ride. To us kids, Knocker was a legend. Eighteen and neck-deep in pussy with a green mohawk, a Willie G. special with a blacked-out engine, and full sleeves.

They got busted by the state police a few miles from the county line. Under the cartons of cigarettes? Five crates of Kalashnikovs. Stones and Knocker both went away on twenty-year bids. Stones died on the inside.

Stones' older sons, Dutchy and Inch, blacked out their Steel Bones ink and founded the Rebel Raiders with the Daughertys.

When Hobs was fourteen, Dutchy brained him with a baseball bat, fixed it so Hobs can't read or remember how to get places. We put Dutchy in the ground. Then Inch attacked Crista Holt. Scrap killed him with his bare hands. We've been the Hatfields and McCoys for most of our lives.

Steel Bones Construction billed over eight hundred million dollars last year, and we're still mired in this back-woods bullshit.

It's past time we put it behind us. Especially now that some of us are starting our own families. We want better than we had comin' up. For the men like Pig Iron and now Dizzy—the men whose women have been hurt—peace ain't an acceptable objective.

While I been recollecting, the conversation has been continuing without me.

"We can call chaos, but that does no good if we can't find their asses," Wall points out. Wall's got two little ones at home now and another on the way. He's got good reason to vote our way.

I steer the conversation back to where we want to go. "When we beat the bushes, we spread ourselves too thin. And we can't drop a dozen bodies. The Feds would have a field day." In all honesty, I think we could pull it off, but it's not the plan.

"So what are you proposing?" Grinder has lost his patience down at the end, and he's directing the question to Heavy. "Cue and Big George won't agree to nothin' that'll blow back on the businesses. Pig and Dizzy want blood. And Bullet probably wants to lure the fuckers out with some kind of box-and-stick trap with pussy in it."

Bullet shakes himself from whatever he's daydreaming about. "Hey. Huh? What?" Then he snickers. "Yeah. That's a good idea."

I look to Heavy, and he gives me the nod.

"We throw everything we have into finding Rab Daugherty. We grease every palm. Stake out every known hangout. We throw every man and every resource we have at hunting his ass down. Nickel, can you bring in Frisco?"

Nickel has a side hustle bounty hunting for a guy in Pyle. Could come in handy.

Nickel nods. "There a finder's fee?"

"Twenty thousand. Cash."

Nickel takes out his phone and starts texting. I wouldn't

be surprised if Rab shows up hogtied in our parking lot within the hour. Frisco is a motivated man.

At the far end of the table, Dizzy's getting restless. His sole concern has got to be destroying the club who dared lay hands on his old lady.

"Why Rab?" Dizzy asks. "Justice needs to be eye-for-an-eye. Rab's an armchair general. We start taking out their foot soldiers, they'll scatter."

Dizzy wants to go after the skinny guy who touched Fay-Lee. Skinny's time will come, but he's a pawn.

"You forget. Rebel Raiders were once Steel Bones." Heavy joins the debate, his great rumbling voice silencing the side chatter and fussing, as it always does. "They ain't cowards. They believe we've instigated a war, and they're on the side of righteousness."

"Rab's the VP." I tag back in. "He'll know where Knocker is. Or at least how to contact him. And Rab's lost his source of income. He's gonna be making moves. He's our best bet. Besides, he's an asshole. Outside of the Raiders, he's not a liked man."

"This what you want, prez?" Dizzy looks past me to Heavy.

"It is."

Dizzy pauses a long moment. This is it. Dizzy's gonna tip this one way or the other. He's the generation that bridges the old timers and our crew, patched in under Slip, but still riding hard. He commands the respect of all. If he nixes it, the plan dies.

Finally, he sighs and says, "Aye."

"Seconded." Grinder elbows Boots who's dozed off again.

"Aye?" Boots sputters, looking to Grinder who gives him the nod.

"This is gonna take all our muscle away from the businesses. You say you don't want us spread thin. That's what this plan will do." Cue's scrubbing his bald head.

"Until we find Rab, Smoke and Steel will stand in for us."

Wall has already called his people in our support club in Shady Gap. They'll cover security until the job is done.

I look to Cue, see if he has anything else, but he's satisfied.

"Vote?"

Heavy inclines his shaggy head.

A chorus of ayes fill the room. That went easier than I'd anticipated. "Get your marching orders from me at 06:00 in the commons. Come packing, and come ready to ride."

As the men file out, there's a general slapping of backs, chest bumping, and chanting of "Steel Bones!" They're already planning how drunk they're gonna get tonight. At 06:00, I'm gonna have to go after half these numbskulls with a hose.

After Boots rolls out, only Heavy, Harper, and I are left. Harper finishes up with her phone and joins us at the big table.

"Well, that went easier than I expected." She drums her long nails on the granite. It's irritating as hell.

"I know we have to enlist Smoke and Steel to work security, but the optics are shit," she complains. Heavy glares at her drumming. She gives it one last, spiteful tap and primly folds her hands in her lap. "Premeditation will be easy to prove."

"I already talked to Deb," Heavy says. "We did some creative invoicing so it looks like we're reallocating staffing for a project."

"Nice. That'll work." She leans back in her chair and

crosses her long legs. "You know what I can't figure? How come no one asked why go for Rab and not Knocker? We're not a curious bunch, are we?"

"We got lucky." Honestly, I thought Grinder would bring it up. Or Big George. Ultimately, it doesn't make sense to go for the VP. The war flared up when Knocker got released. Everyone knows he's behind the attacks.

We're blessed no one asked. Truth is, we don't want to catch Knocker. Not yet. And that information is on a need-to-know basis. Right now? Only Heavy, Harper, and I need to know.

The real plan is not to get Rab to flip on Knocker. We're going to use Rab as collateral to get Knocker to ease off until we're ready to parlay and end this thing, once and for all. The end game isn't to destroy the Rebel Raiders. The end game is to bring them back and make our club whole.

Speaking of ending this thing.

"Where are we on Des Wade?" I ask.

Harper groans and drops her head back to stare at the ceiling. "We? Haven't seen you sucking his dick lately."

Heavy swallows a weird, guttural growl. He's never been a hundred percent on board with this part of the plan, but there's no other way. Until the truth comes out about the blown job, there will be no peace for the club, the body count will keep racking up, and the wrong people will be dying. And we will never end this until Knocker Johnson knows and believes what really happened that day.

Slip Ruth had no idea there were guns were under the cigarettes. He was setup. We were all set up.

Des Wade—upstanding citizen, business leader, philanthropist, and scion of western Pennsylvania's most illustrious family dynasty—setup a small-town biker gang to go down for gun trafficking.

It wasn't personal. Steel Bones was convenient. A bunch of ex-cons, dropouts, and vets down on their luck, the well-known criminal element, not much beloved by the locals at that time.

No one was surprised when Sheriff Anderson Watts busted us running guns, and the pictures in the paper were sure impressive.

Sheriff Watts won the election for county executive handily the next month. Not too long after, Des Wade's contracting company received exclusive rights to develop the downtown waterfront, a deal worth millions that elevated Des from the Wade family kiddie table to carving the Thanksgiving Day turkey.

How do we know?

'Cause Heavy Ruth has spent his every waking moment on three things since his dad Slip died. The club. The businesses. And unraveling what happened that day twenty years ago when Stones and Knocker were pulled over on Route 29.

He's got one of those murder boards on the wall in his suite upstairs. Red string and everything.

But Knocker isn't gonna drop a decades long grudge 'cause we tell him he's got it wrong. We need hard evidence. Which is where Harper comes in. She's our Mata Hari.

Several months ago, she caught Des' eye at a charity gala in Pyle. She saw an opening, and she took it. She ended up doing Charge dirty. They were together at the time, and she didn't get the timing quite right between breaking things off with Charge and getting Des on the line, but I guess all's fair in love and war. And this is war.

"Well?" Heavy raises his eyebrows. "How are things with Des? If you're not getting anywhere, let's pull you out."

Harper rolls her eyes. "I'm getting somewhere. I just

need one of those James Bond doohickeys. Like from *Die Hard*. A thing that can figure out his password."

"We need a tech guy?" I've been arguing that we need to bring in outside help since I came back and took over as VP.

Harper sighs. "Yeah. I've searched everywhere. Des doesn't have his passwords written down."

"Did you look under his keyboard?" Heavy asks.

"Did you look here?" Harper flips him off.

"Some of the guys I worked with at Fort Meade, before I applied for the Rangers? They'd have what we need within an hour." I know exactly who I'd call. All I need is the go ahead.

"No outsiders." Heavy folds his hands over his wide stomach and pins Harper with a stare. "You've been trying to guess? Try birthdays, pet names, whatever he calls his dick?"

"As often as I can without triggering a lockout. I say it's time to do it my way." Harper cracks her neck.

Harper wants to haul Des in and beat a confession out of him. There's a simplicity to the plan that I appreciate, but there's no guarantee Knocker would believe a confession made under duress.

"Des Wade isn't some piece of trash we can gank off the street," Heavy argues. "He'd be missed. You should come home. We haven't seriously considered going after Watts."

"Senator Anderson Watts?" Harper scoffs. "That's a shit plan, and you know it. I'm in this. I'm not coming home until it's time to bury pieces of Des Wade's body under a baby oak tree up on Half-Stack Mountain."

"You're wasting time, sister."

"Oh, brother, 'Let us not grow weary while doing good, for in due season we shall reap if you do not lose heart.'" Harper blinks and flashes him a small, wry smile.

Heavy snorts. My jaw drops a little.

"What? You thought Heavy's the only one who picked up a little King James listening to Mom piss and moan about Dad all those years?" She smiles wider and runs her tongue along her bright red lips, her eyes icy and calculating. "I'm going to stay. Des has been hinting around about the future. Maybe he's gonna put a ring on it."

"Sometimes I think you're enjoying this too much." Heavy gauges her with his own cold eyes. "Don't get too accustomed to the lifestyle. It might be a month or a year, but that man is marked."

Her shark's smile drops in an instant. "Make no mistake, brother. When the time comes, I'm going to cave his skull in with a baseball bat and slip-slide around in his mashed brains."

Neither Heavy nor I speak for a long moment. No doubt, we're both picturing it. Harper's a manipulative, duplicitous witch, but she never makes idle threats.

Harper's the first to break the silence, homicidal madness gone, all fake smiles and sunshine again. "In the meantime, how about I work off my extra energy by running Nevaeh Ellis out of town? I was thinking with all this arson, it'd be easy enough to pin something on her. She's definitely the type who would fire bomb a man's bike."

My muscles bunch so quickly, bolts of pain spear down my fucked-up arm.

"No need," I say. "I've made the situation clear to her."

"What's she doing back here anyway? I'd say she lost her job, but there's no way that woman hasn't lost more than a few jobs before now."

"It's immaterial. She knows where she stands." Heat coils in my gut as I remember her spread across my lap, her ass dancing under my palm, pussy juice smeared on her thighs.

I've never done anything like that before. Maybe a few swats in the heat of the moment, but nothing like what Dizzy and Fay-Lee do. It's just—she was smiling. Ear to ear. Flirting with that ginger asshole like she didn't have a care in the world.

And she didn't care that she was courting real danger. Heavy, Nickel, Creech. They hate her. They blame her for me reenlisting, for breaking up the original crew. They've despised her so long, it's habit. We don't hurt women, but what would they do to encourage her to disappear?

She's not my old lady. No one would physically touch her, but she's not protected when I'm not around. And some of my brothers are devious, vicious motherfuckers. She talks shit, but she's not hard on the inside like Harper or Annie.

And there she was, dancing and laughing it up. Instigating. Giving the club her back. Daring them to run her off.

I've never needed to wipe a smile off a person's face in a worse way.

Now, Heavy's staring at me, deadly serious, his dark eyes unreadable. "Don't underestimate her. She's not some harmless hot mess. She's dangerous. To you. To this club. We let her in once. She used that access to try to tear us apart. She had a temper tantrum 'cause she wasn't gonna be the center of attention for a hot minute."

"She's a brat." There's no denying it.

Heavy nods. "There's the kind of spoiled that's mildly irritating. And then there's the kind of spoiled that poisons shit. I've kept tabs on her."

My chest tightens. I never asked him to do that.

"Did you know there's a video of her fighting some chick in her underwear on PornX? Poor bastard behind the camera begging her to stop. And she got some guy arrested for stealing a car to take her out and show her a good time.

And most recently, she seems to have pissed off Dominic Renelli. He's reached out. Asked us nicely if we've seen her."

My mouth goes dry, and my adrenaline kicks in hard. "What did you say?"

"Nothing. I'm ducking his calls. But I don't have to answer him. She's waltzing around town with Shirlene, not a care in the world. It's a matter of time before someone gives Renelli the heads up."

"No one touches her." I stand up, fists clenched. My chair rolls back and hits the wall in slow motion.

Heavy remains seated, cool and collected. Harper's leaning forward, all ears.

"I'm more inclined to cut her a check. Let her know Renelli's looking for her. Give her a few thousand to get gone." Heavy's voice is even. He doesn't acknowledge that I'm inexplicably about to throw down.

"Why does Renelli want her?"

Heavy lifts his massive shoulders. "She worked for one of his legitimate businesses in Pyle. She probably stole from him."

"She was never a thief."

"She didn't have to be. You gave her anything she asked for. And she betrayed you the first chance she got. She betrayed *us*."

Like I need the reminder.

"Oh, for heaven's sakes, Heavy." Harper rolls her eyes. "She's some loser skank; she's not Judas Iscariot. Run her off. Pay her off. Whatever. Can we get our heads back in the game?"

"She's not club business." I pin Heavy with my coldest stare. He's my brother. I've killed for him. Risked my life for him. But this isn't club business. "No one deals with Nevaeh Ellis but me. Understood?"

The door pushes open, Wash pokes his head in, and he sings out, "Understood! But Veep? You might wanna come out front, then. You got a special delivery."

Wash flashes a gap-toothed grin and ducks back out of the boardroom.

For a long moment, Heavy and I take each other's measure. We've been brothers our entire lives. My earliest memory is sparring with sticks out behind the garage with Heavy, Charge, and Scrap. Before Nickel, it was the four of us. Heavy, the mastermind. Charge, the guy who'd get us out of any scrape with his aw shucks smile. Scrap, the steady soldier. And me. The right hand. The general.

Nothing could tear us apart.

And then I get it. A rush of understanding. "You were tempted. When she came on to you."

Heavy's holds my gaze, but a look I've never seen before crosses his face. Chagrin. Self-disgust. "The flesh is weak, my brother."

"But you didn't touch her." It's not a question; I don't need to ask.

"I didn't touch her."

"She's mine."

"She's heartless. Her father was dying—her brother was hurting—and she didn't come back until the man who raised her was dead."

Harper lets out a loud, blowsy sigh. "Good grief, Heavy, would you drop it already? You're painting her like a Shakespearen villain. Keep going, and I'm gonna start liking her. And besides, the woman herself is apparently out front." She stands. "I'm not missing this. I haven't seen Annie really beat a girl's ass in years. Catch you later, assholes."

Harper tucks her phone in her bra and sashays out the door, hollering, "Prospect! Take me to the trash!"

"We done?" I'm itching to follow her, and Heavy's confession does not rest easy with me.

Heavy lumbers to his feet. "We good?"

I nod, slow. "Always, brother."

"I'll back your play. Every time."

"Doesn't need to be said."

I lead the way out to the main hall, and it's a ghost town. Everyone's out front, except for Wash, who's leaning against the bar, waiting for us to emerge from the back.

"She showed up and asked for you. Won't talk to anyone. The girls went after her again, but Wall jumped in, so it's cool for now."

"What does she want?" Heavy asks. I don't wait for an answer, heading right into the crowd. Folks part like the Red Sea. We've got more people here than usual since the club and our associates are partying close to home due to the recent Rebel Raider attacks. If Nevaeh came to put on a show, she's got a huge audience.

"Oh, you'll see," Wash snickers. "I think she needs some work on her car."

I clear the last of the crowd. I'm in the front parking lot, somehow ending up next to Harper Ruth. There's a beat up red Hyundai idling in the middle of the main aisle. Across the hood, someone has keyed *DIE STEEL BONES WHORE*. The S's are formed with angles, not curves, and the points reach all the way from the windshield to the grill.

"Now where have I seen this before?" Harper's smirking, her eyes narrowed.

Nevaeh's standing next to the car, hand on her round hip, glaring at the sweetbutts clustered nearby, heckling her.

"They got two of them words right," Danielle says.

"Someone got their keys? I'll fix it. Should say Die *Dirty Ass* Whore." Starla spits on the asphalt.

"What? Did you see me down the clinic when they were delousing your pussy, Starla?" Navaeh's popping her neck and puffing her chest. Wall shifts uneasily as six or seven sweetbutts raise their voices and swarm closer.

I glance at Heavy. He reads my mind. "Ladies! Back up!"

It's at that moment Nevaeh sees me. "You! Forty Nowicki! You gonna pay for this to get fixed?"

Her brown eyes spark, daring me. My dick twitches.

I break forward, gesturing to Wash over my shoulder. He jogs close. "Take the car to Big George's."

Then I've got her, close, in arm's reach again, and I can smell her coconut shampoo. There's a loosening in my chest. "Keys."

She has to crane her neck to glare at me.

"Keys."

She huffs and holds them up. Wash nips forward and grabs them.

"You come with me." I grab her by the upper arm and march her through the crowd, glaring at anyone who dares to say shit. Everyone piles inside. No one wants to miss the show.

The sweetbutts are close on our heels, shit talking at the top of their lungs.

"Dumpster's out back, Forty."

"I can teach her some manners for you."

"I say we make her face match the hood of that car."

None of this is setting right. Wash didn't mention anything about her car when he drove past this morning. That means this happened in the past few hours.

I grit my teeth and push her past the bar to the stairs.

"I better not get a bill for that, Forty," Nevaeh shouts over her shoulder, pitching her voice as loud as she can to make sure everyone hears. I force her to take the stairs double time, but there's no way anyone misses a word she says. "I don't have anything to do with this sad little group of tooth-less bitches and mangy old fucks, and I do not appreciate *your* club's bullshit spilling onto the hood of *my* car."

"Shut up, Nevaeh," I growl under my breath.

"If that car's not pristine when I get it back, I'm gonna carve 'limp dick energy' into the seat of every hog out there!"

I slam my hand over her mouth. "Haven't you got any sense of self-preservation?"

"Nope," she mumbles against my palm.

I hustle her down the hall to my room, and it's strange. Her free arm is flailing, and her mouth's running a mile a minute, but she's not fighting me. She's falling into step beside me, keeping close. Like she used to do. Like she's scared.

It's like a signal to my body to fight, my muscles tensing even more. And it all hits me at once. The Renellis. The shit Heavy said. Porno and car theft. The death threat carved into the hood of her car.

She's not leaving my sight again.

Fuck.

Panic sets my heart racing. She could have died. A dozen times over during the past ten years. She's fuckin' nuts, and she has no survival instincts.

She could have died. She hasn't been out there in the world, getting lit and fucking guys, some party girl having a grand old time. She's been playing chicken. I knew guys like that in the service. They had the craziest stories. They always ended up on the missions that went sideways. They weren't mavericks; they had a death wish.

No matter that dated image I have of her in my head, this short-legged woman, half my weight, trying to keep up with me, she isn't a femme fatale, a schemer with no moral compass who got off on crushing a man's heart. She's not the man-eating hellcat I got tattooed on my good arm when I mustered out.

Maybe she never was.

Maybe she's always been this walking disaster, burning out of control. In over her head. Maybe she needed me, and I left. I can't think about that.

We get to my room, and I unlock the door, flinging her forward maybe a bit too hard. She stumbles and lands on the bed, her hair springing and bobbing.

God, I love her hair. It gets everywhere. Until I traded in my old Ford Ranger, I'd find strands of it in the interior. For years.

She rolls until she's upright, kneeling at the foot of my bed, her ass resting on her heels. She's wearing cutoff jean shorts and a T-shirt with a picture of Rosie the Riveter that reads, "¡Sí, Se Puede!"

Her red polish is chipped, and her nails themselves are bitten to the quick. Her cuticles are torn up and red. So messy.

She shuffles forward to get off the bed.

"Stay." I shut the door behind me firmly. She sinks back down and starts picking at her cutoffs, glancing up at me every so often. Each look sends a rush of blood to my cock. And a jolt to my chest.

She gnaws on her bottom lip. "So, what now?"

I don't know. There's something about her on my bed. She needs to stay there.

But this is all wrong. *She's* all wrong. I shake my head to clear the static. This whole situation doesn't make sense. She's not Steel Bones. Why would she even be on the Rebel Raider's radar?

"Where was your car parked?"

"In my driveway."

Ice fills my veins. We didn't check for a tail when we rolled out there last night. The club is on high alert. If a Raider was following any of us, we painted a target on her. I should have had a prospect watching the house twenty-four seven. Not just drive-bys. Careless.

"Did you hear the guys who did it?" Does she even have personal protection?

"Lou and I were both out. He found it when he came home from work."

"You didn't have your car with you? Who were you with?" I take a step forward, and she shrinks back.

"Shirlene."

"What are you doing?" I know she's been hanging with Shirlene. I'm also aware that my tone is uncalled for. Damned if I can help it.

Nevaeh flops back onto her ass, her legs sticking straight out, her feet ticking back and forth like windshield wipers. The dirt from her Chuck Taylors smudges my comforter.

"Oh, you know. Working the corners. Scoring meth. Betting on the ponies?" She scrunches her nose, her lips twitching. "Is it still trashy to bet on the ponies? Or is it classy if I wear, like, a really big hat?"

"You could try telling the truth."

"You can't handle the truth." She says it in the worst Jack Nicholson voice I've ever heard. I have to grind down on my molars to keep my face straight.

"Fine," she huffs. "I'm helping her with the old peeps. She's showing me the ropes. Since I can't seem to get a job in this town, she's hooking me up. It's called companion care."

"Companion care?"

"Yeah. Help old people with chores. Make sure they're

taking their meds. Hang out and chat. Watch a lot of base-ball with the volume turned all the way up."

"You're working with seniors?"

"Yup. Like I said, Shirlene's hooking me up."

I don't know what to say. Heavy put the word out that anyone who wants to do business with Steel Bones would do well not to hire her. It's clear she's *persona non grata*.

Why would Shirlene pick this battle? She's an old timer. Keeps her head down, helps with the cookouts, and spends her time with Boots and his crew, playing spades and talking about the glory days. She and Nevaeh were always tight, though. And Shirlene does what she wants.

Nevaeh makes a show of scanning the room, but she glances back from the corner of her eye. "What? You think I can't do it?"

That's a loaded question, so I ask one of my own. "Why would Shirlene go against the club for you?"

A funny expression flits across her face. Nags at my memory. A softness. A vulnerability. Before I know it, I take another step closer.

"Shirlene's my girl. We're ride or die." Nevaeh tucks her legs to her chest and rests her chin on her knees. I'd forgotten how she does this—constant movement. She speaks with her whole body like some people speak with their hands.

"You two talk?"

Nevaeh shrugs a shoulder. "Every month or so. Mostly she texts me memes and recipes for crap I will never make. Better Than Sex cake. That's a sad name for a cake, man."

This time, I can't hold it back. My lips twitch. She notices, and she flips and bounces so she's kneeling again. Her hair takes a few extra seconds to come to rest.

"So, you were out with Shirlene and Lou was at work when your car was keyed?"

"Yes, detective. You can check my alibi. It's air tight." She winks, and my cock jerks painfully in my jeans.

She knows what she's doing. What she's offering, kneeling at the foot of my bed like that. I want to take it. My body's aching to take it. If this were back in the day, I'd be balls deep in her by now. But this isn't then. And I kind of want to keep talking.

She speaks in circles. She always has. It would drive me nuts, but I loved it, too. She was funny. She still is. And I liked the sound of her voice. Like a chipmunk with a pack a day habit.

I move to my desk, ease out the chair, and sit. She kind of flounces onto her butt and dangles her legs over the side of the bed. I got a California King with storage underneath. Her feet don't reach the floor. Now there's dirt scuffs from her heels on that part of the comforter, too. I could bend her over the edge, and she'd be at the perfect height.

My balls ache. I shift and make it worse.

"So what are we gonna do? Sit here and stare at each other while Big George buffs my hood?"

"Who do you think did it?"

Of course, it was the Rebel Raiders. They either followed me there, they had a man on us last night—which would be a huge problem since that operation ended with blood—or they saw her around town and remembered her from back in the day. With that hair and that ass, there's no mistaking her.

She cocks her head to the side. "I hate it when you do that."

"Do what?"

"I ask a question, and you never answer it."

"Your questions aren't serious."

She blows a curl out of her face. "Do. You. Think. I. Can't. Do. Companion. Care." She drums her heels against the bed base a few times in emphasis. "Question mark."

I don't know what to say.

She glares at me.

"I don't know you."

She rolls her eyes. "This again? Okay. Fine. You *used* to know me. Would I have been good at companion care? Or would I, like, forget something, and then they'd die, and it'd be my fault?"

This isn't an idle question. I take a close look at her face. Her guard's down. The brat, the wild child, the manic pixie dream girl is gone. It's just her now. Nevaeh. Big brown eyes. Pouty pink lips. Dusting of pale freckles across her nose and cheeks. The hint of a yellowing bruise under her left eye.

She's not wearing makeup. And she's squirming now. Eyeing the door. My muscles tense. She's not leaving this room.

"Yeah. You would've been good at that. You never forgot important shit."

It's true. Her lunch, her purse, her keys, her phone, her birth control pill. She was hopeless. But she never forgot anyone's birthday. Anyone's name. When there were kids were around the clubhouse, she'd be the first to notice if a little one was headed for trouble.

And she had this weird superpower of being able to find anything that someone else lost. It's like she could see everything except the thing she was supposed to be looking at.

She's worrying at her lower lip. I used to smooth it with my thumb when she did that. "I've got a list. Shirlene gave it to me. I'm not gonna forget anything."

"Nevaeh." I exhale. "You can't stay in Petty's Mill." Especially not with the Renelli organization looking for her. And now she's somehow found herself in the Rebel Raider's crosshairs.

She juts up her chin, a flash of pain darkening her eyes. My gut tightens. "You can't tell me what to do."

"Why is Dominic Renelli after you?"

Her face blanches pure white, and she jumps to her feet. "Fuck. Did you tell him where I am?"

"He's not touching you." It's out of my mouth before I realize I've said it, but I check my gut, and I mean it. There's no future between us, but there's past, and since she's here, for now, she belongs to me. I know it's insane, but it is the way it is.

"He's Dominic-fucking-Renelli. I need to get out of here." She starts for the door, and I'm up in an instant, blocking the way.

"Move." She shoves at me uselessly.

"Why does he want you? Were you fucking him?" My stomach turns. "You steal from him?"

"I fondled his dick when I was going for some calamari, and then I got into it with my boyfriend—*ex*-boyfriend—Carlo—who I *was* fucking—he's Renelli's money guy, and then I ran into his fist, and he almost killed me, and there were kind of witnesses at the end. Shit. I need to check on Don and Greg. And by the way, I *did* steal his man purse, and I'm not sorry."

What? "Who I was fucking" rings in my ears, and I can feel the vein in my forehead throb.

She starts pacing the room. "I'm in over my head here. I need to get out of town."

Didn't I tell her that a minute ago? It's a little ego bruising. She has no fear of me or my brothers, but some old-timey Italian mob boss from Pyle has her sweating and wild-eyed?

"Sit back down. You're not going anywhere."

"You *literally* just said I can't stay in Petty's Mill."

"What did you do to Dominic Renelli? Talk *straight*." I raise my voice. I *never* raise my voice.

"I accidentally stroked his cock while trying to retrieve a piece of calamari. A circle bit, not a squiddy bit." Her face is flushing, and she's getting louder, too. "And my boyfriend, Carlo the asshole, thought I was aiming to land a bigger fish, and so we fought, and he tried to choke me out, but this guy Don and his husband broke it up before Carlo could kill me, shit in my mouth, and dump me in the river."

"Just the simple truth, Nevaeh!"

"It is *useless* talking to you. You don't *listen*," she shrieks, and reaches into her back pocket, fishing out her phone.

Oh, hell no.

I'm on her in a second, and somehow the phone tumbles to the floor, and she swoops for it. Then, she falls to her knees, and I'm driving my fingers into her thick hair, jerking her head back, and she freezes, eyes huge.

We're both out of breath and still as statues.

Her gaze dips down. Her eyes widen impossibly larger when she sees the bulge of my cock fighting to get out of my jeans. And then her hands are scrabbling at my belt, but her fingers slip, so I push them away, and she tugs her shorts and panties down, jamming her fingers into her pussy while I shove my cock into her mouth.

"Oh, fuck," I moan as she swallows me, taking me so deep her throat constricts around the head of my cock. I figured I must have exaggerated this in my memory, but she's *that* good. "Good girl, good girl. Don't stop." If she stops, I swear I'll cry.

She mewls. Oh, yeah. I don't have to stand here, careful not to thrust, while she takes what she can handle. This is Nevaeh. She always wants more. I let my hips drive forward to meet her bobbing head, and she gags. I freeze. Shit. Maybe I'm not remembering right. Maybe things have changed with her. But then she reaches around and scores her short nails into my ass, urging me on.

Oh God. Yes. I thrust, fucking her mouth, watching my shiny, wet dick part those pink lips, a string of spit stretching between us each time I pull out. Her eyes are watering, and her fingers are working furiously between her legs.

"Give me that." I reach down and grab her hand, bending to shove those slick fingers in my mouth, sucking the tangy pussy juices from them. She lets out an adorable, pissed off growl and snatches her hand back, so I plunge my cock into her mouth again, harder, knocking the back of her throat until she gags, jerks away, and then immediately comes back for more.

She's moaning something, the sound muffled and interrupted by wet slurping and sucking, but I can't make it out. She's okay, though. I remember her noises vividly. She's enjoying herself.

The base of my spine tingles and my balls draw up. It's so fucking amazing. Her lips smack and my dick slides through her spit as she drools, and we're a mess, and I'm feeling no pain, high as a goddamn kite.

"I'm gonna cum," I manage to pant, and I'm expecting her to pull away, but her shoulders are shaking—she's cumming already—and then so am I, shooting hot spurts down her throat, a huge load that goes on and on as this perfect sensation, like sun on bare skin, washes over my entire body.

She swallows, and another spurt jets from my cock. She

swirls her magic tongue, licking me clean, and then she flops onto her butt, cranes her neck, and grins up at me. Her shorts are around her left ankle. Her cheeks are damp and flushed, her hair's all over the place. Somehow one of her shoes came off. It's halfway across the room, under my desk.

She's a mess. The prettiest thing I've ever seen.

And a huge mistake.

I can't turn my back on her. I can't believe her. I can't help her. She won't tell me what's going on with the Renellis, so I need to find out myself, but there's no time for that. I need to coordinate a manhunt to find Rab Dougherty. And then I gotta find out who messed with her car, kill him, and bury him up on Half-Stack Mountain.

That perfect feeling drains away like water in a bathtub.

I tuck my dick away, zip my pants, and buckle my belt.

The corners of Nevaeh's mouth slide down. "We used to snuggle after we made love."

A sliver of guilt niggles at me, pissing me off. I don't have time for this. I have my own problems, and now I've got hers. "That wasn't making love."

Her eyes darken. My chest aches. For a second, it looks like she's gonna let me have it. Instead, she reaches down to pull up her shorts.

"My bad." She hops to her feet, and starts hunting for her missing shoe.

"It's under the desk." I head for the door. I need to finish mapping out assignments. And I need to not be here. "Stay in this room. Don't touch anything." I reach out and pluck the phone from her back pocket and stick it in my own. Then I open the door.

She's standing in the middle of the room, one shoe on, one shoe in her hand. A chunk of hair is sticking out from the side of her head, defying gravity. She's trying to hide it, but hurt shines in her eyes.

Fuck.

"There's a spare toothbrush in the medicine cabinet."

I force myself to look away, head out and lock the door, make my way down to the main floor. My steps are slow. I'm listening, knowing if she calls out, I'm going to turn around.

But she's quiet. So I go back to business.

The club is at war. I need to focus.

I pass Wash on my way to Heavy's office. "Go stand by my door. She asks for food or anything, get it for her."

"Yes, sir."

"Don't let her out."

"No, sir."

"She can pick locks."

"Okay, sir."

I straighten my shirt and rap twice on Heavy's door. "And Wash? Don't touch her. Anyone touches her, they die."

6

NEVAEH

I twist the knob again and bang on the door until the flat of my palm stings. Forty locked me in. That heavy-handed, ungrateful asshole locked me in.

In high school, I always pictured him as a Wild West gunslinger, the dusty man of few words who rolls into town alone, saving the day. His clothes were frayed and faded, his truck was rusted, but what he had, he cared for. He didn't say much, so when he did, you listened.

I guess when you hone that personality with years of military training, you get a cold-hearted asshole. Insert dick in pants. Engage zipper. Mission complete.

There's a spare toothbrush in the medicine cabinet. Jerk.

Like I didn't rock his world. He tried to be all above it at first, but then he let go, and he loved it. I did, too. I thought for a second that this would be it. We'd take it to the bed. He'd snuggle me under his arm like he used to, and we'd talk. I'd tell him everything, and he'd tell me it's all okay.

Nope.

Robo-Forty took my phone and locked me in his creepily clean and orderly bachelor pad.

Don't touch anything.

I think I'll start in the bathroom. I kind of do want to brush my teeth.

I toe off my other shoe—if I'm gonna be here awhile, I'm gonna get comfortable—and I head for the en suite. These digs are pretty fancy for an MC clubhouse. He has a tub with jets and a separate shower. Natural stone tile. There's Lava soap in the dish, though, and off-brand shampoo in the shower.

I open the medicine cabinet. There's the toothbrush, still in the package. There's a can of Barbasol, floss, and a nearly empty bottle of Drakkar Noir. Some things never change.

There are also several bottles of pills on the highest shelf. I have to haul myself up onto the sink to take a closer look. The names are unfamiliar. I could look them up if I had my phone. Lots of warning stickers. *Do not take with alcohol. Do not operate heavy machinery.* The bottles are almost full, and they're old. Filled last year. Pain meds, I'm guessing. There are several tubes of prescription creams, too. He seems to be using them.

They must be for whatever happened to his arm. I haven't seen the damage. Lou told me there was a helicopter accident. That would have freaked me out, but Lou didn't mention it until months after it happened, and Forty was coming back to town.

Uneasiness swirls in my belly. Heavy threw it in my face that Forty was hurt overseas. It can't be that bad. Forty doesn't act hurt. But he wouldn't, would he?

Lou said Forty was in a helicopter, and it made a hard landing. He got burned saving another passenger. The other guys died. It messed up his arm so he couldn't be a sniper anymore.

He can drive his truck just fine. I'm assuming he can ride his bike. He's got to be mostly okay, right?

I bet he didn't listen to the doctors. That's why there's all those expired medicine bottles. He's crap at listening. He decides what's right, and that's what he does. Like enlisting. I told him over and over that I didn't need a house and all of that. We could get an apartment downtown. We'd get jobs. I'm not afraid of work.

But he had it in his head that he needed to provide for me. He thought that no matter what I said now, one day I'd wake up and realize I'd made a shit deal, and I'd bail. Like his mother, I guess.

Which is really stupid, considering I've woken up every day my entire adult life, thought "this is a shit deal," and rolled out of bed to go to work anyway. Is there really an opt out?

I squeeze a big ol' squirt of toothpaste on my brand-new brush and scrub the salty taste of Forty out of my mouth. I don't *like* to swallow, but I was cumming so hard, and he was so into it, I got kind of carried away.

After I rearrange all the stuff in his medicine cabinet, I wander back into his room. I'm gonna touch *everything*. Starting with the closet. The front of my T-shirt is damp with blowjob drool. I need a change of clothes.

Forty's room is in the new annex. This whole part of the clubhouse hadn't been built yet when I left town. It's really modern, but somehow, it fits with the renovated 1930s garage that houses the commons, the bar, the kitchen, and the cramped rooms we used to pass out in back in the day.

Forty's closet matches his fancy bathroom. It's a walk in, with recessed lighting and cedar hangers. It's mostly empty. I start opening drawers. Socks, folded and stacked in neat rows. I shuffle the black dress socks and the white gym socks. Underwear and undershirts, folded and organized by cut. I shuffle those, too. Ammunition.

Ammunition?

Yup. Three drawers of ammunition. Organized by caliber and manufacturer. I leave that alone. Messing with a man's hoard of ammunition just seems unwise.

In the last, shallow drawer, meant for watches and cufflinks, there's a rectangular jewelry box. Inside, there's a gold medal hanging on a green ribbon with white stripes. There's an eagle on the medal, and the letter "C" on the ribbon.

There's nothing else in the drawer. I shut the box and put it back, trying to remember exactly where it was.

My stomach feels funny. Like I'm nervous. But I'm not afraid of being caught. That's not it. I shove the feeling aside and keep exploring. There are plenty of shirts. I help myself to a white button up, and I roll up the sleeves. Then, I randomly reverse the hangers.

Forty has a lot of cargo pants, and he hangs them up by shade of earth tone. Weird. At the back of the closet there's a garment bag. Inside, there's a dark blue jacket with gold buttons and a dozen striped ribbons on the breast. On the left sleeve, there's a badge that says *Ranger*.

That funny feeling comes back. It's kind of a mix of queasiness and dread. The dread makes no sense. The helicopter accident happened. It's over. Forty's fine. Or fine enough. I couldn't have done anything, even if I'd known at the time. It must have been almost three and half years ago. Back when I was working as a receptionist at the day spa that turned out to be a rub-and-tug place and got shut down.

I shouldn't be touching his uniform. I zip the bag up carefully, and I wander out and perch on the edge of his bed.

I was so mad when he enlisted. He'd said he was just

going to talk to the recruiter. Hear the man out. But he came back with paperwork, and there was nothing I could say. He had an answer for everything.

Of course, he wouldn't get killed. What? Did I not have faith in him?

This was gonna be good for us. He'd be able to get ASE certified, and the Army would pay. When he came home, he could work at the Autowerks with Big George. Make real good money.

I had a year left of school. I'd hardly miss him. We'd email. Video chat. He'd send money home. When I graduated, if I wanted, I could go to school. Or better yet, I could get started setting up a place for us. I wouldn't have to worry. He'd take care of everything.

He was excited to go.

Oh, hell. He *wanted* to go. I guess I've always known that, but until this moment? That's not a part of how I tell myself the story.

My heart cracks in my chest, quiet as an eggshell.

Back then, I knew that the instant Forty's horn didn't wake Ed Ellis up every morning, my life was going to go off the rails. I was scared shitless, and Forty was stoked to go make a man of himself.

If I had told him what was going on, I'd have ruined it for him. Forty would have kill Ed, gone to jail, and he wouldn't have been gone two years, he'd have been gone forever.

I could do two years. It would only be a year until I could move out. I could get a gun; I knew bikers. I wouldn't shoot Ed. Just get him to back off. Or I could tell Mom. There were moments. She'd come up behind me, scoop up my hair, twist it into a bun, and tell me how much it looked like

Grandma Ruth's. There were moments I thought maybe she'd help me, if I told.

Around and around in my brain, words teetering on the tip of my tongue. But then Forty was gone, and things flew out of control, and so did I.

But that's not quite the truth, is it?

Forty left, and I was so *angry*. I was gonna make him regret it. I knew he couldn't come home and rescue me. I pretended to fuck around on him because I wanted him to hurt as bad as me. Feel as powerless as me. Because I was mad he needed to leave me to feel like a man when I needed saving right where I was.

I was stuck and scared and hurting, so I decided to make him suffer.

Oh, shit. What a freaking mess.

What am I doing? There's not some long lost love to rekindle here. There's only strangers who once upon a time were two kids who needed to grow up.

I go try the door again. Still locked. I bang until my palm throbs. No one comes. No one even hollers through the door to knock it off.

I can't be here. I need a hair pin.

Forty's not gonna have a hair pin. A paper clip might work. I go to his desk and dump the drawers. I don't need to be in this kind of rush, but I'm still tearing through his shit, whether out of shame or panic, I'm not even sure.

I dump the nightstand drawer onto the bed. A box of condoms, spare batteries, and a miniature copy of the *New Testament*. The condoms are half gone. Ouch. The hits keep coming.

I go back to his desk. There's his laptop. I can email for help. Yes, I can message Fay-Lee. She'll spring me. I shake the mouse, and his screen blinks to life. Please don't be password protected. *Please.*

Oh. Double ouch.

I don't need a password. His browser's still open, and I guess he hasn't set it to automatically log him out. He's on LoveMate.com. Seriously? Who doesn't use the app on their phone?

I've never seen the actual site, but it's easy enough to navigate. Big mistake with the profile pic. It's a headshot. He's not smiling, his hair's buzzed way short, and he's clearly in fatigues. The whole thing screams "backwoods militiaman with no sense of humor and a shit ton of canned goods in his bunker."

His tagline is "looking for a serious relationship."

Well, I'm changing that. I think "looking for a woman who cans fruit and knows her generators" has a ring to it. Fits the picture. Catches the eye.

Okay, so what does all-grown-up Forty Nowicki want in a serious relationship?

I work construction and enjoy rides with my motorcycle club movies and eating out the ideal woman would ride. I spend my free time fishing and like I said on my bike.

I'm getting the feeling Forty doesn't have much free time. Or working knowledge of grammar.

Looking for a woman who is organized loyal with good common sense. Basically someone low maintenance with their shit together. Bonus if you're tall blonde and love monster trucks professional wrestling and motorcycles.

Triple ouch.

I sink into the desk chair, all my frantic energy gone. I am the exact opposite of Forty's perfect woman. Except the monster trucks and motorcycles.

I don't even have the heart to mess with his blurb. Much.

I do add some punctuation. Now he enjoys rides with his motorcycle, club movies, and eating out the ideal woman.

I lean back and spin the chair. This sucks. I've heard about letting go of your ego in order to find inner peace, but mine's getting bulldozed here. I just happily sucked off a guy whose dating profile might as well read *Literally, anyone but her.*

And then a key turns in the lock. I turn to face the door, dread pooling in my stomach.

There's a long pause before the door opens, as if for deliberate effect, and then Heavy strides in, his boots falling like concrete blocks. He has to duck his head to get through the door frame. He eyes the mess before he skewers me with the most scorn-filled glare I've ever been subject to in my life. Which is saying something.

I open my mouth to defend myself—who knows how; I'm always surprising myself—but he interrupts by raising his enormous hand.

"When I've said my piece, I'm leaving, and this door will be unlocked. This is what you're going to do."

Bullet and Creech follow him in and loom silently in the doorway, mean-mugging, flexing their fists.

"You're going to put everything back as you found it, and you're going to walk away. Take the stairs by the exit sign. There's a Ford Focus parked in the back lot with the keys in it. It's yours. There's a check in the glovebox for fifty thousand dollars. Made out to you. You're going to get in that car and drive until you pass out. Then drive for another two days. I don't care which direction. I'll make sure you're in the clear. No Renellis. No Rebel Raiders. Only one condition."

I swallow. My throat's gone entirely dry. Heavy's size alone is intimidating as hell. "Which is?"

"You never come back to Petty's Mill. You never contact

Forty or Fay-Lee or anyone affiliated with Steel Bones ever again."

"Lou?"

"That's your choice. He can stay in contact with you, or he can hang around here. Both isn't an option."

He looms there, glowering, crowding the room. Scary as shit, to be honest.

"A Ford Focus, eh? Not sure how to take that." I giggle, my nerves making me sound on the verge of hysteria.

"Take it. Go. There's nothing for you here. When it comes down to it, Forty will choose his brothers. Not you. He'll drop you. Again. Make the smart choice. Stop embarrassing yourself."

He sneers at me for another few seconds, and then turns. A horrible thought pops into my head, and I call out before he can go. "Would the Renellis hurt him? Over me?"

Heavy looks at me as if I just don't compute. "The Renellis and Steel Bones go way back. We would never war over you. You're not anywhere near as important as you think you are, Nevaeh."

Then he turns up his lip in disgust and stalks off, leaving the door wide open behind him, Bullet and Creech on his heels.

I exhale slowly. This must be how it feels like to encounter a bear in the woods and walk away unscathed. Badass for no good reason.

I scan the room. There's all sorts of crap on the floor. At a loss for what to do, I slide down and start scooping stuff up. It is kind of a dick move to trash someone's place, especially someone who's so obviously anal retentive.

As I straighten up, my visit from the-ghost-of-dickheads-past begins to put a couple things into perspective.

First, and I never would have guessed this, but my price

is apparently higher than fifty thousand dollars. And I know it was supposed to feel like a burn, like I'm a whore who can be bought, but if I'm worth fifty G's, I'm *way* more valuable than I thought I was.

Second, Forty still cares about me. It's as clear as the difference between a locked and an open door.

For the first time in a while, a sense of calm falls over me. I finish shoving a stapler and envelopes into a desk drawer, and I go collapse on his bed. His Army green comforter is crisp and clean and smells like spring fresh laundry detergent.

My brain swirls like it always does, but the loops are lazy and slow. I'm used to riding the ups and downs, but the past hour or so has been one hell of a crazy rollercoaster ride of emotion. It broke my noggin.

My eyes fall on Forty's desk. There are a dozen books lined up by size on the hutch. Frederick Forsythe. *Ben-Hur*. No pictures. The walls are bare. There's nothing on his chest of drawers but a wrench. It's the kind of room that some would say "needs a woman's touch."

I think Forty Nowicki needs a woman's touch.

I don't know what love is. I'm probably as wrong about it as I am about most things. But here's what it feels like to me.

When I was fourteen, I had a bonfire in me, crackling and bright, the kind you dance and laugh around. The kind you get lost staring into. When I was seventeen, Forty left, and the fire was doused by a downpour of freezing rain. There wasn't an ember left smoldering. Not one.

But still, a long time later, there's a place where the fire was. It's a good place for a fire. It's been waiting all this time. There's no love now, but you know what? There should be.

I'm no catch, but I'm worth more than fifty G's.

This is a barren room. It needs warming.

I yawn so wide it cracks my jaw. I grab the comforter and pull it over me like a taco.

Vaguely, I realize it's nuts to ignore a clear threat from Heavy Ruth. But I'm a goldfish. The danger left, I've swum around my bowl a few times, and the fear has already floated off into the babbling in my mind.

My lower back aches, my boobs are sore, and I'm exceptionally horny, so it's probably almost that time of the month. Do I have tampons? Maybe I shoved them in Carlo's messenger bag when I packed. What did I do with the bag?

I left a bucket of dirty mop water in the middle of the kitchen. Lou's gonna be pissed.

I haven't been to monster truck in years. I miss monster truck.

My brain misfires and meanders, and I pick at the loose stitching at the corner of the pillowcase.

This isn't going to be easy. Spitting in the eye of an entire MC. Rekindling a fire from nothing. But I love lost causes.

After all, I am one.

7

FORTY

I t's ten at night when I arrive back in the clubhouse from a fruitless day of searching for Rab Daugherty. I sent the boys out with their assignments in the morning, and I took the local VFWs. You can't roll into those places swinging your dick, so I spent the day slowly nursing light beers and chatting up old timers.

I met some guys who knew Twitch. Ran into a few vets I know from the hospital.

No leads.

None of the other brothers had much luck, either. Gus found a dude who never paid up after he lost to him in a race back in '97, but other than that, day one was a bust. I'm not that concerned. The message about the bounty is out. Now, we wait. Make ourselves visible. Twenty large is a great motivator.

I come back to one hell of a spread. People are still keeping close, the place is packed, and the old ladies have been trying to outdo each other in the kitchen. There's a whole buffet laid out: bar-b-q, all the sides, oysters, casseroles. I make myself a plate and force myself to take a seat at one of the long tables.

My feet want to make a beeline for Nevaeh. She's gonna be spittin' mad at this point. No doubt she's trashed my room. Maybe hurt herself doing it.

I half rise before I realize what I'm doing and force myself to plant my ass back down. She's a grown woman. Wash is on it. He would've texted me if something happened. She's fine.

Danielle sashays up with a beer, and I take it with a nod. She squeezes in next to me, and clinks her bottle to mine. Danielle's a second cousin on my dad's side. She used to babysit me when Mom was still around.

"So, it true you've got Nevaeh Ellis stashed upstairs?" Danielle was one who sent me pics after I left for Basic.

I shrug and chomp down on some pit beef.

"You should bring her down here. We can have dinner and a show."

Starla and Angel are nearby, listening in. They take their cues from the older sweetbutts like Danielle.

"I got an idea," Starla slurs. "We can run the hose out back. Make a mud pit. Bullet can take bets."

"I've been wanting to snatch that bitch bald since back in the day," Danielle laughs.

My back teeth clench. I get why the girls hate her, but they enjoy it way too much. "No one touches her."

A silence falls. "We should still do the mud wrestling," Angel says.

There's a vocal roar of agreement from the brothers at the far end of the table, and clanking of beers on the table, and after some negotiation, most everyone files or stumbles out back to make it happen.

The clearing crowd lets me survey the room. There, at

the bar, is Wash, bellied up without a care in the world, jawing with Boots and Grinder. What the hell? I check my phone. No texts that he's pawned off Nevaeh on another prospect.

I stand, head immediately in his direction.

"Who's on Nevaeh?" I've got Wash by the front of his shirt, out of his stool, before he even sees me coming.

"Peace, man. Heavy said he had it under control."

Heavy? Hell no.

I stride for the stairs, Wash on my heels. What did he do? My boots pound the floor, and brothers wisely clear out of my way. If she's gone, I'm gonna—

I jog down the hall. When I get to my room, the door knob turns easily in my hand.

She'll be hours away by now. She could be dead. Done by a Renelli or a Raider. What they did to Crista... Fuck! She's got no weapon. My heart's slamming against my ribs, gut churning as I rush in and careen to a halt.

She's passed out on my bed, in my shirt, on her belly with her legs spread and her ass hanging out. Her hand's cradled under her cheek, and there's a box of condoms and my copy of the *New Testament* beside her. Wash wisely hangs back in the hall.

Nevaeh snorts, startles, and then fights the blankets until she's sitting up, cross-legged. I can see her pussy lips puffing from her panties. My cock is instantly rock hard and throbbing.

She blinks and pushes her hair from her face. It springs right back forward again.

"Forty?" She rubs her eyes. "I'm hungry."

I glare at Wash over my shoulder. "Did you feed her?" This fucker is not getting a patch. And Heavy and I are gonna brawl.

"I'm sorry, man. Heavy said he'd take care of her. I do what the big man says, you know?"

Nevaeh must realize she's giving me a show—and I must be staring—because she blushes and draws her knees to her chest.

"Go get her a burger. And sides. Bring a six pack." Wash beats feet back downstairs. "Domestic!"

I slowly approach the bed and sit. You never know with her. Her temper comes and goes so quick.

She crawls over and perches next to me, dangling her bare legs over the edge. There's a few inches between us, and we're both facing the door. Guess she's cool.

I keep my back straight and my shoulders square as she yawns and rests her head on my bicep.

"What did Heavy say?" I ask.

"It was more of an *offer you can't refuse*." She does a cheesy mobster impersonation. My lips quirk. Clearly, Heavy doesn't remember Nevaeh all that well. She's more than capable of ignoring a word to the wise.

"What was the offer?"

"Fifty thousand dollars, a used Ford Focus, and a brand-new life!" She does a game show host voice.

"In exchange for?"

"Getting lost."

"But you stayed."

She shrugs, glancing down at her lap.

"Why?"

She completely ignores the question. "I want to see your shoulder."

This girl can give your brain whiplash. "Why?"

"I want to see where you got hurt. The rest of it."

"Why would you want to see that?"

"I just do. Come on. Take your shirt off." She starts tugging at my flannel.

"You can't just ask someone to show you their scars."

"Why not? You do. *Why are you here, Nevaeh? What's your game? Why, Nevaeh? Why? Why? Why?*" Now she's mimicking me. She's making me sound like one of the big, dumb Muppets.

"You never give me a straight answer."

"Okay. I'll give you a straight answer if you let me see your arm."

I raise an eyebrow. She narrows her eyes.

"Okay. Deal."

I take off my cut, fold it, and place it behind us on the bed. Then I unbutton the red plaid flannel underneath. She jumps to her feet and comes to stand between my legs. For once, she's inches away, and I'm not hard enough to pound nails. Instead, my stomach churns.

The burns aren't pretty.

Fuck. If she wants to see, she can see. I peel off my shirt, and I bring it to my lap to fold it, but Nevaeh snatches it from me before I can. She tucks it under her chin and starts rebuttoning as she eyes my tats.

"You got a full sleeve?"

I rotate my shoulder so she can see the work on my tricep. Creech did it. He's an artist. My dick twitches. I don't mind her looking at my ink.

"Is that a long-haired black cat eating a human heart?"

"Yeah."

"Is the cat leaping out of a bomb?"

"Yeah."

"Is that me?"

There's no sense in denying it. "I asked Creech to make you a rat, but he thought this was more badass."

Her mouth turns down. "That's mean."

Yeah. When we joked about it years ago, Nevaeh was in the past. Saying it now...I feel like an asshole. "I'm sorry. That was a dick thing to say."

Her brown eyes flick up to meet mine. "It's okay. If I got a tattoo animal of you, it'd be an enormous ass."

"Fair enough." I picture all the glimpses I've had of her naked. I haven't seen all of her, but I don't think she's got any ink. "How come you don't have any tattoos?"

"I was gonna. When I turned eighteen, I was gonna have Creech put your name on my left tit. The number, not the letters. That kind of fell through, for obvious reasons, and it occurred to me that maybe I'm not a lifetime commitment kind of girl."

"Seriously?" My dick's almost at full mast now, imagining my name on her pale skin.

"Seriously. You can ask Creech. Good thing I didn't, though. I'd have had to tell every person who saw my titties that I'm really into malt liquor."

I snort. Funny girl. She reaches out and traces the outlines of my other tats: the Steel Bones skull and hammers, the Army eagle perched on a sniper's crosshairs, the POW-MIA profile set against an American flag, the engine block on my bicep.

My abs clench. It's getting hard to sit still and let her explore, especially since she's biting her lower lip in concentration, oblivious to me.

"What are these for?" She strokes the scales, the nickel, the handcuffs, the wrench, and the Roman numerals XL.

"That's the crew. Heavy." I tap the scales. "Nickel. Charge. Scrap. And me."

Nevaeh trails her fingers over my shoulder to my collarbone, and my cock throbs. "You gonna get more?"

"Maybe. Creech finished the full sleeve a few months ago. I like having it finished."

Her fingers reach the outline of my burns. There goes the hard on. I shift.

She startles and jerks her hand away. "Oh, shit. I'm sorry. Does that hurt?"

"No. It's fine. You can touch me."

She peers into my eyes and resumes her exploring, testing to see if I'm telling the truth. I am. The pain is in the bones where the pins are holding me together.

She finds the scar from one of the surgeries and traces it down my forearm. "You broke your arm?"

"Yeah. Broke my clavicle and shattered my proximal humeral bone and my elbow. There's some nerve damage. I've got a decent range of motion, though."

"How did it happen?"

"Helicopter."

"I know that. What *happened*?" She's got my forearm and my bicep, and she's bending it and straightening it like the doctor, her forehead furrowed. I let her.

"There was a hard landing."

"Did it land on your arm?" She huffs. "*What happened*?"

She wants the details? All right. Fine.

"The tail rotor control linkage broke. We went into a tail-spin, and we crashed into a paved lot. I reached out to brace myself, but with the spinning—" I stop because my mouth is suddenly bone dry. Her eyes are glued to mine. She nods for me to go on, so I clear my throat. "I ended up landing on my own arm and crushing it against the metal seats. The seats are welded to the frame. They don't give."

She's holding my hand now, fingers interlaced. Her palm is clammy. "How did you get burned?"

"I crawled out. There was lot of bent metal, but no

smoke. I was alone in the far back. I circled around to help, and it burst into flame. So I tried to get the men out, and I got the co-pilot, but then my jacket caught on fire, and by the time we put that out, there was... We had to retreat."

Her hand tightens on mine like a vise.

"He died? The pilot died?"

"Yeah. Him and another passenger. But two of us survived. That's not common in that kind of accident."

"What do you mean?" Her eyes are turning to shiny pools.

"In a crash like that, usually there are no survivors."

And then she bursts out in tears, slamming her free hand against my chest. I grab her wrist. "You could have died!"

Her tits are heaving. There's snot. I don't know what to do. Nevaeh doesn't cry. "It was almost four years ago."

"You could have died, and I would have never seen you again, and that would have been the end!"

"I didn't. I'm fine." If you disregard the scars and the chronic pain. And I'm only accurate to six or seven hundred meters now.

She wipes her snot with the sleeve of my white button down, but the tears keep coming. "You were hurt! And I didn't even know until Lou happened to mention it!"

"Nevaeh. Calm down."

For some reason, that makes her cry harder. Her breaths are coming all jagged. Should I whack her on the back? Before I can decide what to do, she gags and bolts to the bathroom, kneels in front of the toilet, and pukes.

At that moment, Wash walks in with two plates piled with burgers, baked beans, and devilled eggs. He's got a six-pack tucked under his arm.

"Thought I should bring dinner for two, boss." His grin falls when he hears Nevaeh wretch. "She okay?"

"She's fine."

Nevaeh flushes the toilet.

"Uh. Sure, boss. You need anything else?"

"Close the door after yourself."

I set the plates on my desk—she rearranged all my shit —and I take her a beer. She's brushing her teeth. I press the cold bottle to the back of her neck. She yelps, but then she relaxes into me.

I wind an arm around her waist. I don't question the impulse. She needs to be close to me.

I need her close to me.

"You feel better?"

She sniffles and taps the toothbrush against the edge of the sink. "I feel horrible."

"You look pretty." I gaze at her in the mirror. Her hair's wild, her skin's pasty white, and her brown eyes are eating up half her face. She squirms, her thick ass brushing my thighs. My hard-on comes raging back.

"Don't tease me," she says. "I'm emotional."

"I'm not teasing. I love it when you look like a mess."

She snorts. "Oh, yeah?"

"Yeah. You look freshly fucked. I love that."

I unscrew the beer and offer it to her. She shakes her head. I take a swig.

She wriggles in my arms. "Let's go eat."

"We had a deal. I showed you my scars. Now you answer a question."

Her jaw clenches, and her eyes darken. She knows what I'm going to ask. She stops squirming and meets my eye in the mirror.

"Okay," she says softly. "We had a deal."

Her eyes are pleading with me not to ask. My cock wants me to leave it alone. It would be so much easier to drop it. Feed her and fuck her and figure out what to do with her later. I don't need to listen to her lie to my face again.

But maybe I'm a fucking optimist. Maybe if she cares whether I live or die, she'll tell the truth.

"How many men did you cheat on me with?"

She drops her head. "None," she says into the sink. "I didn't cheat. I messed around where I knew people would talk. What you got pictures of? That's all I did."

I tighten my arm around her middle, and lift her chin with my hand. She can look me in the eye while she lies.

"Just tell me the truth, Nevaeh. Tell the truth, and we can get past this. How many?"

Her gaze darts around the bathroom, like there's answers in the corners.

"How many?"

Finally, she opens her mouth. At first, nothing comes out. I drop my arms to my side.

Then she says, "Five."

"Five?" The word is a fist driving into my gut. "Who?"

She chews on her bottom lip. "I don't remember their names."

"The Rebel Raider?"

"Yes. Him."

"Who else?"

"I don't remember." Tears are streaming down her face again. She's not pretty. She just a mess. I step back.

"Why?"

She finds my eyes in the mirror. There's hurt there. And anger. No remorse.

"The deal was one question. I answered. Do you feel better now?"

"No."

She sighs. "Yeah. Me neither." Then she slips past me and crawls into the bed.

I stand in the bathroom doorway for a long time, waiting for her to say something. She huddles on the far edge of the bed, silent.

"You're not going to eat?"

"I'm not hungry," she says, quietly. "Can you turn the light out? I'm tired."

I flick the switch. I should go downstairs. Drink a bottle of whiskey, clear my head.

Instead, I sink down on the foot of the bed.

Nevaeh's still sniffling every minute or so.

"We were so young." It's weird, talking with the lights out. How you hush your voice.

She doesn't answer. I suppose it didn't require a response.

"I'm sorry," I say.

"For what?" Her voice is muffled by the sheets.

"I should have asked you something else." I mean to stop there, but there's something about the darkness that draws the words from my mouth. "I should have asked you if you thought about me at all these past years."

There's a rustling of cotton. "Did you? Think about me?"

"Every day." Despite myself. I did. A dozen times at least.

There's a quiet that stretches long, and then Nevaeh flips the comforter and pats the mattress. "You can have this side. Don't be poking me in the ass with your dick in the middle of the night."

My lips twitch as I bend to unlace my boots. "My bed. My dick goes where it wants." I peel off my clothes and drop them in the hamper.

"You've been warned." Nevaeh flounces to her side, and I climb in next to her. "Are you wearing underwear?" she asks.

"Nope."

She harrumphs and rolls onto her belly, tucking her arms underneath her. I smile in the dark, remembering. She's a stomach sleeper. I rest my hand on the small of her back, and she sighs, already dozing off.

There's a sharp ache in my chest and an uneasiness. Five. It was a quick answer. Certain.

Had the unmistakable ring of bullshit to it.

There's also the warm scent of woman, and the soft sound of her slow breathing as she resettles herself to line up her side and mine.

I think I've been asking the wrong questions.

Why was she so upset when she heard about the accident?

Why did she stay when Heavy offered her an easy way out?

Why is this the most at peace I've felt since she the last time she was in my bed, stealing the covers and babbling away?

And how do you get Nevaeh Ellis to tell the truth?

8

NEVAEH

When I wake up, I'm surrounded by Forty Nowicki. His hard dick is poking the small of my back, his arms are wound tight around me, and a muscular leg is thrown over mine.

His chest is hot against my back. My head is tucked under his chin.

There's so much sensation. The weight of him. His earthy smell. The quiet sound of his breathing. And all the memories of waking up here in the dead of the night, in a room much smaller and danker than this, climbing on him, riding him until we both cum and pass out.

It's not quite sunrise. The room is growing gray. The hall outside is finally silent.

Suddenly, Forty draws in a sharp breath and sits straight up. I shriek. His alarm clock goes off. He slams his hand down, and it stops.

My heart is in my throat.

"What was that?"

"Time to go."

He's already swinging his legs over the side of the bed.

Somehow, I feel foggier now than when I woke up. I rub my eyes, and he's already in the bathroom.

"Be ready to go when I get out," he calls over the flush of a toilet. "We need to be on the road in thirty."

We? Road? Thirty? What is he talking about?

I struggle out of the sheets and pad into the bathroom. Steam is filling the room, and he's already hidden behind the glass door of the shower. I slip my panties down and pee.

"Are we going somewhere?"

"Yup."

"Where?" These panties are not fresh enough to put back on. I kick them into a corner.

"You don't need to know."

"If we're going somewhere, I'll know where we are when we get there," I point out around a jaw-cracking yawn.

"Can't hear you."

I flush, wash my hands, and wipe steam off the mirror. I don't look so good. A shower would be nice. Doesn't sound like that's part of Forty's mystery plan.

Screw that.

I unbutton the shirt I slept in and let it drop to the floor. That'll drive him nuts. Then I slide open the shower door and step in.

Forty turns to me, suds in his hair, eyes round with shock. And then they rake down my front.

My nipples pebble. Spray from the stream hitting Forty dampens my skin.

I try to act cool, like it's nothing, like I hop in showers with guys all the time, but I really don't. And Forty? He's not any guy. He's huge, filling up the space with his broad shoulders. The water sluices off his chiseled pecs, his muscles rippling as he squares his shoulders and stiffens into his soldier's stance. It turns me breathless and awkward.

I grab a bar of soap, and it squirts from my hand.

I'm not bending over for it. It's all the way by the drain. Between Forty's legs. Under his hard, veiny cock. That's pointing at me.

"Here." He grabs my hand and rotates me so I'm under the showerhead. Hot water chases away my shivers. I stoop and swipe up the soap.

Forty's hair is rinsed, now. He seems finished, but he's not stepping out.

"You can go. I'll be quick." I soap up my hands. His gaze is traveling, roaming all over me. My tits. My pussy. Down my legs to my chipped, pink toenails. Up to my face. My body heats.

It's a weird time to get bashful, but I'm a weird girl.

"I can manage on my own." I jerk my chin toward the shower door.

Forty grabs his cock, strokes it slowly.

"Okay. Let me see you," he says.

"See me what?"

"Manage it on your own."

My breath catches. I don't know how I got here. I just woke up. I haven't had my coffee. I leapt before looking. Again.

"We need to roll out in seventeen minutes. Come on, Nevaeh." He snaps. "Time's wasting."

A throb starts between my legs. I run my soapy hands down my arms. Then I cup my tits, slide my slippery palms over my aching nipples. His breath quickens.

"Put your foot up on the side," he orders. His strokes are firmer now. And his gaze is focused between my legs.

I do what he asks. My pussy opens for him.

"Spread the lips. Show me your clit."

I use my fingers to open myself up. My clit pops from the hood. I graze it with the pad of my thumb, and shivers shoot up my belly. I whimper. Forty falls to his knees, his shoulders bracing me wide, his head delving between my legs.

And then his mouth is on me, sucking my clit, his tongue teasing, lapping, and I buck forward, chasing what I want. He isn't having it. He grabs my hips, pins me in place, and then he sucks my clit again, breaking only to circle it with the point of his tongue and blow hot breath over it.

He's learned a few things. I hate the thought, but I love his mouth and the way he's working me, so intent. I love his grip, firm and unyielding. He's doing what he wants to me, and I want him to.

An orgasm is coiling in my belly, tighter and tighter, and I'm sweating as the hot water pounds my back. I dig my fingers into his hard muscles.

"Make me cum," I pant. "Forty, please."

"You want to cum?" he murmurs between long licks.

"Yes!" I have to, or I'm going to explode. "Please!"

Forty stops, stands, and grabs my chin. "I want the truth. All of it. This isn't just sex." He kisses me lightly, firmly on the lips. I can taste myself. "And until you're ready, I want to go find a Rebel Raider and beat the shit out of him until he talks. You're comin' with. I can't trust you here alone. You move my shit around." Then he slaps my ass, slides open the shower door, and hops out.

"You got about two minutes of hot water left," he calls over his shoulder as he heads into the other room. "And we're leaving in eight minutes whether you're ready or not."

Joke's on him. I finish myself off in thirty seconds flat, and I'm ready to go a minute early, hair pulled back into the world's poofiest, messiest bun.

It was easy. My steps are light. I'm fizzling with happiness.

Whatever this is, it's more than sex. And I'm comin' with him.

As he walks down the hallway to the stairs, I fall into step beside him. As soon as we hit the commons, everyone does a double take and stares with contempt in their eyes. Heavy Ruth purposefully turns his back and stalks out of the room.

Guess my scarlet A is bright and shiny this morning. They can think what they want. I don't care.

Forty's by my side.

I'm right where I want to be.

~

FIVE HOURS LATER, I have changed my mind. I haven't done any long runs on a motorcycle since I was a teenager, and after several hundred miles doubling back and forth all over the tri-county area, my inner thighs are burning and my ass is numb.

Apparently, we're looking for something. Or someone. Forty won't say. Club business. We've been to honkytonk bars, tattoo parlors, package goods, the Elk Lodge, the Moose Lodge, the Optimist Club, the Oddfellows, both gun ranges, three community ponds, and two public fishing piers.

We're definitely looking for a man.

Forty tells me to stay by the bike, and while I hang out in the parking lot, he pokes around, talks to whoever he finds. I'm kind of impressed. Forty was never very gregarious, but he's bullshitting with all types.

Around one, my stomach starts growling audibly, and

Forty pulls into Duck's Diner on Gracy Avenue. Duck's has been around forever. It's a Petty's Mill institution. The décor has never been updated—plastic booths and no A/C—and neither has the menu. You can get a real cherry soda where they add the syrup.

I don't wait for Forty to mess around with his bike. I'm getting a little sick of him barking at me to stay like a dog and ignoring me otherwise. I know he's aware it's me riding bitch with my arms wrapped around him. He has to adjust his dick at each stop.

I drop my helmet on the seat, and bound inside, leaving him to catch up. The wooden screen door slams with a satisfying thud. Nothing smells as good as Duck's. The counter is polished wood, so old it has that mellow shine and the lemon scent from Grandma's house.

The place is packed, but no one bothers to look up. I nip back to the bathroom, do my business, and glare at my hair in the cloudy mirror. A helmet and seventy mile per hour winds have not improved the situation. At least my cheeks are pink. I pat my curls 'cause there's nothing else to be done and shake out the Steel Bones T-shirt I borrowed, trying to dry the sweat under my boobs.

It's a hot day for spring, inching towards eighty-five degrees. I can't wait for summer in the country. Summer in the city isn't the same. No real cherry soda. No swimming at the lake. No tubing down the river.

Forty and I used to do all that. We'd be outside every minute we could, and by July, I'd have hundreds of freckles, and he'd have every tan line you can imagine. Socks. Hat band. Short sleeve and tank top.

I want to do that again. Maybe I can convince Forty to take a break after lunch. Go to the bend in the river where we tied up the rope swing. See if it's still there.

First, though, I'm getting a Rueben with extra meat. Forty better be paying. I think my purse is in my car. Which is in the shop. Or did I leave my purse at home?

I rush back to the dining area, smiling, imagining how cold the river will be, and how wonderful it'll feel to sun ourselves naked on the bank after taking a dip. I can see it, feel it, and—

Forty's standing in the entrance, talking to a woman. Trying to smile at her. I think that's what this is. Kind of looks like a raccoon baring his teeth.

Her hand is on his arm. She's animated. She kisses his cheek. His hand presses briefly to the small of her back to steady her. She's wearing six-inch heels. In Duck's Diner.

She's tall. Blond. Wearing a perfectly-tailored, navy blue business suit. And coral lipstick.

Now she's introducing Forty to the guy she's with. He's short and thin with a collared shirt and a sweaty hairline. His handshake is quick and floppy.

They must be co-workers. She's about two thousand fathoms out of that guy's league.

And she's Forty's perfect match.

They banged. The way she's leaning in to talk to him. How he squared his shoulders? They definitely banged. Crap. Now I'm not hungry anymore.

I guess she's the ideal woman. Organized, loyal, with good common sense.

I hate her.

But that's unfair—and besides, maybe she's his realtor or something—so I make myself go forward, hand stuck out, friendly grin plastered on my face.

"Hi!"

The man with her startles.

She blinks at me. She has big blue eyes and killer lashes.

She kind of cocks her head and shoots Forty an expectant look.

"Amelia, this is Neveah."

She blinks a few more times, and then she grasps my hand. She has a firm grip. "Nice to meet you. I haven't met any of Forty's friends yet."

Oh, good. So maybe they've only banged once. "We're not friends."

"You're not?" Blink. Blink.

"Definitely more like enemies at this point." I stretch my lips until it feels like I'm at the dentist. "I'm Nevaeh." I grab the guy's hand, and he jumps and mumbles *Mike*.

"Mike! I've met a Mike before." I laugh, and he laughs, high-pitched and nervous, like a hostage. His gaze is careening from Forty's cut to his biceps to my hair to Amelia. She's got eyes for no one but me, though.

"I've never met a Nevaeh," she purrs. "Such a unique name."

"It's heaven backwards."

Blink.

"Heaven spelled backwards." Mike helps me out. "N-E-V-A-E-H. Heaven." Mike is inordinately pleased with himself. He relaxes a little and sips from his cup.

"I'm sorry I haven't returned your call yet." Amelia's done with me and my name, and she's aiming those freakishly blue, blinky eyes up at Forty. "The system went down. Again." She cuts a look at Mike. He sips so hard on the straw he hits bottom.

"Refill!" He holds up his cup and lopes off to the lunch counter.

"No worries." Forty shifts slightly on his feet. Oh, he's sweating this. Good.

"I had a really great time the other night. That steak

was the best." Amelia's not looking at me at all, but I'm picking up what she's laying down. She's staking her claim.

Forty grunts.

"It's so strange. Seeing you in your vest." She trills a giggle and strokes a finger down his cut. Oh, gross.

Forty's jaw tightens. He doesn't know what to say. The situation has short-circuited his brain.

"On the phone. You mentioned doing something this weekend? Maybe you could finally take me for a ride on your motorcycle."

Come on, Forty. Tell her you can't. You're with me. Take her aside. Let her down easy. Or grab my hand. Rest your arm across my shoulder. Come on.

There's a painfully long pause, the kind I usually leap into with reckless abandon, but I'm biting my bottom lip so hard my nose itches from the pain.

"I, uh. That's not gonna work out."

An awful heat blooms in my chest. My face burns. And I've got that feeling. That end of the rope, about to let go, crazy, wild feeling. *That's not gonna work out?*

"So." I smile with all my teeth. "Did you two bang yet? Or am I reading this right and you guys are still in the *will they, won't they* phase?"

Mike has rejoined us with his drink, and he's mid-sip when he does a spit take.

I hold up my palms. "Don't let me get in the way. I'm just the ex who woke up to his dick in her ass this morning."

Mike hacks so hard he has to lean for balance on the bubble gum machine.

I cover my mouth. "Oops. That came out wrong. His dick wasn't *in* my ass. It was nestled *against* my ass."

Amelia's mouth is hanging open. If my heart didn't feel

like it just got stomped by a boot, this would be really entertaining.

"I mean, his dick has been in my ass plenty in the past. But not this morning. Just wanted to clarify that."

"Nevaeh," Forty growls in warning. Fuck him. I don't have to play nice with the corporate ladder climber he's trying to nail.

I don't have to play nice with him, either. You know what? I don't have to play with him at all. Where is this getting me? Not back to my man, the one who'd never in a million years leave me alone in parking lots or let there be a single doubt in anyone's mind that I belonged to him.

That man doesn't exist. Maybe he lives in the past. Maybe only ever in my imagination.

My head swirls as all my blood sinks to my feet. Reality glares at me, her neck set back, nose wrinkled in disgust, coral red lips pressed into a thin, disapproving line.

But there's no white knight rushing to save me. Not from monsters or mobsters or being embarrassed as hell in Duck's Diner.

There's just this man. Stuck in his pride. Can't see what's in front of him. Likes me well enough on my knees, but doesn't think I'm quite worth it in the broad daylight.

Yeah, fuck that.

"Did you drive?" I ask Mike who's finally managed to breathe again.

"Uh. Yeah. I have a Hyundai."

"All right. I like Hyundais. Can you give me a ride somewhere?"

Mike's eyes fly to Forty. Fuck *that*, too. "You don't need his permission."

"Nevaeh." Forty's voice is an octave lower. Oh, he's serious now, is he?

"It's your lucky day, Amelia. Forty here can give you a ride on his motorcycle, or you can ride along while Mike gives me a lift. Your choice."

"Uh, the, uh, server. I really need to get back to work —*We* really need to get back." Mike's physically cowering, and all Forty's doing is raising an eyebrow at him. "Uh, maybe you could call a ride share?"

Oh, Mike. You disappoint me.

This day is turning into a shit sandwich. No ride. No Reuben. I'm sure as hell not asking Forty to front my ten bucks so I can get something to eat while he firms up a date with his tall, blonde, ideal rejection of everything I am.

No glimmer of hope that I can mend something, make something work out for me finally.

Well, at least my feet work.

"Nevaeh, wait for me at the table." Forty jerks his chin at a booth. Oh, he still thinks this is me making a scene and him playing the put-upon, long-suffering man.

I flip him the bird as I walk out the door.

As the screen door slams, I catch a glimpse of Amelia getting up in Forty's face, as she starts, "You never said you were—"

I jog through the parking lot and down the block, heading toward the waterfront. Hopefully, Amelia buys me some time. I don't want to do this anymore. I don't want to keep reaching out, opening up, just to get slapped back down.

Why did I think this was going to be some healing journey? God, how did I not see that all I was doing was giving the universe a wide-open shot to grind me down once and for all?

My eyes are burning, but I'm not gonna cry. I'm gonna go sit on a bench at the promenade, and I'm going to let the breeze off the river cool me down, and when I'm not falling apart anymore, I'm going to start the ten-mile hike to Lou's house.

No. Better yet. I'm going to go to the Steel Bones Clubhouse and get that Ford Focus from Heavy. I'm gonna drive to someplace I've never been, maybe the mountains, someplace where the sun doesn't beat down on you so hot in early spring.

I cross the street, still hustling, and I'm panting now, sweat trickling down my back.

I'm planning it all out, Denver or Boulder or better yet Telluride, when I remember Shirlene. I promised her we'd start work on Ray's basement this weekend.

I slow to a walk.

Shirlene tries to hide it, but her knees are really giving her trouble. She won't be able to haul stuff up and down those steep steps by herself. And we've got to clear the basement. The mice are nesting down there. It doesn't matter what we do on the first floor if those little fuckers are having baby-making orgies downstairs.

I can't run away. They need me.

A calm swells in my chest. It's not a soothing calm. Awfulness is still sloshing around inside me, but my mind is clearing. I'm centering.

When I get to the Promenade, I'll ask someone to use their phone. I'll call Shirlene to come get me. She will.

I'm not alone.

And that's when I hear the roar of Forty's bike. I consider ducking into an ally, but there's none convenient. Besides, I stand by that middle finger. I am absolutely willing to repeat myself.

Hell, maybe he's going to whiz by with Amelia riding bitch. Maybe he'll be alone, and he'll just keep going.

I stiffen my spine and school my face.

He pulls up parallel to me and shouts something.

I can't hear him over the engine.

I keep walking.

He duck walks his ride along Gracy Avenue. Cars swing around him. None of them dare honk.

"Nevaeh! Get on the bike!"

I heard him that time. I roll my eyes and keep truckin'.

"Goddamn it!" He passes an open parking space and pulls in.

I'm nearly a block further when he jogs up behind me, boots clomping on the pavement. He grabs my upper arm. I jerk my elbow forward, and his grip's tight, so I end up digging his fingers into me. A small whimper escapes before I can swallow it.

He instantly drops my arm. "Nevaeh, stop."

I start walking again, picking up my pace.

He sighs and falls into step beside me.

"Where are you going, Nevaeh?"

"Doesn't concern you."

"You're not safe walking around on your own."

"Noted. You can fuck off now."

"Come back to the bike. I can drop you back off at the clubhouse."

"I'm not going back there."

"Goddamn it, Nevaeh." He stops in his tracks, spearing his fingers through his hair. I keep marching. He huffs and trots to catch up.

"I didn't fuck her."

"I don't care."

"You're acting like you care."

"I don't. It's not my business."

"Nevaeh." He sounds exasperated as hell. As if I'm a

child having a temper tantrum, and he's the reasonable one. That's always been his position. And didn't I oblige?

I take a deep breath, and I stop by one of those pretty benches they added when they redeveloped downtown. I exhale slowly.

"Listen. This is a mess." I wipe sweat off my forehead with the collar of my T-shirt.

"I just broke things off. We'd been on a few dates. That's all."

I shake my head. That doesn't really matter. I sink down on the wrought iron bench. There's a huge maple tree behind it, so the metal is cool against my thighs. Cars shush by. Across Gracy Avenue, there's an old church with a red door, its front yard filled with hydrangeas.

Shirlene told me something interesting about hydrangeas once. Their colors depend on the pH of the soil. The ones across the street change from blue to purple to pink.

Forty stands, looming, back straight and face hard, as if he's waiting for orders.

I draw my knees to my chin, wrap my arms tight around my calves.

Finally, he lowers himself next to me. His jaw's tight. He's radiating tension.

"You want the truth. All of it." I hug my arms tighter. "Okay. Here goes."

I don't know where to start. So I start at the beginning. "The night I came home from the eighth-grade dance, my stepdad came in my room and jacked off on me and told me if I didn't say anything, he wouldn't tell my mom that I came onto him."

Forty makes a strangled sound beside me. I wait. He doesn't say anything.

I'm staring straight ahead at those hydrangeas. A light breeze is rippling the blossoms. "He kept doing it, with like, variations, and I didn't tell anyone, and I pretty much pretended in my mind that it wasn't happening. Except for when it was. And then I met you."

He's breathing heavier, pained breaths.

"I wish I could say he stopped, but he didn't. He said what would your boyfriend think if he knew what a dirty girl you are?"

The rotting ball of shame and fear, the ugly thing that lives in my chest, rattling around, sucking blood and weighing me down, it rises and sticks in my throat like tar.

"And then you decided to enlist. And I knew it was going to get worse. I tried so hard to convince you not to go. But when I was a kid, I was also really good at pretending things weren't actually happening. I think I was genuinely surprised when you left."

I remember waking up and thinking *what are Forty and I gonna do today*? And then I remembered driving him to the airport the day before, and I had a panic attack in the shower.

"I never really cheated on you. But I tried to make you think I was. It was childish. You were right."

Forty is motionless beside me. I don't dare look at him. I don't want to see the disgust on his face.

"Anyway, I was a mess. But in the end, it was good, you know? I lost my mind, messed around with all those guys when I knew there was a sweetbutt there to take a picture. It was like I was blowing up my own life. When Annie and Harper beat my ass, it was permission to leave. I should thank them one day. They gave me the push to save myself."

I lay my cheek on my knee. "So that's the truth. All of it.

You can go now. We're good. We're done. It's settled. I don't want to do this anymore. You can go now."

I exhale. There's a hot prickle in the corner of my eye. I watch the cars go by. Whatever he's going to say, I don't want to hear it. *I wish I could kill him. You should have told me. How could you let him do that? Why didn't you tell?*

Maybe he'll make one thing in my life easy and stand up and just walk away.

I count thirty-two cars before he finally makes a move and stands. Reflexively, I look up.

His face is grim. Shuttered. His jaw is tight. Every muscle in his neck is standing out.

He holds his hand out to me, palm up. And he leaves it there.

I search his face. I can't read it at all.

"Come on," he says. "Let's go home now."

I stare at his calloused hand. It's huge. I shouldn't take it. I can't trust it.

I never really tried, though, did I?

"I'm not gonna hurt you, Nevaeh. Not ever again." He's not pleading. He's promising.

If I was a different woman, if I was wise or tough like Shirlene, I'd walk away and keep walking. But I'm Nevaeh Ellis. For good or ill, I can't be anyone else.

I take his hand. It's rough, and he squeezes too tight.

It feels good. Leaping without looking. Hope placing a wild bet against experience. It feels crazy and risky and dangerous.

It feels right.

~

I DON'T ASK where he's taking me. We head out of town, up toward the bluffs. I hold on around his waist, but unlike this morning, he covers one of my arms with his, twining his fingers in mine and pressing my hand to his hard belly. This is how we used to ride when we were kids.

The sun beats down on my helmet, and my scalp is itching from the sweat. I think I'm getting a sunburn. I feel wrung out and nervous, and my stomach's growling.

I need a break. If we pull up to another social club or package goods, I'm quitting. There are no businesses up this way, though. Only renovated farmhouses and a lone rancher here and there as the elevation rises. We've hit the Petty's Mills equivalent of the 'burbs.

And then there's a fake stone wall with a sign that reads *Gracy's Corner*. What are we doing where the rich folks live?

Forty lowers his speed to the posted twenty-five, and he waves at the man in the gatehouse. The gate rises before we get to it. I guess they know him.

I've been to Gracy's Corner a few times in high school. The rich kids always like to party with the delinquents. We had weed. It was always clear, though, that when Daddy got home or the cops showed up, they didn't know us.

We circle the roundabout with the pretty gazebo in the middle and head uphill. The street names are super cutesy. Ever After Court. Riverwatch Lane. Rocking Horse Circle.

Who does he know that lives here?

Finally, he turns down a cul-de-sac—Loewen Tree Terrace—and drives up to the house at the very end. It's enormous. There's another McMansion on one side and an empty lot on the other. There's a view of the wooded valley that the Luckahannock runs through.

Double garage. Brick. Huge windows. Wraparound front porch. The lawn is so green and thick and perfectly cut it looks like AstroTurf. This place must be over half a million, easy.

He cuts off the engine and helps me off the bike.

"Who lives here?"

"I do."

"Bullshit." There's properly mulched landscaping filled with lush green shrubs, hot pink peonies, and rhododendrons about to blossom. "Those are your flowers?"

He shrugs as he unbuckles my helmet. I swat his hand away and do it myself.

"The HOA has a guy. He's got a company. I pay him."

"You have an HOA?"

"Pain in the ass. Can't work on my bike in the driveway."

I don't get it. "I thought you lived at the clubhouse?"

"Most of the time, yeah. But I got this place, too. Come on." He grabs my hand and leads me to the front door. He keeps glancing down, watching my face.

He's probably thinking about Ed Ellis in my bedroom. My gut churns.

"You hungry?" he asks as he unlocks the front door.

"Nope." I want a shower. And a nap. And a time machine. Is he just not going to say anything? I'm into denial as much as the next girl, but it feels...anticlimactic. I guess I thought he'd be mad. Or something.

The only thing that's changed is that now he has a tight grip on my hand.

"I'll show you around."

I shrug. So far, there's not much to see. A roomy foyer with high-ceilings, natural light streaming in from those big windows. No furniture. It's open concept, so I can see the living room. There's a leather sofa and an enormous TV mounted on the wall. That's it. The kitchen is on a two-step rise. A breakfast bar with stools and a fridge bigger than any closet I've ever had. Nothing on the countertops.

"Do you like it?" He's standing at attention at my side, staring at the kitchen with me.

"Dusting must be a breeze."

"I got a service for that."

His phone rings, and he gives me a *wait a second* finger, heading into the other room to take the call. I poke in his cabinets while I eavesdrop on him arguing with someone, telling them to send Mikey or Bucky, he'll check in later. He's got the bare minimum in his pantry. Pasta and sauce. A box of Au Gratin potatoes.

The kitchen has two ovens, though. One next to the other, and two ranges on top with a griddle in between.

Forty ends his call with a grumpy "figure it the fuck out yourself" and wanders back in. I'm fiddling with the superoven. It's bright blue on the inside. Fancy.

"How come you're rich?" I'm just gonna come out and ask. There's no way the Army pays this well.

"Steel Bones Construction. All patched in members get an annual dividend."

I whistle. "Business must be booming."

He doesn't answer. This must be getting uncomfortably close to "club business."

"Come on." He tugs me toward the stairs. There's a landing halfway up and a railing along the upstairs hall like in a movie. A fancy chandelier hangs in the middle.

"You swing from that?" I nod up.

He grunts. He's not amused.

"This is a spare room." He opens a door and shows me an unfurnished bedroom with the vacuum marks still showing on the carpet. There's a walk-in closet and a communicating door opens to an en suite.

He leads me to the next doorway. "Spare room."

This bedroom must connect to the other's bathroom.

He rests his hand on my lower back and urges me on. I lean back into the touch. It's firm. Soothing.

"Let me guess. Spare room?"

"Library."

This empty room doesn't have a closet or en suite. Nor are there any books. But it does have a wall of built in shelves. Bare except for a lone can of WD-40.

"Very nice."

He's still touching the small of my back, and now his arm is crossed in front of him like a square dancer so he can hold my hand, too. I'm tangled up in him. The hollowness in my chest that erupted on my walk down Gracy Avenue shrinks a little.

"Half bath." He nods at a shut door.

He leads me to the open doorway at the end of the hall. "Master bedroom."

"So this is where the magic happens?"

At least this room is furnished. There's a California King-sized bed, neatly made with a gray silk comforter and at least six pillows, not counting the decorative ones. There's a heavy, dark wood chest of drawers, mirrored dresser, upholstered chair and ottoman, and a bench at the foot of the bed.

I wriggle my fingers until Forty drops them, and I wander in. French doors lead to a kind of balcony-veranda thing. His backyard is enormous. It goes for at least an acre before it slopes down a steep incline towards the woods.

"Sledding," he growls in my ear.

"Jesus!" I nearly jump out of my skin. He crept up behind me. "What?"

"That's why I picked this house. That hill. It'll be perfect for sledding."

I crane my neck up, a smile softening my lips. We used to go sledding at the community college. They had a great steep hill, and you had to keep your wits about you, or you'd end up sailing onto Route 12. I ate a lot of snow, tackled by Forty at the last minute before I went sliding into the path of a car.

"Have you been? Is it awesome?"

"Not yet." His lips are quirking up in the corners. He's meeting my eye instead of glaring at my face. Finally, he's looking a little less like I killed his dog. "Come on."

He opens the French door and guides me down the stairs to one of those outdoor living spaces they have on home improvement shows. It's almost five; the sun's inching down. The sky's a cloudless, vivid blue, the color that makes it feel low and thick.

"Pergola. Fire pit." He points past the deck area. "Hot tub."

"Hot tub!"

There's a hot tub! And it's gorgeous. It's round and set in a low wood deck with benches built in. I'm already kicking off my shoes. "Turn it on."

"Seriously?"

I'm peeling off my jean shorts. He keeps his eyes level with mine. My heart cramps. That's one of the reasons I never told any boyfriends about Ed Ellis. That look on Forty's face right now.

Screw him. There's a hot tub, and I'm sticky and gross and saddle sore. I'm taking a dip.

"Crank it up," I say as I pull my T-shirt over my head, slip off my bra, and work the elastic band out of my hair. Of course, my hair's knotted to hell, and I take a good clump out when I finally get the tie free.

It looks like Forty uses the hot tub a lot more than the rest of the house. He gets the cover off in no time, and it's steaming and ready to go.

"You bring the ladies here a lot?" The thought turns my stomach, but not enough that I don't dip my toes into the bubbles.

"It helps my arm. Keeps it limber. My physical therapist recommended it."

Oh. I glance over my shoulder. Forty's still keeping his eyes glued above my neck. Ugh.

"You coming in?" I step down into the frothing foam, and it's *amazing*. It's so clean and the perfect temperature, warm enough to make the air seem cool, but not so hot as to make you sweat.

"Do you want me to come in?"

Double ugh. I float in the middle, let the jets hit me from all sides.

"You asking me now? You didn't ask me on the picnic table behind Sawdust. Or at the clubhouse. Or at any point today."

He stiffens to attention on the deck. He stays frozen for a long moment, and then he shrugs off his cut and lays it on a lounge chair. Then he bends over and unlaces his boots, setting them neatly side-by-side under a bench. Finally, he shucks his T-shirt and jeans, folding both and resting them on top of his cut.

I watch him, arms crossed and resting on the side of the hot tub, lazily kicking my legs behind me. It's a symphony of sensation. Streams of water massage my sides, and when I twist just so, they nail my pussy. Wherever my skin emerges from the bubbles, the cool air nips, and the sunset's turning the distance purple and orange while the sky overhead seeps into a deeper blue.

Crickets are singing in waves, and in front of me, Forty's unwrapping his beautiful body, inch by inch. His tattooed arm. The scar and the burns. The chiseled stomach muscles and his sculpted back. His firm ass and his hard, veiny cock, bobbing in midair.

Well, nice to know *he* doesn't see me any differently.

Finally, he steps into the tub and takes a seat opposite me. I lay my cheek on my forearm and let my legs float. A jet tickles my belly.

"You comin' over here or do I need to come get you?"

I glance over my shoulder. Forty's eyes are glittering and dark.

"You want me over there?"

"Yes," he growls.

I make him sweat it for a few seconds and then I push back and let go, drifting over to him. He scoops me up and nestles me on his lap. His cock is blazing hot against my hip.

I'm exposed to the evening air from the waist up now. Goosebumps pucker my arms, and my nipples harden into achy points.

Forty doesn't paw at me. He holds me very, very tight against his chest, resting his chin on the top of my head. We both stare into the distance where the sunset casts its colors against the black outline of trees.

"I don't know what to say," he finally says low, right into my ear. Little shivers zip down my neck. Warm breath against my chilly neck. My crazy brain is anchored to the moment. "If I knew the right words, I'd say them. But everything I think to say—it's wrong."

I rest my head on one of his pecs. His body is amazing. He's so strong. So solid.

"Say whatever you want."

There's a jet pounding the vertebrae right at the bottom of my spine. It's making the spot tender, but it feels too good to shift.

"I would have killed him."

"I know."

"You could have told me."

"Nope." I drop a kiss right above his nipple. I let my lips linger to see if I can feel his heartbeat. "I couldn't tell anyone. Not for years."

"I should have known. Fuck. I should have made you tell me." His body's tensing underneath me. Priming to fight. His arms wrap more tightly, and he's surrounding me. As if he's trying to protect me.

"You couldn't have known."

"You went crazy. I left, and you went crazy. And I never fucking asked why." His voice breaks. It's an ugly sound.

"You did ask. *What the fuck is wrong with you, Nevaeh?* Like a dozen times."

"Why are you trying to let me off easy?"

"Why are you trying to beat yourself up?"

"'Cause I fuckin' deserve it. Goddamn, Nevaeh. You were *everything* to me."

"Nah." I keep my voice gentle. I don't want him to think I'm blaming him. "You wanted to see the world. Make a man of yourself. You wanted me, too. Sure. But you wanted that for yourself. That's okay. Kids grow up. That's what they're supposed to do."

"You think you weren't the world to me?"

"It's water under the bridge."

"No." Suddenly, Forty shifts me until I face him, my legs straddling his thighs, and he grabs my chin and makes me look him in the eye. "You were my whole goddamn heart. All these years since? Just me tryin' to keep living without one. I reenlisted 'cause there was nothing for me here. I bought a house. I want a family. But I can't put anything in it. It's *your* house. I go out with women; they're nice—"

Oh, yuck. I don't want to hear this. I try to cover his mouth, but his enormous arms are blocking me.

"—They're not you. I don't even remember their names."

"They must love you."

"Don't make a joke out of it, Nevaeh. Do you know what I thought about on that helicopter? When I was falling out of the sky, and I knew I was gonna die?"

I muffle a soft cry by smushing my lips closed, and I dig my fingers into his biceps. I hate that image. I don't want it in my head.

"Your face. Your wild hair. Your huge smile. Your beautiful face. Goddamn it, Nevaeh. Why didn't you tell me? I wouldn't have had to be mad all these years."

"You didn't have to be mad," I whisper.

"You didn't have to stay gone." He wraps his arms around me again, crushing me to his chest. "We're both stubborn as hell."

"Yeah." I smile into his damp skin.

"Do you like the house?"

"It's all right. Could use more of a view." The sky's exploding in pastels now, every color of rainbow sherbet, and a smattering of stars are twinkling overhead.

"Nevaeh." Forty runs his fingers in my hair, holding my head in place. He searches my eyes. "Always tell me the whole truth. Trust me. Promise."

Heat gushes between my legs.

"Okay." I tilt my hips forward so my clit grazes his cock. It's now tucked between us, pointed straight up. I whimper and buck. The stretch in my hips, the bubbles on my toes. It all feels so good. My eyes drift shut.

"Nevaeh." He shakes me—gently—and I open my eyes again, but I keep grinding, slipping my slick pussy against his wet cock. I'm swollen, almost unbearably tender. "Are you focused?"

Nope.

I nod yes.

"Are you, uh. Does it bother you? To have sex?"

Bother is a weird word. I stop rubbing myself on his cock.

"All evidence is to the contrary, Forty."

I don't want to talk about this with him. I know I'm... sexually glitchy. Some people, they can't stand to be touched. I went the other direction. I tried to erase everything with Forty, and after him, with whoever I was with. My brain misfires sometimes, and I'll strike out without warning—kind of a startle reflex—or I get the panic sweats sometimes. But not often. And I can make myself cum. I figure I'm as good as I'm gonna get.

I don't want to be thinking about this. Not in a hot tub.

And Forty's getting soft against my belly. And I'm cold.

"I have trouble getting hard sometimes."

What? Record scratch.

Forty sniffs and stares over my shoulder. "After the accident, I was on a medication that fucked with my erections, and I stopped taking it, but I'm still like, fifty-fifty."

I cock my head. Just 'cause I can't believe he's telling me this. Forty Nowicki is not the kind of man who shares. Well, he wasn't. I guess I don't know the man he's become all that well.

"All right. More like sixty-forty," he amends.

"I wasn't doubting your percentage!" It probably looked

like I was. Oh, I'm a jerk. "Both are very good odds. Like, the Lotto is millions to one."

He cracks a wry smirk. "The ladies do feel lucky."

I slap his wet chest, making my palm sting. He chuckles from the belly.

"No one wants to hear about the forty to fifty percent of the dates that you banged."

He snorts, still laughing, and he stands, cradling my bare ass, as if my weight is nothing. He steps out of the tub and heads for the back door.

"Hey! We were hot tubbing!"

"We can hot tub again after."

"After what?"

"After you get lucky."

"Oh, I'm getting lucky, am I?" With each step, I'm bouncing against his dick, and it's hard again, like steel, and I wrap my legs tight against his waist, let my slickness coat him. Butterflies go crazy in my belly. This is it. This is happening.

He carries me up the grand stairs, down to the master bedroom.

"If you feel like you're gonna freak out, tell me. Slap my head or something."

"Slap your head?" I giggle as he drops me on the bed and does a push up over me, urging my thighs to part with his knees. He strokes the inside of my arms, drawing them up beside my head, and he drops light kisses down the blue vein that runs from my wrist to my elbow.

I squirm. The head of his cock brushes my clit. I moan.

When his mouth reaches my shoulder, he nips it, and I shriek. Shivers zing up my neck and race down my spine. I'm covered in sensation. The heft of his body pressing me into the comforter. The smell of him and the scrape of my nipples across his chest every time I draw in a deep breath. The dimness of late evening, and the chilly breeze coming through the French door we left open.

The wanting, hungry grunts he makes as I writhe, chasing his cock, working my knees higher so he'll fill me up where I ache. I want to be lost. Totally. Utterly. In him.

"You can do it. It's okay. I'm good." I'm begging him, urging him with my rolling hips, and he's lazily kissing my neck and stroking his rough fingers down my side, tickling me gently 'til I wriggle, and then roaming with his hands over my belly, cupping my tits.

"Come on, Forty. Do it." I'm panting. I'm dripping cream, and I can't reach my clit because he's taking up all the room.

"Do what?"

He nibbles the crook of my neck and nudges my pussy with the head of his cock. I buck to take him in, but he draws back, and I can't follow because his chest is pressing mine, and our fingers are entwined above my head, and he's kissing me, tasting me with his tongue.

"What do you want me to do?" he murmurs into my mouth.

"Fuck me. Please. Forty. Please."

And he cradles a thigh, lifts my leg to open me up, and slides home, slow and steady, stretching me, and it feels so good, so right, and he's kissing me in time with his thrusts, and in between, he's whispering in my ear.

"I love you, baby."

"Does that feel good?"

"I missed you, baby. So goddamn bad."

"You're so beautiful like this."

"I love you."

"I love you."

My heart fills up and overflows, and as the coiling in my

belly tightens and bursts, and I squeeze his cock, and he cums inside me, I think *I love you, too. I always have. I never stopped. I never will. Not ever.*

I'll tell him about the car tomorrow. He'll understand. I had to do it. He wasn't going to give me a chance. It was only a dumb prank. A ruse to get him to give me the time of day. He'll understand. He's different now. I'll tell him I was the one who carved up the hood of my Hyundai first thing in the morning.

I'll feed him first. He'll be cool about it. It'll be a laugh, not a betrayal.

He holds me for hours, tickling me, teasing me, and we nap, and then we wake up and do it again. Around eleven, I fall into a deep sleep.

An hour or so later, a loud thwack and crack, followed by another and another in rapid succession, startles me awake. The bed is empty. I run to the French doors, grabbing my dirty T-shirt from the chair where Forty folded and stacked it neatly with my jean shorts earlier.

The moon is high, and it's almost as bright as day in the backyard. Forty's at the fence separating his house and the empty lot. He's chopping it down with an ax.

Moonlight glides along the rippling muscles of his arms. Thwack. Crack. Splinter. A patch of fence sways and then falls, dangling from a post. Thwack. Crack. There goes the post.

I pad down the stairs and cross the lawn, cold dew numbing my bare toes, until I get a few yards away.

He's got his earbuds in. I can hear the death metal from where I stand.

His expression is pure fury, his teeth bared, sweat dripping down his temples, his hair poking up all over as if he's been driving his fingers through it.

I bend and grab a shard of fence and toss it gently at his bare back to get his attention. He turns, taps off his phone. His chest is heaving.

I work my arms inside my T-shirt and hug myself for warmth. "So. You, ah, doing a little demo work?"

He lowers his gaze, chagrined, and he tries to school his expression but rage is etched in every line of his face and in the burn in his eyes. "I'm giving you more of a view."

He's managed to knock down a good eight feet already.

"You need help?"

"You don't have shoes on. You'll get splinters in your feet. Go back to bed."

"I can't sleep. There's an idiot demolishing a fence out here."

Forty's head drops back 'til he's staring blindly at the sky. The ax falls with a thud in the grass. "I can't stand it. I can't stand that I didn't stop it."

"Yeah. Me too. I'm sorry."

"Don't ever be sorry."

"Don't try and boss me." I stretch the T-shirt over my knees and sit, cross-legged, on the ground.

"I left you." His voice hurts me; it's so tormented with guilt.

"You didn't know."

He shakes his head as if that doesn't matter at all. "Why didn't you tell me?"

"Lots of reasons." I pick through the wreckage from that time, try to pick what will hurt him the least. "Mostly I didn't want you to stop loving me."

"I would have never stopped loving you."

I don't know. He wouldn't have *wanted* to feel differently. "Maybe. Maybe not."

"No. I wouldn't have." He stoops, grabs the ax, and swings at a board.

"How do you know?"

Thwack. Slats crack. "'Cause I love you now."

Well. Okay. I rock back, T-shirt stretching as it hugs my knees. My butt's wet and cold, but my chest is glowing.

"Are you gonna tear this whole fence down?"

"Yeah." He pauses mid-swing. "Unless it bothers you."

"No, go on. I'll watch."

"You'll watch me knock down the fence?"

"Yeah. You said you're giving me more of a view. Go on. We'll be able to see the sunrise across the valley."

"You're gonna freeze your ass off sitting on the ground. Go get one of those chairs with a cushion."

"What did I say about bossing me, Paul Bunyan?" I hop up and go for one of the deck chairs. It is too freezing on the ground.

"Get a blanket from inside!"

Thwack. Crack.

I slip inside and grab a throw and a beer. There's not much in the fridge besides condiments and a six pack of IPA. I'll have to get creative with breakfast. Or have him ride us into town.

I go back outside and curl in a chair, sipping the beer. I chat away as he tears down the fence, telling him all about nothing, chattering away like I used to. He answers every so often so I know he's listening—he always listened—and his strokes become more rote, less rage-filled.

Of course, me being me, I can't stay seated very long. I wander off to take another dip in the hot tub, and I go upstairs for my shoes. I roam around the house, poking in closets and drawers. I watch Forty from the windows. At one point, the neighbor's outside lights come on. I guess they think better of fucking with the ax-wielding biker 'cause the lights go off again a few minutes later.

I keep returning to Forty, though. I bring him a beer. I ask him for the password to his computer. It's Beretta92.

And I watch his fury ebb and flow, his powerlessness rise up and drive him to swing that ax harder and harder. Tear boards with his bare hands. I watch him get tired and keep going.

I don't want him to feel like this.

I don't want to feel better because he feels like this.

But there's no one on the planet except Shirlene and two or three others who know and care. If I called my mother right now, she'd hang up on me. She knows. But she picked her husband over me a long time ago. He's gone, but her choice lives on.

There's something about Forty's rage that tethers me down. That reaches into the past and shines a disinfectant light. This thing happened to me. It wasn't right. Every swing of that ax, every board that comes down, it's testimony.

Ed Ellis had no right to do what he did.

I deserve vengeance.

I deserve a white knight to ride to my rescue, even if he's years late, and I already saved myself ages ago.

I just hope I can keep him.

This beautiful, prideful man.

Busting down boards with his fists, letting the sunrise in while I tell him all the things I've been keeping for him, deep down, where love still lingered in the corners, waiting for me to be brave enough to come and get it.

9

FORTY

I love coming home. Nevaeh's here.

These days have been long. Four a.m. to four p.m.

Rab's in the wind, and it's felt like a wild goose chase since day three, and we're on day fourteen? Fifteen? Beating the same bushes for twelve hours a day on shifts, chasing down false leads. Word about the bounty has gotten out, and we've got several players from out of town combing the same ground, muddying the waters.

Frisco conducts his business with some suavity and professionalism, but the same cannot be said for the other dumbasses rolling in from Pyle and as far as Jersey and Detroit.

I'm spending as much time with locals smoothing ruffled feathers as I am checking in with our boys and following up on the more promising leads. Heavy's found himself some mysterious tech genius who's working some magic, so we're reasonably confident Rab hasn't left the area. I'm beginning to suspect Rab's one of those men just really good at keeping his head down and staying in one place.

As I pull into my drive, I understand the mentality. Every minute on the road I'm thinking about being back here. And as soon as I see my big ol' empty house at the top of the street, my whole body thrums with adrenaline.

Nevaeh's here.

And as soon as I open the door, she's gonna come running. Every time. I have to position myself so my bad arm doesn't take the brunt of her weight—she's put on a little since she used to do this in high school—but I'm never going to tell her to stop. I'm gonna catch her every time.

She's goin' a little stir crazy, but I think I've impressed upon her the seriousness of the situation without going into detail. She knows she can't be running around. The Raiders have targeted her, and she can't be traveling the countryside with Shirlene.

Nevaeh keeps trying to argue, tells me she has to talk to me about that, but then she ends up not having anything to say. And nine times out of ten, we end up naked with me balls deep in her sweet pussy.

I'd forgotten how it is with her. In a messed-up way, it's like pain. I can remember that right after the accident, I hurt worse than any physical pain I'd experienced before. By a factor of a hundred, at least. But now, I can only remember the fact of the pain. Not the sensation.

It's a fucked-up comparison, but that's what it's like with Nevaeh. I remember loving her. Being happy. The fact. Not the feeling. But the feeling—it's a million times better than the memory. There's nothing like it in the world.

All these years, I tried to convince myself I was young. Hormones. First love. But the reality is there is nothing that suits me better than Nevaeh Ellis.

I'll put it this way. I'm a soldier. I march. Straight ahead, mission focused, locked on target. I'm efficient, and I'm good at my work, but it sucks ass as a way to live. Nevaeh's a butterfly. Or one of those birds that flit from flower to flower—a hummingbird, giddy and bopping around for the sheer fun of it. Beautiful. She makes the marching mean something.

In the house, she doesn't go far, but she never stays in place. She buzzes around, saying crazy shit, leaping at me out of nowhere, all smiles and shrieks.

The way she fucks...she climbs me like a tree, or she gets obsessed with my biceps or my balls, and she hyper-focuses, her eyes going dreamy and dazed, and it's like she's starving, and I'm exactly what will satisfy her.

I make her happy. She doesn't have to tell me. It's written on her face.

Making her happy unknots the tangled-up shit inside me. I'd pretty much accepted I was gonna have to schlep it around until I die. But contented Nevaeh eases me. Gives me peace.

And about a week ago, when I got home, she didn't come running. I found her standing in the living room, staring at the TV, fists balled, white-knuckled, hyperventilating. The local news was on. They arrested some guy in Pyle for rigging up cameras in the changing room at a department store.

She was wild-eyed, rocking back and forth. She started telling me about this perv, and then she started in on Ed Ellis, and the floodgates opened, and I stood there, and I listened. I don't know how I didn't go dig that fucker up and burn his corpse, but I listened. And I didn't know what to say. The guilt... It claws at my guts.

I made her mac and cheese, and I poured her a whiskey. She got drunk and puked and fell asleep on my chest. I called Heavy at four in the morning to tell him I was out until later in the day, and he gave me shit.

He's not down with me getting back with Nevaeh. I haven't told him what happened to her. It's not my place. He'd better figure out this is my call and change his tune, though, 'cause my girl is where she belongs.

I wasn't there for her back then, but I'm not blinking this time. I know it's not gonna be a smooth ride. Hell, she's got the Renelli crime family after her, and the Raiders too, somehow. But she's mine.

She's where she belongs.

"Baby, where you at?" I come in the front door, and I'm greeted with beach towels hanging from the upstairs railing like United Nations flags.

"In here!" she calls from the living room. No running footsteps. My gut clenches, uneasy, instantly relaxing when I see her smile.

She's laying on her stomach, heels kicked up, in the middle of the floor next to Fay-Lee, Dizzy's old lady. They're watching TV and lining up empty pop bottles like they're on a sugar bender. Ah. She has company.

I didn't see a car in the drive. Dizzy must have dropped Fay-Lee off. She's still got the bruises from her run in with the Raiders at Twiggy's bar. Even as ornery as Fay-Lee can be, I don't see her flying the coop with things as tense as they are right now. She's an instigator, but she's not stupid.

I go and straddle Nevaeh's ass and start rubbing her shoulders. She moans and drums her heels against my back. I'm instantly hard.

"Why's there shit hanging from the bannisters?"

"Slip and slide."

I check out back. Oh, yeah. There's the tarp I use to

cover my bikes in the winter, nailed down the incline into the empty lot, covered in suds.

"You do that yourself?"

"I commandeered the prospect you've got watching me."

I put Boom on her. He's not as dumb as the rest of his crop. And he's a good shot. We've been to the range together a few times.

"You didn't let him slide, did you."

I like the guy, but I will kill him if he got slippery with my woman.

"I invited him, but he declined."

See? He's smart.

"Dizzy drop you off?" I nudge Fay-Lee's side. My opinion of her has changed these past two weeks. She's good people.

I really like that Nevaeh's making a friend. She doesn't think she's good at it, but she enjoys people. Me, I don't care. But I like her happy. She bounces and giggles when she's happy. It's cute as hell.

"Yeah. I told him if he kept me locked in the house one more day, I'd break out."

"It's dangerous out there now." I say it for both their benefits.

"No shit, Sherlock. A Raider tried to kidnap me." Fay-Lee swings her foot and whacks me in the side. "I almost got murdered."

My blood runs cold. The Renelli problem is close to solved. Heavy's in contact with Dominic Renelli, and he says it's personal between his moneyman Carlo and Nevaeh. He wants a call if his guy shows up so he can talk him down. He's got no interest in Nevaeh outside of keeping his man out of trouble.

The Raiders are a different story. Somehow, they got

Nevaeh in their sights. Most likely they had a man on me who followed me to her place from Broyce's that first night. The Raiders aren't businessmen. They're a cult set on doing Knocker Johnson's bidding, and Knocker came out of lockup a madman. Nevaeh's not safe until they're neutralized.

I lean over, let my weight press her back, and I whisper in her ear. "You stay inside or out back. Promise."

"Promise." She wiggles her ass and blood floods to my cock. "Ease up."

"Later, when Fay-Lee leaves, we'll drive out to the clubhouse, and we'll do some target shooting. You need a gun."

"That's a terrible idea," Fay-Lee pipes up from the kitchen. She got up to get herself some chips.

The cabinets are stocked now. I had Nevaeh use a delivery service. I think she ordered alphabetically and got distracted. We've got apples, bananas, chips, doughnuts, and eggs. And no meat, milk, paper towels, et cetera.

"How so?" I back up, sit on my ass, and draw Nevaeh into my lap. She nuzzles her head in the crook of my neck. "Nevaeh and I used to shoot cans up at the reservoir all the time. She's a decent shot."

"Not talking about the gun. Talking about the clubhouse. Steel Bones is not exactly friendly toward your woman, Forty. You know that."

I do, and it pisses me off. Harper Ruth cheated on Charge. Grinder cheats on Ernestine on the regular. Wall cheated on Mona back in the day, took him four years to fix his fuck up. It's bullshit, and it's because Heavy won't give her the nod. The club follows his lead.

When this shit with the Raiders is over, Heavy and I are gonna have a reckoning. He's my brother. But he ain't my big brother.

"They'll have to get over it," I say.

"You want to hang out at the clubhouse?" Fay-Lee asks Nevaeh.

I can feel her tense. I wrap my arms around her middle. She nips at my collarbone. "Not particularly, but I'm sick to death of this house. No offense, Forty. Besides, we won't be there for long. There's not gonna be that much light left when we get there."

She falls quiet. I wait.

"It would feel good to shoot shit," she finally says. "Okay. Let's go." She pries my arms loose and hops up.

I didn't really mean right now. I wanted to haul her upstairs and work out this hard on until she cums on my cock. Get a shower. Eat.

But Fay-Lee is here. I don't care, but Nevaeh wouldn't want to be rude. If we go to the clubhouse, I can save Dizzy a trip up the hill. I can also get Nevaeh a piece better suited to her hand. All I have in the house are square butt revolvers, and she needs something smaller.

"All right, ladies. Get in the Jeep."

Takes 'em both a good half hour to find their shoes or whatever, but by five, we're pulling into the clubhouse. The parking lot's about half full.

Most our men are out looking for Rab or getting some Zs, so there's been more women around the clubhouse these past two weeks. This is painfully obvious when we walk into the commons, and two dozen females either turn their noses up at Nevaeh or turn their backs.

That's the last time that's happening.

I make note of which old ladies decided to make their opinions known so I can beat their old men up later.

I drape my arm over Nevaeh's shoulder. Fay-Lee sticks to her side after flipping some sweetbutts the bird. Yeah. I like her.

I leave Nevaeh with Fay-Lee at the bar while I grab a compact 9mm and eye and ear protection from the armory. Leaving her in the commons is intentional. It'll only take a minute, and I want someone to approach her. I feel like laying down a lesson.

When I come back, though, all is copasetic. Crista's working the bar. She's come over to chat, and everyone else is steering clear.

Good. I'll accept that for now.

"Ready, baby?"

Nevaeh kneels up on the bar stool to give Crista a hug—startling the hell out of her before she laughs and goes with it—and then my girl jumps down and leads the way out back.

"You coming, Fay-Lee?" she asks.

"Nope. I'm gonna hang with Crista here and get caught up."

I follow, watching her ass twitch in her tie-dyed booty shorts. She's wearing a matching cropped hoodie and white tennis shoes and ankle socks. Her hair's a wild bramble, she's tanned from hours lounging on the back patio, and toned from marathon sex, and from what she tells me, sessions in the home gym while I'm gone.

As soon as we shoot off a few rounds, I'm taking her upstairs, pulling those shorts to her knees, and eating her out 'til she pulls my hair. She loves oral to a point, and then all she wants is cock. She's not shy about letting me know what she needs, either.

I adjust myself in my jeans as I jog over to the recycling to grab a few bottles. There's a clearing at the far side of the yard that leads to a gully overrun by a thicket. There's no dirt bike trails or hunters back that way 'cause the terrain is impassable until you hit the base of the foothills a few miles away. We use it as a range when we can't get to the one in Shady Gap.

I set the bottles on the closer stumps. Nevaeh used to be a decent shot, but I don't know if she's kept up with it.

"When's the last time you shot a gun?"

I put flat to flat and slide the magazine home. Then I rack a round into the chamber, take the magazine out and put another round in so she's loaded plus one.

"When's the last time you took me to the range?"

"You remember the rules?"

"Point the muzzle in a safe direction."

"Yeah. And?"

"Don't rely on the safety."

"And?"

"Assume it's loaded. Know what's beyond your target."

"You're forgetting the important one."

"Make sure the barrel's clear?"

"Yes, but?"

"Oh. If I shoot, make it a kill shot. Don't stop shooting."

I sigh. She's rusty. As soon as this shit with the Raiders is put to bed, we're putting in some hours at the range.

"Put your muffs and glasses on." She covers her ears and eyes while I line up a shot. Thirty yards. Once upon a time, I could make the shot lefthanded with one eye shut.

I use a two-handed grip and exhale as I squeeze the trigger. A bottle explodes. Lucky me, it was the one I was aiming at. These days, I need more than a few shots to warm up.

"Your turn." I hand her the gun, and I take a step back, but I stay close and alert. Nevaeh needs to know how to protect herself, but she's also still Nevaeh. A cute squirrel comes running past, all bets are off.

She's different now in some ways. When we were kids,

she was always on to the next thing. Nothing could hold her attention.

Now, she gets serious about something, she doesn't let it go. Like she was gonna cook me dinner, have it ready when I got home from huntin' Rab. First day, she forgets to defrost the meat. We order pizza. It's not a thing. I don't expect dinner. I'm not my father, bitchin' that he's got to wait a few minutes 'cause plates aren't on the table the second he walks in the door.

Well, she tries again the next day. Meat's defrosted. She's gonna make burgers and corn on the cob. She's shucking the corn on the porch when I get home. Smiling and chatting, happy as can be. Cuts up onions and makes the patties from scratch. Smells amazing. She forgot the buns. Which is weird 'cause it starts with a *b*. She gets mad, kicks a kitchen cabinet, and hurts her foot.

Anyway, she's kept at it, and we've had a few good meals and some more take out. So, that's different. But she still has that distractible thing. I don't think she can control it. And with a weapon, you need to be focused.

In normal times, I wouldn't want her armed, but the Raiders are a real threat. I think what they did to Crista all those years ago...I think Scrap showed restraint by only beating the man to death. I would have ripped him limb from limb.

Nevaeh lines up her shot.

"Exhale as you squeeze the trigger."

"I can't do two things at once, Forty."

Sweet Lord.

She shoots and dings a stump. There's no bottle on it, but it's right next to a stump that does have one, so there's that.

"Are you lining up the sight?"

"Yes."

"Are you aiming with your dominant eye?"

"Are you gonna nag me the whole time?"

"You gonna hit the target?"

We're shouting at each other due to the ear protection, but we're also smiling. I love it when she gives me shit.

She takes her time on the next shot, and she takes a chunk out of the stump with a bottle on it. Her grin goes from ear to ear.

I take a turn, nail a bottle on the farthest stump, in the tree line. I shouldn't be proud of such an easy shot, but my chest does prickle a little. Nevaeh claps and hoots.

She's doing better with each shot, and we've got a good hour or so of daylight left, when a prospect comes pounding up behind us from the clubhouse.

It's Wash, the idiot who did such a shit job of keeping an eye on Nevaeh before.

"Boss! You gotta come back. We found him!"

"Found who?" Nevaeh takes her eye off the target to ask me. The gun's still aimed downrange. This is what I'm talking about. Distractible. I gently press her arm so she lowers the weapon.

"No one." I don't mean to be a dick, but she doesn't need to know. It's my job to make sure any shit that goes down can never blow back on her, legally or otherwise. Wash shouldn't have said anything in front of her. He and I will have words.

I take Nevaeh's gun back, release the magazine and clear the chamber. "We got to go back. You can hang in my room."

Her face falls. Yeah, I don't like it either.

"Do you need to go back out?"

"Probably."

"When will you be back?"

"I don't know."

"Give me your keys. I'll drive myself back to Gracy's Corner."

I'm shaking my head before she finishes her proposition. If we have Rab, the rest of the Raiders are gonna mobilize. She's safest here. Besides, I sent Boom home when we left for the clubhouse. There's no protection at the house.

"It's not safe. You stay here."

"They hate me here."

"Stay in my room. They'll leave you alone."

Her brow's furrowing, and she's getting fidgety. "Take me with you."

"It's club business." I say it without thinking. My dad said it to my mom all the time.

We're trekking back to the clubhouse, and she stops in her tracks. I turn, exasperated. I don't want to be leaving her either.

She's trying to keep her face blank, but her eyes are sparking. She's pissed. "What am I?"

"What do you mean?" There isn't time for this now.

We're ten feet from the door. We've been searching for this guy for two weeks straight. I want to get this shit settled. Get back to normal so Nevaeh's safe, and I can give her more than a few hours at night when I'm exhausted as hell.

She jerks her chin at the clubhouse. "That's business. What am I?"

"Nevaeh. Please. We got to do this now?"

"I just want to know where I rank. Which place do I get? Am I second to club business? Third?"

"You're being dramatic."

She grits her teeth and sucks in a huge breath to let me have it. I'm happy to listen, but not now. She can rip me a new asshole after she's safe from the Raiders.

"Listen." I grab her upper arms. "I don't want to fight. You know old ladies aren't involved in club business."

Deb and Harper are exceptions. And it's not a sexist thing—not anymore. It's about plausible deniability and protecting our families from the shit that isn't legit.

Nevaeh's not saying anything. Her lips are pressed together in a thin line, her hip's cocked, and she's glaring at me like I'm supposed to read her mind.

"You'll be fine. I'll be back soon, and we'll talk. I need you to trust me on this." I loosen my hold and smooth my hands down her arms.

She narrows her eyes and wrinkles her nose. I can't help it. I drop a kiss on the tip. She huffs.

"Trust me. Okay?"

She draws in a deep breath and forces the corners of her lips up. "Okay. I'll wait in your room. When you come back, we'll talk. I'll trust you."

She starts back toward the clubhouse, her steps calm and measured. I should feel reassured. That's what I wanted to hear.

But a trickle of dread runs down my spine, and as she disappears through the door, the feeling strikes me again, an old, forgotten sensation from those last days before I left for Basic.

I'm missing something.

But Heavy and Nickel are heading toward me, expressions deadly serious. I will fix this when I get back. In the meantime, she's safe.

10

NEVAEH

I last four whole hours sitting alone in Forty's bedroom, lonely and bored, feeling like I'm sixteen and grounded, before I decide to take my chances down in the common room. Fay-Lee or Crista might still be around, and there are pool tables and darts. And I'm so freakin' hungry. All I had to eat today was chips and pop.

I'm also deeply uneasy, and each time I nail down the source of my anxiety, my brain skips to another thing to freak out about.

Forty probably just headed into real danger. Fay-Lee is not discreet; she drops little nuggets all the time. This war with the Rebel Raiders is no joke. Fay-Lee and Story were both attacked and a prospect was nearly beaten to death. There are rumors about a standoff behind a gas station on Gracy Avenue, men disappearing.

Forty could get hurt. He could be killed.

I still haven't told him that it was me who messed up the hood of my car. I've started to tell him a dozen times. I even wrote down what I could say. I thought about leaving him a voicemail or texting or sending an email.

Then I'd hear him in my head saying *You know what Nevaeh? You're trash. We're done.* And I'd figure I could give it another day. Bang him so good and love on him so hard he won't even care.

He'll care. He'll hate me.

So maybe he doesn't need to know. Maybe one secret won't ruin everything. Again.

The whole thing makes my stomach ache. And that's before I think about how when duty called, he bailed on me without blinking. No discussion. Club business. Boom. Gone.

I'll only be gone two years. I have to do this. I'll be back before you know it.

I don't think he even knows he's full of shit. I'm his heart. His whole world. Yeah. Until duty calls. Then I'm a woman. And *old ladies aren't involved in club business.*

Maybe I'm being unfair. If this is life and death, if this is really important, aren't I being overly dramatic, moping around feeling sorry for myself? I know what the Raiders did to Hobs and Crista. They deserve justice.

Ugh. I need to get out of my own head. Find someone to talk to. I finish tying my sneakers, and I hustle on downstairs and head for the bar. It's late, but Crista might still be working.

It takes less than a second to realize that she's not here, and the vibe is definitely very, very different than it was earlier.

There's a cloud of smoke hanging in the air—pot and vape—and there's top 40 on the jukebox. Probably because after a brief scan of the place, I only see a handful of men. Grinder, Big George, Gus, Hobs. I wish Boots were here. He'd be a friendly face.

There are at least a dozen women, though. Danielle,

Cheyenne, Angel, and some other sweetbutts. No Fay-Lee. Dizzy must have come for her. No Shirlene, either, but I doubt she'd be out this late. She gets up at the ass crack of dawn.

No Deb or Ernestine or any of the older ladies. Annie Holt's here, though, shaking her ass on the dancefloor. She ended up marrying Forty's older brother, Bullet, and had a few kids. Bad choice. Bullet's a gambler and a drinker, and he's been working steps and falling down them since long before I met him. They're split now, but they still bang. So Fay-Lee says.

And there's Harper Ruth, bellied up to the bar, dressed like a villainess from an 80s soap opera. Half-dollar-sized, red fan earrings, sparkly black one-shouldered blouse, pencil skirt, and six-inch heels with bright red soles.

She's drinking straight from a bottle of wine as she scrolls through her phone. She hasn't noticed me. No one has. The lights are low, and I don't think anyone's sober going by the volume of laughter and reek of hops.

The door to the kitchen isn't too far from the bottom of the stairs. I'd need to scoot past the hallway to the offices, pass a few prospects playing cards, and duck on in.

I'm so hungry, I'm starting to feel light-headed. I'll just stroll on over there, slip through the swinging doors, make myself a sandwich, and take it back upstairs. I'm not completely reckless. This is not a good scene for me.

I make it *six damn feet* before Annie Holt shouts, "What are you doing out of your room, you dumb whore?" At the top of her lungs. While pointing at me. Just to make sure everyone knows who she's talking about.

Harper's gaze locks on me and a dead smile curls up her lips as she slithers out of her chair. Oh, crap.

Annie, Cheyenne, and Danielle march over. Grinder's

crew swivels so they don't miss the action. The ladies crowd me, almost toe-to-toe, in a boozy, sweaty, smudged eyeliner and dragon-breathed half circle.

I swallow, and it gets stuck in my throat.

Harper saunters over, bottle dangling from her hand, and they shuffle back, make room for her.

"Who let the dog out?" Cheyenne calls over her shoulder. A smattering of drunk voices woof in response.

I can't take all four of them. A decade ago, I got in a few decent licks before Annie and Harper left me curled up in Finnegan's parking lot with chunks of my hair missing, but I haven't been brawling much these past few years. And all four of these bitches are taller than me. Cheyenne outweighs me by fifty pounds, easy.

Annie cracks her knuckles. "I say we drag her ass up these stairs, throw her back down, and tell Forty she tripped."

"Good plan," Cheyenne says as she grabs my collar and yanks. I jerk back, try to get loose, and strangle myself. Panic rises as I fight for air, focusing my glitchy brain like a spotlight operated by a drunk guy.

Harper has inch-long, almond-shaped blood-red nails with Swarovski crystal flowers at the cuticles.

I scrabble at the hand on my collar, flashing back to Carlo, those fingers squeezing, and a surge of pure fear steals the rest of my breath. I swipe wildly for Cheyenne's eyes.

"Let her go." Harper lays those nails on Cheyenne's forearm. Cheyenne shoves me back, and I fall on my ass on the bottom stair.

"Stay down," Cheyenne widens her stance and sneers down at me.

I tug the neck of my hoodie until it loosens all the way, and I drag in a deep breath.

My body screams at me to run, fight through these bitches, or turn and bolt up the stairs, but they're a solid wall, and some animal part of me knows I won't make it an inch.

And besides, I can't tear my gaze from those nails. Harper wraps them around the neck of her wine bottle and takes a swig.

She's still smiling. Shivers shoot down my spine.

"Cheyenne, be a dear and go get my purse, will you? It's on the bar."

Cheyenne shuffles off; Annie and Danielle spread out to block the opening she left.

Would they go after me if I sprinted up the stairs? If I threw a few punches, maybe grabbed Harper's wine bottle, I could get the element of surprise.

Who am I kidding? I'm in the middle of a football huddle of drunk biker bitches. I'm not getting the upper hand. I'm gonna take a beating.

Whoever throws the first punch, I'm going for Annie. Harper's the ringleader, but Annie's her muscle. Also, I kind of hate her for letting Crista fade away after what happened to her.

I brace myself, waiting for it. Instead, Harper says, "Hey, Annie?"

Harper's smile widens. She stares down her nose at me with her gray cat eyes. I swear she blinks a tenth as often as a normal person. It's unnerving.

"Yeah?" Annie snaps her gum.

"Do you remember when Forty left for Basic, and Nevaeh here tried to fuck every loser and Rebel Raider from here to Pyle?"

"Oh, yeah."

"Remember when Forty finished Basic? How you and Bullet and Eighty flew out for Family Day and graduation?"

"Yeah. Nevaeh should have been there, but you know—" Annie shrugs. "Slut."

"Remember when he deployed? The first time?"

"Yeah." Annie flashes me a smile oozing spite and malice. "We sent him a picture of all us ladies with our tits out. For morale, you know."

"All of us but Nevaeh," Danielle adds.

"Because Nevaeh had long since bailed. At the end of the day, she didn't care if Forty lived or died," Annie spits. "He wasn't around, so she had no use for him."

"Ernestine put his name in the book of intentions at church, so everyone would pray for him," Harper says.

"Shirlene and Deb sent him care packages." Annie's eyes grow shiny. Guilt collects thick in my chest. Smothering. Sapping away the adrenaline I was operating on.

"When he came home, we had that huge party," Danielle says as she makes room for Cheyenne who's returned with Harper's purse. "You and me and Story and all the girls from The White Van gave him an evening he won't forget." She winks at me.

My stomach lurches.

"I know I'm never gonna forget. The Army did that man's body good." Cheyenne smirks and licks her lips.

Harper takes a step forward until the pointy toes of her high heels are almost touching the rubber of my sneakers. The others shuffle forward, and lean over me, crowding as close as they can without touching, their hair dangling like curtains.

My blood pounds in my veins. I'm about to take a beating, and I keep getting stuck on random details—Harper's nails, the freckles on Cheyenne's chest, how Annie's rubbed off the blue eyeshadow on her left eye—while my broken, record-scratch brain tries to handle the guilt. The shame.

"Remember when he came back after the accident?"

"He was in so much pain."

"He could have died."

"He almost got addicted to those meds."

"He kind of gave up there for a while. Until Heavy took him and the boys on that camping trip up the mountain."

"We weren't gonna let him give up." Annie's crying now.

"Where were you, Nevaeh Ellis?" Harper bends at the waist and rests her index finger on my chest, flicks the tie to my hoodie with one blood-red nail. "Getting internet famous for cat fights in your panties? Joy riding in stolen cars? Seeing how close you could get to mobsters before you got burned?"

She waits for an answer.

She can keep waiting.

I don't owe Harper Ruth shit.

But damn if everything she says doesn't crank open that spigot of self-loathing wide, and I'm cowering on this bottom step while in my head, I'm flailing around in a flood of all the horrible things my brain accuses me of whenever I stop long enough to listen. *Dirty. Foul. Weak. Coward. Ruined. All your own fault.*

"Forty was risking his life for his country. What were you doing, Nevaeh?" Harper cocks her head. "Yeah. I'd have nothing to say for myself if I were you, either." She grabs her black leather purse from Cheyenne, roots around in it for a second, and pulls out a set of keys.

"Heavy says he offered you a Ford Focus and fifty thousand?"

I grind my teeth so hard they ache.

"He's so smart, but he doesn't understand women. Here. Take my Audi. It's parked out front. Drive wherever you want. Sell it. Keep it, if you want. It's paid off. It's a gift. To make starting over easier. But it's not a payoff."

Harper drops the keys into my lap and crouches until she can speak directly into my ear. "'Cause you're not going to leave because I asked you to. You're going to leave because you know Forty Nowicki deserves better. He deserves someone who cared whether he lived or died. And he deserves better now than a lying little attention-whore who vandalized her own car."

She steps back. My heart's slamming against my chest. I can barely swallow past the shame in my throat.

"There's about a quarter tank of gas left. Registration's in the glovebox."

Then, she spins on the ball of her red-soled shoes and struts off to the bar, swinging her wine bottle. Cheyenne swats the side of my head, and then turns to follow, Annie and Danielle on their heels.

My ears are ringing. The commons are totally silent. Grinder and the other old guys are staring at me, pity on their faces.

I need to get out of here.

And I have car keys, and my legs work, and fuck this. Fuck them. I get to my feet, and I jog toward the door, and then I'm sprinting, cackles, hooting, catcalls following me, but not into the parking lot.

When the door to the clubhouse slides shut, it's quiet. There's a full moon, and streetlights, so it only takes a second to find the Audi. Harper parked in one of the closest spots.

I'm not keeping this car. But I am getting the hell out of Petty's Mill.

I was crazy to think I could come back here. Make things right. What a joke.

The car is a stick, and reverse is in a weird place, top left. I strip the gears as I pull out onto Route 12. The interior reeks of gardenia perfume and strawberry air freshener.

Ah, shit. I can't ditch this car. Mine's still at Big George's garage. I'm going to have to start a new life in a car that smells like my grandmother's bathroom.

I head for the house on Barrow Road. I only have some spare clothes and my cosmetics bag at Forty's place, and besides, I don't have a key. I have enough stuff at Lou's to tide me over.

My face is burning, blood whooshing in my ears. I press the gas, accelerate into the curves as I navigate the back roads to my old house.

What am I doing here?

I wanted to go back to the beginning, fix things, and like every time travel movie ever made, it didn't work.

Instead, I ran head first into the immutable fact that every choice I make blows up in my face.

I peel into the driveway on Barrow Road, brakes squealing. There's no sign of Lou's truck. Thank God. I don't need to explain things. I can leave him a note, drop his keys under the bucket on the front porch, and he'll understand.

I fiddle with the front door lock—turns out Lou left it open—and I hustle to the room I'd been using, not bothering to turn on the lights. I know this house like the back of my hand. I click on a lamp and grab my duffle bag from under the bed, throw it on top. Then I scoop up armfuls of clothes from a chair, and dump them in, shoving them to one side to make room.

That's when I see the necklace.

It's in the middle of the floor.

It must have fallen from my cosmetics bag. I keep it in an outer pouch that snaps shut, the same place I keep extra cash when I have it.

The pearl and gold band are so small, the chain so thin, I could have so easily missed it.

I plop to the floor and pluck it up, rolling the pearl in my fingers.

Forty gave me this ring. We were at the river. Just the two of us. He'd found two, heavy-duty, rubber tubes and lashed them together. We'd floated for hours in the sunshine, clear blue sky, the water perfectly cool when our skin overheated.

I'd been basking in the sun, head tilted over the edge of the tube, hair floating in the river when he grabbed my hand. He slipped the ring on my finger and said, "I'll get you a diamond as big as your head once I get a decent job."

The ring was too loose. I spent the rest of that afternoon with my hand curled closed so it wouldn't fall off into the river. By the time we got back on land, my knuckles throbbed from holding on so tight.

Later, he bought me the necklace from the pawn shop in Shady Gap. I slide it over my head now, untangling it when it gets stuck in my curls. I exhale, and the pressure bearing down on me slips, gives me the smallest room to breathe.

I never got the diamond. But I held on to the pearl this whole time.

I'm forever losing things. Some things I run from. Some things have been taken from me.

Some things I'm not wise or tough enough to keep.

I don't care if I don't deserve Forty Nowicki. I haven't deserved half the shit I've gotten—or been dealt—in my life.

It's not about what I deserve or didn't deserve.

It's about what I can hold onto. And I'm not letting Forty go. Not this time.

I grab my phone and shoot off a text. *I'm at Lou's. I'll be here.*

I just press send when the phone goes flying from my hands and a body slams me into the ground, cracking my head off the metal bed frame.

Pains spears through my skull, my vision blurs, and I can hear my phone crunch as Carlo snarls in my ringing ear, "Where's my bag, bitch?"

11

FORTY

"How do we get a message to Knocker Johnson?" I get real close to Rab Daugherty's slack-jawed face.

Rab didn't come easy. He lost his dentures at some point. Makes his smartass leering extra creepy.

He's not even that old. Forty-five. Fifty at the most. Guess he's led a rough life. He's an asshole, but I'll give him that. He's tough as hell. Roughed up but unbroken and unbowed.

"Fuck. Yourself. And your mother." Rab turns to Heavy. "And fuck your dead whore of a mother, too." He hocks blood onto the concrete floor of the barn.

Heavy's squatting on an overturned bucket. He doesn't blink.

I get right back in Rab's face. "We're not asking you to roll over on your guy. We're asking how to get a message to him. He got a phone number? He got a fuckin' email?"

I'm trying to reason with him, but Rab's next-level squirrelly. Our intel said he was on meth, but he's showing no signs of withdrawal. He's just got that meth personality.

"Don't try to bullshit me. You'll track him down. GPS. IP

address. 5G." He shakes his head with its shock of wild, gray hair, and so help me, he looks a grizzled, redneck version of that alien guy from the memes.

"You can walk out of here, Rab. Just call him on your phone."

"You've got my phone."

Heavy's mysterious new tech genius has already been through Rab's contacts. We got a few new leads, but so far, we've come up with nothing.

I'm getting impatient. I don't like how I left things with Nevaeh. I don't particularly like *where* I left her, either. No one at the clubhouse will hurt her, but given the chance, they'll fuck with her. Nevaeh's always been able to hold her own, but this isn't how I wanted to introduce her back into the club.

I was planning to bring her around. Show everyone how it is now, how it's going to be. Ease the transition.

I got such little time with her, though, spending all my daylight hours hunting down this asshole. I didn't want to spend an evening opening a can of worms. And maybe I'm a weak man. She comes running when I open the door, and there is no place else on earth I want to be.

My brothers know better than to say shit to my face, but I catch the looks when she calls. Or when they want me to have a beer after a wasted day, but I head home.

I'm gonna need to bust someone's head over this before they understand that Nevaeh's my old lady. And it's probably gonna be Heavy. They'd all adjust if he gave the nod, but he's holding his line, whatever the fuckin' reason.

I grab Rab by the front of his flannel shirt, shake him a little. "Come on, Rab. Quit dickin' us around. How long do you think it's gonna take us to visit every one of those contacts in that phone? You want Steel Bones rolling up on your women?"

The answer is less than three hours to visit the four women on Rab's rotation. He's got no wife, no kids, and no teeth, but he's not hurting for female companionship.

"You roll up on them, they ain't my women anymore. At that point, the jig is up," the old coot cackles. "Unless you guys is discreet."

I roll my eyes and step off. Heavy brushes his hands on his jeans and lumbers over to take my place.

Heavy and I have been at this for almost five hours. Charge and Nickel have been here for seven, almost eight. It was Mikey, a brother who usually works construction and keeps a low profile, who wound up running into Rab at the super store on route 12, buying tackle.

Charge and Nickel brought him in, but Nickel's been sitting this part out. He's trying to reform himself, be less aggressive. That's kind of like asking a fish to breathe air, but I got no problem doing what needs to be done. We're not gonna kill Rab. This is a waiting game.

We apply pressure, then we ease off.

We sent Mikey to get him some burger and fries. We'll have Charge feed the guy, take the gas off, be the good cop, and then Heavy and I will roll back in with the threats. If need be, we leave him to sweat it out alone for a day or two. He'll break. It's basic psychological warfare.

It's a waste, too. We told Rab the truth from the get go. We want a meet with Knocker. And in the meantime, we want a ceasefire.

Rab told us he wanted a three-titted woman, and in the meantime, we could lick his ass.

Heavy's looming over Rab where he's tied arms, torso, and legs to a crappy plastic beach chair, reminding him that his trailer can burn as quickly as his tattoo parlor did, when my phone chirps.

I'm at Lou's. I'll be here.

What the hell? I told that woman to stay put. Goddamn. There's no one on Lou Ellis' house. She's a sitting duck.

Go back to the clubhouse. Now. I type as I stride over to Rab, and then I grab him by the bristly chin.

"Do you have men on Nevaeh Ellis?"

His brow furrows. "Who?"

Heavy gives me the eye. I'm off-script. We agreed to save this line of questioning for after we got a location on Knocker.

"Do you have anyone on Lou Ellis' house?" I dig my fingers into his jaw as I pull my revolver from my waistband with my other hand, cock it, and press the muzzle to his forehead.

"What the fuck are you talking about, man?" Rab's voice wavers, an octave higher.

"Brother." Heavy shakes his head.

"Talk."

"I don't know no Ellis. No Lou or whoever you're talking about."

I dig the muzzle into his temple. "I have no problem splattering your brains all over this barn. Your brother Book's still kicking around, isn't he? Down in Florida? I make a phone call, I have ten men at his condo in Jacksonville in less than sixty minutes."

"I don't know no Ellises man!" His voice is high-pitched, panicked. His bravado's gone.

"Brother." Heavy gently lays a beefy hand on my shoulder. "A word."

I can't tell if Rab's speaking the truth, but I wasn't going to pull the trigger anyway, so I reengage the safety and back off slowly. Charge takes my place. I follow Heavy though a side door, out into the moonlit night.

An ember burns a few yards away where Boom smokes, standing sentry with Scrap. An owl hoots in the distance.

I start for the van we rode up in. "I need the keys, man. I gotta go back into town. Nevaeh left the clubhouse. She's at Lou's place."

I check my phone. No reply. Damn it.

"Keys!" I snap.

Heavy stands there, arms loose at his sides. He's outlined by the light spilling from the open barn doors, a still, shaggy giant.

"There's no time to do this with you now, man." I fight down a wave of rage.

"She's fine."

"Fuck you. Give me the keys."

"She's fine, man. The Raiders didn't have anything to do with her car. She did that herself."

What is he talking about?

"Just give me the keys, man."

"Listen, brother." Heavy scrubs a hand over his face. "I was waiting for a time to tell you. Shit's been so crazy. Harper's the one who noticed it."

"Noticed what?"

"The S's. In *Die Steel Bones Whore*. They were pointy, looked like dollar signs."

"Yeah?"

"Nevaeh drew her S's like that."

"What the hell? Tons of people draw S's like that."

"I had Big George check out her keys. There was red paint residue on them. Man, she did that to her own car."

I draw in a deep breath and close my eyes. Ridiculous. Having Big George go all crime lab on Nevaeh's keys.

It's totally something she would do. That's what she's been trying to tell me. Crazy woman.

"She can't be trusted, man. I'm sorry." He steps forward and reaches out to clap me on the back.

I shake him off. "What's your problem with her? For real."

"Seriously? She *lied* to you. Her shit distracted us from the mission. You're fine with that? The fuck, man. What's with you and this bitch?"

"You never call her a bitch again."

"Or what?" Heavy's drawn himself up, and there's probably few men who wouldn't blink, confronted by a literal giant. But I need those keys.

"I don't have time for this." I snap. "Keys."

"Or what?" He repeats himself, slower, and he holds up the keys, clenched tightly in a giant hand. "We have Rab Daugherty in there." He gestures to the barn. "We break him, we bring Knocker to the table, we *end* this shit. We put two decades of senseless bloodshed behind us. And you gotta bail now? 'Cause some gash texted you? You'd betray your club, your brothers for that *lying bitch*?"

Yes.

He makes it complicated, but it's not. I learn from my mistakes.

She's first. On her best day and her worst day. She's first.

"Last chance. Give me the keys."

"We're your brothers."

"Hand me the keys, *brother*."

Heavy throws them, pitches them overhand into the field.

We run at each other, and we meet midair as I slam my fist into his nose. Blood squirts, sticky warm splatters on my face. And it's on.

He comes back with a kidney shot.

We grapple. I nail him with an uppercut, but his massive bush of a beard deflects the impact. He's grunting in my ear, and we're clutching each other, working in body shots.

Boom is shouting, and I catch Nickel approaching in my peripheral vision.

"Shouldn't we break 'em up?" Boom yells.

"Don't really want to die tonight." Nickel grunts as he squats to watch.

We're slowing down. I clock him in the jaw, and his head snaps back. It takes him a few seconds to come back, and his reflexes are shaky, but he commands so much mass, he takes us to the ground.

We're at an impasse. Heavy has forty pounds on me, and he doesn't have a messed-up arm, but I've got years of combat training, and I don't spend so much time on a computer.

We're rolling now, occasionally getting in jabs, but mostly wrestling, vying for an upper-hand that neither of us can keep; we're too evenly matched. Neither of us is giving up. Blood's streaming from his nose. I'm holding a rib in place with my left arm.

He tries to piledrive me. I use his momentum to throw him into the ground, but he twists, dragging me under, and I get a huge hunk of his hair in my mouth. As I spit it out, my knee connects with his nuts.

And then a corner of the barn explodes.

The sky lights up. Shrapnel and dust flies in a plume, yards into the air.

Mikey's standing in the headlights of his SUV with a rocket launcher in his hand. "Shit. I was aiming for the tree."

"Jesus Christ! I'll tell you whatever the fuck you want to know!" Rab hollers from the intact half of the barn.

I squint at the weapon. "Is that the RPG I gave you back when you were a prospect? That time we went after that drug dealer for Wall?" That was shortly after my discharge. Three years ago.

"Yup," Mikey says. "You never asked for it back. I kept it."

"You ever fire it before?"

"First time." He grins. "Has more of a kick than I expected."

Heavy and I look at each other, and just like when we were kids, we crack up at the same time, doubling over.

My arm and ribs are throbbing. Heavy's hacking. His nose is definitely broken.

The laughter dies off, and he slaps the keys into my hand. "You'd really pick her? Over your club?"

"You'd really make me?"

Heavy shakes his wooly head. "No." He sighs. "I don't understand. But I back your play."

"After this, you make it clear that Nevaeh is one of us."

"Aye." Heavy leans back, cracking his spine, tilting his head to stare up at the empty sky. "I do not get what you see in that woman."

"Yeah? I bet Mikey gets it." I clap Heavy's shoulder. "She's got more kick than you'd expect."

Heavy snorts. "Call if you need back up."

"I just need to put her back where she belongs. I'll be an hour. Two, tops."

As I hop in the cab, I try Nevaeh again. By some miracle, my phone didn't get damaged in the melee. There's no answer. The hackles rise on the back of my neck.

"You sure you don't want to take Mikey and his RPG?" Heavy asks. Mikey's poking around the wreckage, grinning like a kid on Christmas.

"Nah. She's probably just kickin' a fuss 'cause I left her at the clubhouse. I'll text when I'm on my way back."

"Drive safe." Heavy slaps the side of the truck as I pull off.

I start the drive back to town, navigating the potholes on the unpaved road leading to Heavy's cabin, and I try Nevaeh again.

She doesn't answer.

Odds are she's fine. Renelli isn't coming after her. The Raiders are going to be focused on finding Rab, and if they decide to go for collateral, they'll go after someone with a strong connection to the club. Rab didn't even know the Ellis name.

She's giving me the cold shoulder.

She's never been one for the silent treatment, but plenty of women are.

It's so late, she could be sleeping.

There's no need to panic.

But what about the ex? The money man that Renelli would prefer we don't drop if he shows up.

I call Wall. He's not at the clubhouse; he's home with his old lady and the kids. I ask him to go over to Lou's. Make sure Nevaeh's okay. I feel like an asshole asking him to leave his family, but cold chills are trickling down my spine.

I press the gas to the floor.

12

NEVAEH

"**Y**ou dumb bitch!"

Carlo spears his hand into my hair, grabs a clump, and tries to pull me to my feet.

"Stop!"

I fight for balance, grab his forearms, my scalp screaming and everything tilting and careening as he shakes me like a rag doll and then throws me on the bed.

"Where's my bag?"

"I don't have your bag." I scramble to the far side of the bed, huddle against the wall. For some reason, he doesn't follow. He paces the room.

"You have my bag. God, you're so *dumb*. You didn't even notice I was sitting in the goddamn living room! I tossed this entire house, and I was on the sofa with a gun aimed straight at you." His voice cracks, hysterical, and he waves a pistol above his head. I whimper and search the room wildly for something, anything.

There's nothing but pillows and sheets. Lou's weights are on the other side of the room. So's the lamp. My duffle has nothing but clothes in it.

I could throw a pillow at him. Distract him. Run.

I lunge, but he's faster than me. He grabs me by the arm, hauls me across the bed, and jams the muzzle under my chin.

"I could blow your face right off."

I freeze. Every particle in the air, every molecule in my body freezes.

"Your loser brother would walk in, and all he'd see is this hair and a big, bloody hole."

I slowly raise my hands, palms wide.

Piss trickles down my inner thigh.

I need to get him out of here. I don't know where Lou is. He could come home at any time.

"You gonna behave?"

I can't nod. Metal is boring into my chin, clamping my mouth shut.

"Yeah, you're gonna behave."

He lowers the gun and backs off. I stay exactly where I am, kneeling on the bed, hands raised.

Carlo does not look well. He's dressed to the nines as always, but his jacket's unbuttoned, his shirt's untucked, and his wingtips are muddy. He's got stubble, and the whites of his eyes are veined red, the pupils blown huge and black.

He's high. Coke, probably.

"Where's my bag?"

It's in the upstairs bathroom. It's literally sitting on the floor behind the door. I took it up there to unpack my shampoo, and then I kind of forgot about it. He must have missed it. I know I kept not noticing I'd left it there.

I can't tell him it's there. He'll kill me.

"It's not here."

"Where is it?"

Oh, God. Think. Think. I could tell him it's at Forty's, but there's no one there. Why does he even want the bag so bad?

Where would the bag be if it wasn't here?

"It's in my car."

Carlo straightens his arm and levels the gun at my head. "Take me to the car."

Shit.

"I can't. It's not here."

There's a click as he cocks the gun. "I heard you drive up. Stop lying, bitch."

"It's not my car. It's an Audi. You can look."

"Where's your piece of shit?"

I can't tell him it's in the shop. The shop's closed. No one will be there this time of night.

"It's at the clubhouse."

"What the fuck's The Clubhouse? Is that a bar?"

"The Steel Bones MC clubhouse. It's a local riding club." There's an outside chance he's never heard of them, right?

"Yeah, you would be hanging out at a biker bar. Slut." He pretends to spit. It's one those mannerisms he picked up from mafia movies. I met his folks; they're middle class people from Long Island.

Oh, brain, focus. What if Lou comes home? I have to get Carlo out of here now.

"I can take you to it."

"Yeah." He gestures with his gun to the door. "You try anything, when we're done, I'm coming back here and putting one in little brother's head and one in his chest. Capisce?" He taps the barrel once against my temple and once between my breasts.

I raise my hands higher, nodding. "Can I move?"

"Yes, you can fucking move." He sweeps his gun toward the door. "After you."

I slowly get off the bed and walk to the front door. Carlo follows, the gun jammed between my shoulder blades.

My breath comes shallow, and waves of nausea and dizziness keep rising, making my steps wobbly. I'm going to trip by accident, and he's going to shoot me. I walk so deliberately, he digs the gun harder into my back.

"Speed up."

Now that I'm actually paying attention to my surroundings, I see that the place is trashed. The coffee table is overturned, and the couch and chairs have been slit open, upholstery ripped from the foam cushions. The TV is face down on the floor. Lou is going to be so pissed.

I should never have come here. I didn't think I'd be putting him in danger. Like always. I didn't *think*.

Carlo nudges me out the front door.

"Go right." Oh Lord. The moon's still shining bright. How did I not notice his car is parked on the side of the road, a few yards from the house?

I missed it.

This time, I really am going to die from my own stupidity.

The car chirps, and Carlo opens the back door. "You drive. You try anything, I shoot. I need that bag. I've got nothing to lose."

What is up with that bag?

"I took everything out. I left it at your place."

"Get into the fucking car and drive Nevaeh. Or we can wait for little brother to come home."

I slide into the seat, wiping my sweaty palms on my shorts. It's cool, no more than sixty degrees, but I'm flushed and clammy.

"Drive!" Carlo sits behind me and leans forward to prop the gun next to the headrest.

"I don't have the keys!"

"Shit." He fumbles around and then drops them in my lap. "You try anything, the last thing you see is gonna be your brains flying out of your head."

That makes no sense. I put the car in drive. It's a Beamer, an automatic. I've actually never driven Carlo's car before. He did all the macho things—always drove, ordered my drinks, helped me on with my coat. I thought it was quaint. But that's how you treat a doll, isn't it? Someone who's not quite a person. Schlep her around, feed her, dress her.

This epiphany is coming a year too late.

"Faster," he barks in my ear.

I'm doing the speed limit. I press down on the gas as gently as I can.

I don't know what to do. When Carlo gets the bag, I'm done. Obviously, there's something in there I didn't see. Maybe a false bottom like in a spy movie?

I could just drive to the police station like they say to do if you're being followed. Is he crazy enough to shoot me in front of a police station? He'd never get his bag then.

But what if he just ran when he saw where I was going? And went after Lou? Carlo's alone, but what if he has people with him, and I didn't notice them? I didn't see his car. Or him. Or the trashed house.

I was so hyper-focused on my drama. I hate my brain.

"Whatever you're thinking, don't," Carlo snarls, his breath hot in my ear. "Be a good girl. All I want is the bag. I get it; I leave."

"What's in the bag?"

"Immunity." He laughs, bitter with an edge of hysteria.

Oh, shit. He's flipping on the Renellis. Whatever is in that bag, it's his ticket out. And he wouldn't be talking if he had any intention of letting me live.

My brain's a buzzing, jumbled mess, and I try to sort it, make it flow in a direction, but Carlo's breath smells like spearmint, and there's a faint rattling sound coming from underneath the car, and it's worse when we come to a stop, and it wasn't there the last time I was with Carlo, the night he choked me in his apartment. I bet he ran over something wrong, and why do I care?

I need a plan, but the car keeps rattling. He's leaned back in his seat, but I know the gun is still aimed at my back.

Tears gather in the corner of my eyes. I don't want to die now. Forty needs me. He probably doesn't know it, but he does. He needs to take care of me, and he needs me to love bomb him until all the stiffness in his body and the rigidity in his soul melts, and he laughs as if he's surprised. Every time. He laughs like he's surprised.

I make him happy. Too serious, uptight Forty Nowicki. *I* make him happy. And he makes me happy. I'm going to survive this.

I don't know what I'm going to do, but my brain's whirling and glitching as my body drives itself down Route 12 until I'm turning in to the clubhouse. It's getting close to five in the morning. It's still dark, but it's a thinner dark. You can see yards away, but the world is gray.

There's still the dull thud of bass coming from the clubhouse, but there's only a few cars and a half-dozen bikes. I don't know how many brothers are bunking here now, or how many might still be awake. If it's like it used to be, anyone still up will be three sheets to the wind.

"I don't see your car."

"It's in the garage."

"Why is your car in the garage?"

"It got keyed."

He snorts. "Of course, it did."

Carlo gets out of the car and opens my door, slipping his gun into his jacket pocket. "Go. Walk in front of me. If we run into anyone, we're just picking up your car. You scream, you do anything, you're dead, and so is anyone who wants to play hero."

"You don't have to do this. You can just leave. I can get you money. Fifty thousand dollars." Shit maybe there's a Ford Focus around here somewhere with a check still in the glovebox.

Desperation is seizing my chest. I'm babbling nonsense. When he realizes my car's not here, he's going to kill me.

He's going to shoot me, and people will come running, and he'll kill them, and it'll be my fault. Oh God. I search the lot for a trike. Shirlene cannot be here.

I'm scanning, panic rising, when I see it. My red Hyundai backed into a spot in front of the garages. The hood is buffed and painted. It's a freakin' miracle.

Carlo sees it at the same time I do.

"Go." He shoves me forward, and I stumble, tripping on loose pebbles.

I have no plan. I walk as slowly as I can toward my car. My brain whirls and clicks and churns out nothing. Just stupid, random thoughts.

Where is my necklace? It was in my hand when Carlo knocked me into the bed frame.

Big George did a good job on the hood. I had some fender damage from accidentally bumping into a retaining wall, and he fixed that, too.

This early, you can smell dew in the air, and you can almost feel it, too, on your skin.

I don't have the keys to the Hyundai. Will Carlo shoot the windows out?

Mad panic swells behind my eyes again, and then there's

a crunch of tires on asphalt. A car door slams, and boots are pounding toward me. A distraction. I can run.

I lunge, but at the same instant, Carlo seizes me, spins me, and oh no. Oh shit. It's Forty. I'm facing him with Carlo's hand clamped around my neck and a gun jammed into the small of my back.

Forty skitters to a halt twenty feet away. He's aiming a gun at my head, both arms straight, one hand cupping the other.

"Let her go."

No. He's not aiming at me. He's aiming at Carlo.

I start to shake, shivers coursing all down my body, and I move to hug my arms around my waist, but Carlo yanks up on my throat, tilting my chin in the air as he burrows the gun so deep I'm forced to arch my spine.

From where he stands, Forty can't see the gun at my back. He can only see the hand around my throat.

That's where his eyes are trained. Carlo's head. My throat. They're scanning steadily between Carlo's forehead and where his hand squeezes my neck.

Forty's stance is sure. He's a soldier. He's calculating, lining up his target. He's not going to see the gun at waist level in time. Carlo isn't going to wait for him to choose his shot. He's going to swing his arm from behind me and shoot. I'm his shield.

"Last time. Let her go." Forty's hair is mussed. He's wearing his cut and a white T-shirt stained by drops of blood scattered down the front. He has grass stains on his jeans. He's been fighting.

His square jaw is tensed, but his lips are slightly parted. His chest rises and falls. He's breathing deeply, exactly like he taught me to do. So he's totally oxygenated when he exhales and pulls the trigger.

He's so beautiful.

I'd go for him again, any day. I was right when I was fourteen, and I was right last month. He's the one.

I was made untethered, like a bird or a butterfly or a balloon that slipped its string. He was made steady and firm, like solid earth or a strong hand.

Made for me in the same way I was made for him.

I smile. I want him to see me smile.

"Baby?"

"I love you." I inhale the rich, early morning air. "He has a gun at my back," I say, and I fling my arms wide, throwing all my weight backwards as I wrench my torso, twisting into the metal digging right above my hip.

Bang.

Bang.

Carlo collapses, and I crash on top of him, pain ripping through my side. The silence echoes.

"Nevaeh!"

Shouts come from the clubhouse, feet pound. I'm sprawled on my back, and my hip feels wet. The bone burns. I whimper. It hurts.

Carlo is lumpy underneath me. He's not moving.

"Baby." Forty's there, kneeling over me, shirtless, pressing hard on my hip. It hurts. "What did you do?"

I mean to say stop, that hurts, but my tongue's not working right.

Why is he not wearing a shirt? Every time my eye catches on his tattoos or his scars, my gaze slides away.

I can't focus.

I'm lying on something awkward and cold. Carlo. It's Carlo.

"Is he dead?"

"Yeah, baby. Hold on. We'll move you."

There's more shouting. There's been shouting. I don't know how long. There's a bunch of people, and then there's a stretcher. Where'd they get a stretcher?

Wall and Grinder are lifting me into the back of a van while Forty keeps pressure on my hip.

The gorge rises in my stomach. I turn my head and wretch, but there's nothing in my stomach.

"Give her water," Forty barks.

There's a girl in the van with us, early twenties. She has dyed blonde hair, and her tanned face is blanched white. She's a sweetbutt. I don't know her.

"Angel!"

"Yeah!" The girl fumbles with a water bottle, holds it up to my lips. I try to sip, but it dribbles down my cheek. "Sorry," she whispers.

I try to smile. It's okay. I'm getting tired, though.

"She's freezing." Angel presses her palm to my forehead.

"I need shirts. Cover her up."

There's a bustle, and then they're heaping flannels on me, and it all smells like beer and man sweat, and I wish Forty would stop leaning on my hip; it hurts.

"Shouldn't we take her to the hospital?" Angels asks, tentative. Yeah. That's a good question. Why am I in a van? I need an ambulance. Drugs. Good drugs.

Wall answers her. "The nearest ICU is in Shady Gap now. The Dentist is way closer. And he has more trauma experience than any doctor outside of Pyle."

"The dentist?" I definitely don't think I should be going to the dentist. I mean, I haven't been going like I should, but now?

"You know. Sunny's old man."

Oh, I remember Sunny. Story's mom. A real hippie chick. I liked Sunny. When did she hook up with a dentist?

This is too confusing, and I'm really tired. I let my eyes drift shut.

"Oh, no you don't. Nevaeh!"

Forty is shouting at me. He doesn't have to shout. It's a small van.

"Shut up. Let me sleep."

"Nevaeh!"

"That's my name. Don't wear it out." I chuckle weakly. Lou and I always used to say that to each other. Oh, Lou. He's gonna be so pissed when he gets home, and the TV's on the floor.

"Nevaeh, you need to stay with me, baby. We're less than five minutes out. Just hold on. Everything's going to be okay. Stay with me."

"I'm right here." I manage a small smile. His face is utterly serious, totally severe. There's something in those brown eyes I don't think I've seen before. Fear.

Oh.

I'm dying.

I force myself to smile for real. "Forty?"

He's staring at where his hands are clapping a bloody, wadded up rag to my hip. Is that his shirt?

"Forty."

Finally, he looks up and meets my eye.

"I carved that shit into my car."

"I know."

I chuckle. It comes out a cough. "And you came anyway?"

He frowns. His face is so strained. He looks old. Like someone's dad.

"Of course, you did. You love me, don't you?" I hope he's someone's dad one day. He's going to be the very, very best at it.

"With everything I am." He's so solemn. It's a vow.

"I love you, too."

"Why did you do it, Nevaeh?" His voice disintegrates mid-sentence, cracks wide open.

I try to shrug, and there's a piercing pain, but I don't think my shoulder moves. "I saved your life. I didn't let the bad guy win this time."

"Goddamn, Nevaeh." His eyes darken.

"I saved the day."

Me. The girl too scared to open her mouth. The woman who ran every time the going got tough. Who could never figure out how to get things to work out her way.

In the end, I got the boy.

And I saved the day.

It's a good story. The best.

I drift off, and there's shouting, but the voice is deep and familiar, and it's a beautiful sound to hear as I float away into the dark.

13

FORTY

There was a moment—a matter of seconds—in the helicopter when the rotor broke, right before we went into the tailspin. We had been going vertical, moving slightly southeast, and then we stopped. In midair. No more than a few seconds. Probably a fraction of a second.

Our momentum was arrested, gravity blinked, and we were floating.

That's what it feels like when Nevaeh closes her eyes. The world is over.

Wall crouches at her head, fingers on her pulse.

"It's weak but steady, man. She probably passed out from the pain. It's better that way."

"Fuck, man. We should divert to Petty's Mill General." I want to inspect the wound, but I know better than to ease up on the pressure.

Wall was a firefighter back in the day, and he has extensive trauma experience. He said go to the Dentist. He said if it was Mona, his old lady, he'd go to the Dentist.

We're already past the gatehouse in Gracy's Corner. The

Dentist lives a few streets over from me. He's got a setup in his basement. Most of us have spent time there, most recently Roosevelt recovering from the beatdown he got from the Raiders. Steel Bones buys the Dentist whatever he wants. Right now, he wants an assistant, so Angel here is going to nursing school on our dime.

"I wouldn't do it, man. The bullet hit no major arteries. The bleeding is staunched. She's showing signs of shock, and the Dentist can handle that. Time is of the essence. Petty's Mill General is a glorified clinic now. If we take her somewhere, take her to Shady Gap. But I know those folks. The Dentist is better, man. He's knows combat medicine."

By the time Wall's done, it's a moot point. Gus is pulling up behind the Dentist's house and into his attached garage.

Sunny throws open the van doors.

"On three?" Wall assumes position at her head. Grinder's already by her feet, and Gus and Sunny are ready to receive.

"One, two, three." They lift her while I keep pressure on. The bullet went into the fleshy part of her upper thigh, right under her hip bone. There's no exit wound.

It's not a mortal injury. If a guy got this in combat, he'd try to limp to the medic. The logical part of my mind knows this, but the rest of me has not received the message.

I've done everything wrong. What if I'm fucking up this call, too?

"Bring her through here."

Half of the Dentist's finished basement is a family room, big screen TV, overstuffed sofa, bar, pinball machine. Go through a door, and the other half is a dentist's office on the right and fully-equipped surgery suite on the left. He's got a heart monitor, all kinds of equipment.

There's a hospital gurney in the narrow hall between the

two rooms. We ease her onto it. Her eyelids are twitching. She moans as we resettle her, but she doesn't wake up.

Maybe she lost more blood than I calculated.

Fuck.

The Dentist is snapping on gloves. "All right, friends, I'm going to take over for Forty here, and everyone is going to go wait out there except Angel and Grinder. Angel, scrub up, take Grinder across the hall, and tap a vein in case we need it."

Hold up. "I'm not leaving her."

"Then go scrub up." The Dentist jerks his chin toward the double-sink at the end of the hall.

And why is Angel tapping Grinder's vein?

Grinder notices me staring. "Type O neg, dude. Universal donor." He grins, shirtless, from the dentist chair. "Happy to help."

Jesus fuck. That man has at least three side chicks at any one time. They're not putting his blood in Nevaeh.

If she needs it, we don't have a choice.

Impotent rage floods my chest as I rush to the sink.

I've made every wrong choice. I was going to be a better man than my father, and damn if I didn't make every mistake he did. My woman needed me, and I had my head so far up my ass, I couldn't see it. I was so intent on doing things *my* way—and I was so sure it was the *right* way—I let her go.

I was so fuckin' positive she'd wronged me, and that's unforgiveable, right? I never tried to fix things. I was willing to miss her for the rest of my life 'cause I couldn't bear letting go of a grudge.

It's so goddamn obvious now that she's pasty white and limp on a fucking gurney.

I am just like my father. I can hear Dad muttering, *years*

after Mom left, *she could have hocked your Grandma's rings. But she wouldn't. She'd rather you kids starve.* And Mom had been gone *decades* at that point. And you know what, *he* could have gotten a goddamn regular job. I could have picked up the goddamn phone.

All the scales are falling from my eyes, too late. Nevaeh can't die.

I'm a shell of a person without her.

I've fucked up so badly.

"Forty? Can you come in here? We need to make some decisions." The Dentist calls me from the surgery. I finish rinsing my hands and forearms, and I head for Nevaeh.

I'm not leaving her again. Whatever happens. We're in this together.

I WALK THROUGH THE DOOR, and her brown eyes are wide open, blinking at me.

She smiles. "There you are."

I rush to her, push the curls out of her face. Her pupils are huge.

The Dentist has an IV ready. He's got a tourniquet on her arm, and he's palpating a vein. Her feet are elevated. She's covered in a heavy wool blanket, and Sunny's at her side, keeping pressure on the wound.

"You're awake." I feel her forehead. She's cool and clammy.

"I'm not dead."

Pain spears my chest. "No, baby. You're gonna be fine."

Her eyes flick to Sunny. "Are you keeping my insides from falling out?"

Sunny laughs. "No, sugar. I'm just keeping pressure on the wound 'til Larry can clean you up."

"Who's Larry?"

"That'd be me. Now, there's going to be a little stick." He releases the tourniquet. She squeezes her eyes shut.

"I hate needles. I can't stand things sticking in my skin."

"Hate to tell you this, but you have a bullet stuck in your thigh." Larry finishes up with the IV and moves over to a locked cabinet. Weird, I've known the guy since I got back, but I never knew his given name.

Nevaeh's eyeing him warily. She seems more alert. "Are you gonna take it out?"

"Sure am, but there's bad news."

"I might die?"

"Nope. I'm gonna have to stick you with another needle. Local anesthetic."

"This sucks."

"It's gonna be okay." She's so slight under the blanket. People don't notice 'cause her hair's so big, and she's so loud and full of energy, always in motion, but she's a small woman.

I shouldn't have left her.

I got to the house on Barrow Road, and I knew instantly there was trouble. Harper's car was in the drive, and the front door was unlocked. Wall was in the living room, on the phone, calling for back up.

The place was trashed. Nevaeh's phone was cracked on the floor of a bedroom, and the pearl ring I'd given her when we were kids was lying in the carpet.

It's in my pocket now.

She kept it.

It's such a cheap little thing. It was one month's salary

when I bought it, but one month's salary running black market smokes was peanuts.

I threw her away, and she kept this piece of crap, all this time.

"Hey." She's turned back to face me now, her brow furrowed. "What's wrong? Are you lying to me? Is it really bad?"

"No, I promise. It's a flesh wound."

"Then why does your face look like that?"

"Like how?"

She struggles for words, and finally, she sighs. "Like I broke you," she says.

"Here. You're making me nervous." Larry rolls a stool by Neveah's head. "Sit," he orders. Then he wheels his own stool next to Neveah's injured side, relieving Sunny.

I sit, and slide as close as I can, leaning over to rest my forehead on hers. She reaches up for my hands. I grab them and rest them at the top of the gurney.

"Scissors." Larry holds out an open palm. Sunny hands them over.

I drop a kiss on Nevaeh's temple. "I'm fine. And you're going to be fine, too."

"We're both fine."

"Yes." It's not true, but I am going to make it so. "After this, I'm going to take you home, and I'm never letting you leave."

"Okay. But I'm going to need to make some changes."

"Like what?"

"I want a swimming pool."

"You can have the biggest swimming pool they make."

Her lips curve, and then a shadow passes over her face. I glance down at Larry. He's unpacking the wound, but he's being careful. Gentle. He better.

"Does it hurt?" I would take it from her if I could. And I'd take everything back.

She ignores the question. "When I say we stay together, we stay together. From here on out. If you can't do that, there's the door. You don't know what's best for us. We decide. Both."

"I am never leaving you again."

"It's settled then." She squeezes my hands. "We're getting a pool with a slide and a swim up bar."

"I love you," I murmur in her ear. I need her to know. I am a stubborn man, and I make the wrong calls, but I know a gift when I'm given one.

I'm not stupid enough to squander a second chance.

And I can recognize heaven. Even backwards.

14

NEVAEH

There's a quarter-sized patch of raw pink scar tissue on my upper right thigh. The flesh is a little dented, but all-in-all, it's not so bad. It's nowhere near as bad as Forty's. It's not even sore anymore, but the skin feels tight, and it itches sometimes.

Fay-Lee pokes it. I float away.

"Does that hurt?" she asks.

I half-heartedly splash her, but she's already wet and thoroughly buzzed off her third margarita. She flips me the bird and spins herself in her pink flamingo inflatable.

"Yes, that hurts. Come here and let me put my finger your eye. See if that hurts." I'm exaggerating. Like I said, all considering, I got off easy.

"I'm tappin' a kidney. You ladies want anything?" Shirlene swings her legs over the side of her chaise lounge and gives herself a minute before she stands. I finally convinced her to take a day off. She works herself too damn hard.

"More margarita!" Fay-Lee calls from her flamingo.

"I'm good."

"Spray down that chair with a hose while I'm inside,

will you?" Shirlene plucks her white bikini out of her ass crack. I want her confidence when I'm sixty-whatever. "The plastic's startin' to cook me like a George Foreman grill."

"Aye, aye, Captain." I give her a salute. She rolls her eyes.

When she's inside, I splash her lounger the best I can from the pool. I'm not gettin' out, dragging the hose over, coiling it back up so Forty doesn't pitch a fit. I'm an injured woman.

When I was first recovering, everyone spoiled the hell out of me. Shirlene was over every night cooking dinner, Ray and Boots made Charge drive them over, and Angel, Grinder, Larry, and Sunny all dropped by. Lou came over to watch TV almost every day after work. It was an amazing week or two. Now people poke me and ask me to hose off their chairs.

Of course, Forty's still going strong with the spoiling. Right now, he's tilling a strip where the fence used to be so I can plant a vegetable garden. He's shirtless, tanned, and his pecs are shiny with sweat. I squeeze my thighs tight. My pussy's still sore from this morning, but I could go again. I really want the garden, though. I want to grow tomatoes and basil and make pasta sauce from scratch. Forty loves spaghetti.

I'm not sure if we can grow anything before the first frost, but it'll be ready to go for next year.

Overall, life is pretty good. There's this brand new salt-water pool in our backyard. With Steel Bones Construction' connections and some greased palms, it was done in no time.

And beside my pearl around my neck, there's a fat diamond on my ring finger. I hold it up and admire it for the one thousandth time.

"No one likes a show off," Fay-Lee calls from across the pool.

"Does it blind you when I hold it like so?" I stick it up high in the air.

"I've got a big-ass rock, too. I just don't like wearing it in public."

"You pawned it, didn't you?" Fay-Lee was raised dirt poor. She has a thing about stashing away cash, hoarding food, that kind of thing. Her stories about growing up always make you laugh, and then later, they break your heart.

"I did. Dizzy bought it back, though. He hid it in his sock drawer. He thinks I don't know. He's probably got an elaborate plan to teach me a lesson."

"You gonna pawn it again?"

"Most likely."

We fall quiet, and Shirlene pads back out, dropping a fresh margarita for Fay-Lee on the side of the pool. I stretch in my floating lounger, dipping my feet in the cool water.

Larry gave me the okay for baths and the pool, but Forty thinks I still need to keep the wound dry. The lounger is a compromise. I've got a spray bottle to cool me off and ice tea in the cup holder.

After a long work week, it's heaven.

So far, in addition to our daily rounds of the old peeps, Shirlene and I have cleared out Ray's entire basement. Now we're working on his garage. We started making progress a lot faster when we put Boom to work. I've got a permanent bodyguard now, even though I'm in the clear with the Renellis.

That was a crazy story. Apparently, the Feds had gotten Carlo to flip. The deal was that Carlo hands over the Renellis' books, and he gets immunity and witness protection.

The Renellis found out and cut off his access. Carlo had a contingency plan, though. A shadow ledger sewn into his messenger bags. Oops.

Carlo had to shake his tail to come after me, so there were no Feds to witness what happened in the parking lot. The Renellis' problem disappeared, and they all had air tight alibis. So basically, the Renellis owe us a huge favor.

Sometimes I think I should feel bad about Carlo. It's hard to keep my mind on the right and wrong of it, though. My brain skitters to the feel of his hand collapsing my windpipe. So I banish him to the same shadowy corner where I shove Ed Ellis. Damn if they don't refuse to stay there, but I don't have to look them in the eye all the time, so maybe it's the best that can be done.

Forty wants me to go to a therapist. Apparently, Nickel has one, and now he's into Zen and yoga or something, and he's a changed man.

I don't know about that. Story and Nickel were over here the other day for bar-b-q, and a hornet was bothering her, and he slammed that critter so hard he broke a patio table. Crushed it like a can and then casually plucked the sticker out of his palm.

I told Forty I'd go to therapy if he'd go with me. He has nightmares about the helicopter crash still. And Lord knows he has mother issues. Don't we all.

Anyway, overall, everything would be almost perfect except Forty wants to go to the clubhouse tonight. There's going to be a party. He wants me to make nice with Heavy, Harper, and the others.

It's been two and a half months since Larry pulled that bullet out of my chub. I've managed to avoid the clubhouse since then.

It's not because I'm afraid to see where I got shot. It's

because I love my fantasy world where I'm the queen and Forty's king and no one can come between us.

And as soon as I see Heavy and Harper and the others, that fantasy's busted. From all the way over here, I can make out the tattoos on his arm—the scales, the nickel, the handcuffs, the wrench, and the XL. And there's me. The insane cat exploding from a bomb.

I guess my fantasy world's not totally intact, even hiding out here. Forty's gone at least ten hours every day on club business. Sometimes he gets calls in the middle of the night. Sometimes he doesn't come home. He always picks up his phone on the first ring, and I'm not worried he's cheating or anything. At least, not with a woman.

It kind of feels like the SBMC is his side chick, though. And that sucks.

"Forty wants me to go to the clubhouse tonight."

"Yeah?" Fay-Lee perks up and paddles closer. "For Roosevelt's thing?"

"Is that the occasion?"

"Yeah, he got his patch. The private party was last week. This is the big shindig. Everyone's invited."

I've run into Roosevelt at Larry's while we were both getting follow-ups. Roosevelt was almost killed by the Rebel Raiders when they tried to kidnap Fay-Lee. He's a nice guy. An Italian from Pyle. We knew a lot of people in common.

"Think I should go?"

"Hell, yeah. I keep telling you that you're welcome at the clubhouse."

"I keep telling you that you're wrong."

"Okay. Say I'm wrong. You okay with that? Your future husband belonging to a club that doesn't want you around?"

"I'm not gonna ask him to choose between his friends

and his family and me." For one, it's messed up. For two, I'm not sure who he'd choose. He might not know either.

"I think you should roll up like a boss bitch, and when Harper or Cheyenne or whoever runs their mouth, pop 'em in the face."

"Solve it with violence?"

"It has worked for me in the past." Fay-Lee taps her nose. "Strength respects strength."

"I haven't won a physical fight in my life. And I have been in more than a few." There have been some draws, like when Aaron's ex and I figured out he was videotaping us, and we joined forces to beat his ass—that didn't make it onto PornX, of course.

"You'll have back up this time."

"Aw. You'd fight Harper Ruth with me?" My chest warms.

"I've been itchin' to snatch that bitch bald for years," Fay-Lee snickers.

"What bitch?"

A shadow falls over me. I spin the lounger, squint into the sun.

No freakin' way. It's Harper Ruth. She snuck up on us from the side of the house. And she brought her whole squad. Annie Holt. Danielle. Cheyenne.

Forty's heading toward us. He looks as surprised as I feel.

A pit forms in my stomach.

Fay-Lee paddles over to me. Shirlene perks up in her chair. They're lined up on the edge of the pool, a row of hard-bitten mean girls with their impeccably styled queen bee. Harper's bright red lipstick and smoky eye are flawless. Her shimmery white tank tucks smoothly into red capris that perfectly match the shade of the soles of her high-heeled shoes.

She is so overdressed for a pool party.

"You," I answer her question. "You're the bitch."

Her eyes narrow.

"And this is a private party. You can see your way out."

Forty's made his way to the pool, and he stands by the ladder, face stone, arms crossed. Guess he's leaving this up to me. I don't feel abandoned, though. If I say the word, he'll throw them out on their ass. He's mine again. If they test it, they're gonna learn.

Harper draws in a long-suffering breath. "We were instructed to come make nice with you. So you'll grace us with your presence this evening at the clubhouse."

I wait. That's it. She doesn't have anything to add.

"Non-apology not accepted."

Fay-Lee holds up a palm. I give her the high five. Shirlene snorts.

"Listen. We're all adults here. Except you, Daddy's Little Girl." Harper flashes Fay-Lee her freakishly white teeth. "We don't have to like each other. But we do have to get along."

"I see no reason. I can happily continue existing without you in my life."

"As could I, I assure you. But for the greater good, we are asked to come to some sort of truce."

"No one asked me."

"That's because no one expects *you* to do what's best for the club."

Shame burns a path through my chest, and for a second, I feel sorry. Screw that. When I needed them, did the club do what's best for me? Nope. They cut me loose.

"Then you're wasting your time, aren't you? You can leave now. You're blocking my sun." I sip my tea for effect.

"You really are a self-centered little bitch, aren't you?" Annie Holt spits. Forty's shoulders stiffen. He's about to lose it.

I have my mouth open when Shirlene snaps, "Oh, hell no!"

She sticks out her hand. Forty helps her up, and she stalks over, gets right up in Annie Holt's face. Annie doesn't know what to do. Shirlene's nothing but tanned, wrinkly skin and bones, but she's scary as shit when she's mad. Shirlene's got her finger up, and she's poking it in Annie's chest.

"Don't you dare open your mouth and call anyone else spoiled. Where are your kids right now, Annie Holt? They sure aren't with their father. He's down the OTB. Which was where he was when the first was born. And the second. And the third, as I recall. I will bet you a hundred dollars those kids are with Crista or Deb. Again. And don't you think it's self-centered to keep having kids you and their father have no intention of raising?"

Shirlene pauses to take a breath. Annie's face is almost purple.

"I'll tell you what, Annie. Bullet would take that bet."

Fay-Lee whispers, "Oooooo."

"Cheyenne and Danielle. I don't even know what you're doin' here, but I will get to you in a moment." They both kind of shuffle backwards. They want no piece of Shirlene Robard.

"Shirl—" Harper starts, and that's where she does wrong.

Shirlene's eyes flash. "Not a word from you. Not a word." Shirlene holds up a finger, and she turns back to Cheyenne and Danielle.

"I know what I want to say." She points at me. Her thin arm's shaking. "You all think you're tough? You pull some hair when you're drunk, you think you're bad? This girl—" She chokes up. "This girl is *tough*. You don't need to know what she's been through. It's not your business. But this girl has picked herself up and dusted herself off more times than I can count."

My eyes burn. I grit my teeth so my chin won't wobble.

"This girl rescued herself when all of you turned your backs on her. This girl gets knocked down, and she comes back, fighting for what she wants. For better. She's got *heart*."

Shirlene turns her gaze to Harper, her mouth screwed up in disgust. "What are you fighting for, Harper? You fucked around on Charge, traded up to Des Wade, but that's fine, that's forgivable, 'cause it's *you*, right? You walk around that clubhouse like you own it, terrorize these girls, talk like you do it all for the club, but what are you fighting for, Harper? You're drowning in a bottle, and you seem to think if you throw up enough drama, we won't notice. Friend, *everyone* notices. What are you fighting for, Harper? What's all the manipulation and plotting for? 'Cause you ain't fighting for yourself."

Harper is a statue. Her cold, gray eyes are locked on Shirlene's.

"You've got no heart, Harper. When you get knocked down, you're not gonna be able to get back up again."

In the ensuing silence everyone can hear my straw when I run out of my drink.

"I need more tea," I mumble.

"Ask Shirlene," Fay-Lee murmurs back. "Look like she's got it *all*."

There's an odd moment when Shirlene and Harper seem to take each other's measure and come to some unspoken accord.

Shirlene sniffs and says, "I'm gonna go get some suntan lotion." And she shuffles off into the house.

"Harper? Annie? You need anything for those burns?" Fay-Lee snickers.

Now that the tension's broken, Danielle opens her mouth like she's gonna spout off, but Harper raises a hand. I wouldn't say she looks chastened, but there's a thoughtfulness to her plastic face.

"The old bitch has a point."

We all wait.

Forty steps closer to me, casts me a worried look. I give him a small smile. I'm okay.

Finally, Harper sighs, having figured out something in that spider-webbed dark pit of a brain.

"Come to the clubhouse, Nevaeh. The past is the past. You're family now."

And she turns on a red sole and stalks back the way she came, taking her posse with her.

~

"You okay, baby?" Forty eyes me uneasily.

"Yup." I flash him a big ol' fake smile as I tug down my tank top. It's black with an elaborate sequin skull across the tits. I paired it with a pair of black leggings 'cause denim irritates my wound, and I finished off the ensemble with thick-soled shitkickers. In case I need to kick some shit.

Gnarly butterflies are careening around my belly. I'm nervous, and that's pissing me off. I don't need these people to like me.

After Harper's visit, I said I'd come. Just because she and I are cool doesn't mean the brothers have changed their minds. The President still hates my guts. It's not exactly a welcoming feeling.

"Let's head on in." The clubhouse doors are slid wide, air conditioning spilling out into the hot-as-hell late summer evening.

A wall of music, voices, and smoke rolls toward us. We head in and bodies part. The place is packed. There are a lot of SBMC cuts and familiar faces, but they're outnumbered by other folks. I see some Smoke and Steel cuts from the support club based in Shady Gap. Creech's crew is here in all their sideshow glory. My eyes are dragged from a fully tattooed head to a girl with dermal piercings down the back of her neck.

I catch sight of Lou by the pool tables. He's only got eyes for Bucky. They're playing each other, and it looks like it's down to the eight ball. Bucky's showing Lou how to line up a shot. Well, that's interesting.

Forty's ushering me through the crowd, hand firm on my lower back, and my nerves ease a bit. There are so many people here, I might go the whole evening without running into an unfriendly face.

And then I realize where Forty's steering me. There's a table by the bar. Unlike every other inch in this place, there are no bodies smashed together within several feet. Like there's an invisible rope. Heavy's sitting at the head.

Nickel's to his left, Story on his lap. Charge is there, but his old lady Kayla's nowhere to be seen. She has a young kid. She's probably home. Harper's across from Charge. She greets me with a subtle chin lift.

Scrap is the only one not staring at me. His eyes are glued on Crista, working the bar. Annie Holt's perched on a stool, Bullet Nowicki's hand on her ass.

There's an empty chair at Heavy's right hand. Right between Heavy and Harper.

Oh, hell no.

I stop in my tracks, and Forty's hand on my back kind of propels me forward. I trip. He grabs my elbow, steadying me.

Great. Very smooth. My face burns.

I shake my elbow free.

Pretty much everyone is staring at me now. Heavy lounges back in his chair, a head taller than everyone else at the table, black hair wilder than mine. I feel like a peasant come to beg at the foot of the king.

Let me back in.

Like me.

Decide I'm worth something.

Fuck that.

I'm the hero of this story. Not the victim. Not the villain.

How do I get one of these assholes to fight me? I took a bullet. I'm invincible.

I ball my fists as I look for a drink to throw. And then Harper pushes up from the table.

She's always dressed to the nines and perfectly made up, but she's dialed it up to a hundred tonight. Her smoky eye makes her gray eyes look like mirrors, and pearl combs hold her hair back.

"Well, folks. This reconciliation promises to be emotional and all, but I've got a date with destiny." She tugs up her black bandeau top. It's made to look like a bow. I'm one hundred percent into Forty, and I hate her, but I'd untie her given half a chance.

Heavy's chair screeches, and a hush falls. He is truly a freakishly-sized individual. I don't know what the exact qualifications are for a giant, but he's got to be close.

"You don't have to be the one who goes."

Harper glances around at all us listening and raises her eyebrows. There's a definite sense that these two are speaking out of school. "We decided."

"Are you packing?"

"Where would I fit a gun in this outfit?" She smooths her

hands over her round hips. She's wearing her trademark palazzo pants. You could totally fit an ankle holster under them.

"Harper." It's one word, and it's the most vulnerable I've ever heard Heavy Ruth sound. "I'll go."

"You don't send a man to do a woman's work." Harper pops her bright red lips. "And this is woman's work."

"If you don't call in twenty-four hours, we move in."

"If I don't call in twenty-four hours, tell Hobs I love him. And burn everything in my beside table drawer before anyone gets a look at what's in there." She winks, turns, and sashays away.

Heavy balls his fists.

"Where's she going?" I whisper to Forty.

"She's going to have a conversation with Knocker Johnson."

I blink. I'm not sure what surprises me more—Harper has apparently volunteered for a suicide mission or Forty told me club business like it was nothing.

"She's our Mata Hari," he adds.

We watch Harper disappear into the crowd.

"You know they shot Mata Hari, right?" I whisper under my breath.

"You. Nevaeh," Heavy barks. I startle. I was wondering what Harper Ruth keeps in her bedside table. "Come on. I got to show you something."

He's beckons me to follow him and ambles off toward a back room, the one where they hold church. I've never been in there. Back in the day, I never would have dared. That's where Slip and his officers did club business. They were terrifying guys, very old school. Except for Boots, I don't think one of them knew my name. And I'm not sure about Boots.

Forty follows me. The room is dominated by a granite or marble conference table and fancy leather office chairs. The furniture makes the room look like a high-class law office on TV, but the walls totally ruin the effect.

It's so much; I can't take it all in. There are flags. American, POW-MIA, Army, Marine Corp. There are dozens of framed pictures. None of the frames match. Police blotter clippings and mug shots. There's Cue, the flash reflecting off his bald head. There's a whole row of Charge. His beard and hair get longer and shorter and longer again, but his ridiculously gorgeous smile remains the same.

Then there's the pictures of bikes. And naked women on bikes. Is that Shirlene? That's Shirlene. Whoa, she had perky tits.

There are engine parts mounted like in a faux-country restaurant, vintage motorcycle license plates, a display with old striped medals and patches. Maybe war medals from Vietnam and Korea? A lot of brothers have served.

I'm getting a high from these walls. I'm already touching, running my fingers along the smooth edge of frames. My eyes skate to Forty every so often. Does he see what I'm seeing? His lips curve. His body's tense; it always is when we leave home, but even so, it's clear he's proud of this place. That it's home to him.

My heart plinks. I don't want Forty to be torn between this home and ours.

Oh, wow. There's a funeral card next to a blurry photo of a shaggy haired man on a bike, arms high on his ape hangers. It's Twitch. He's my age in the picture and handsome as hell. The arms wrapped around him must be Shirlene's.

This is amazing. I almost forget Heavy's looming in the doorway. I startle when he speaks.

"Look over the head of the table. On the far wall."

Holy crap. There's a human bone hanging there. Whoa. That's a whole leg from the knee down. Tibia. Fibula. Toe bones.

"Is that Boots' amputated leg?"

"Yup," Forty answers. He's come up behind me. He gently tilts my chin down a hair. "Look right underneath."

There is a bullet mounted on a shiny wooden plaque.

"Is that my bullet?" I kept thinking I should ask Larry where it went, but then I'd forget.

"Yeah." Heavy stomps over until he's standing beside us. Forty winds his arms tight around my middle.

Whoever made the plaque carved pretty vines and flowers around the edges. It's sweet. And creepy.

"Who made the plaque?"

"I did." My gaze flies up to Heavy. He raises his bushy, black eyebrows.

"You do woodworking, too?"

"I do whatever needs to be done for this family. Go look at it closer. Get up on a chair."

Okay. I roll one over and climb on up. It's not until I'm inches away that I see it. My name—Nevaeh—written out in curling vines.

I trace it with the tip of my index finger.

"If it's up there, it don't come down." Heavy sniffs. "You're in, Heaven Backwards. If you'll have us. Anyone gives you any shit, punch 'em in the face."

"That was my plan."

Heavy chuckles, deep and rumbly.

"Hey, Heavy?" I can't tear my eyes away from the plaque.

"Yeah."

"I'm sorry I tempted you with my hot body when we were kids. I was trying to make Forty jealous."

Heavy stiffens. I swear, the temperature in the room

drops. Maybe I wasn't supposed to have noticed how long it took him to ask me to cover up when I flashed him back in the day.

Maybe in Heavy's mind, he wasn't supposed to be the kind of guy who struggled for a minute to do the right thing.

"I'm sorry I came between you and your brother," I say, quiet. "I won't do it again."

Heavy dips his chin in acknowledgement, and then his eyes start twinkling. "I wouldn't rule out anything yet. Shit do get weird around here late on a Saturday night."

Forty growls, and Heavy laughs.

"I'll be in the commons." Heavy slaps Forty's back and heads out.

Forty has eyes only for me.

"You're gonna fall off that chair, aren't you?"

"It's really unsteady." I rock my hips, get it to roll back and forth, squatting like I'm on a surf board. "Would you catch me?"

"Yes." His brown eyes sparkle, following me as I sway, entranced. A smile plays on his lips. "Would you fall on purpose?"

"You're onto me." I wind my arms around his neck and wrap my legs around his waist, hooking them at the ankles. He carries me the few steps to the conference table.

He lays me down gently, ass at the edge, and pulls down my leggings, somehow working them over my boots. Then he draws up my knees. "Does that hurt?"

"Nope. The stretch feels good."

He unbuckles his belt. "Do you like your bullet?"

"Yeah. Was it your idea?"

"Nope."

Forty unzips his jeans and shoves them down. His thick,

red cock springs free. My pussy gushes hot while the marble table freezes my bare ass. Ah, sensation.

"It was Boots' idea. They were trying to figure out how to get you to come around. Boots figured no woman can resist —" He gestures to the bullet on the wall.

"That man understands women."

"Only one of us who does." Forty smiles, intertwining his fingers with mine, and slides home, filling me up, stoking a fire that smolders in me every waking hour.

He lightly touches his nose to mine.

"Bet I can make you cum in twenty strokes."

"I'll take that action."

We get distracted, though. In the end, I don't know how long we're there, exploring each other, the most familiar strangers, newly in love for the second time, the world and everything else ahead of us.

THE STEEL BONES MC series continues in Heavy.

A NOTE FROM THE AUTHOR

Will Ernestine ever take Grinder back?
Will Creech ever find someone who can love him?
Who was Boots' "California Girl' and why did she leave?

I have no idea! But you will be the first to know if you sign
up for my newsletter at www.catecwells.com.

You'll get a FREE novella, too!

ABOUT THE AUTHOR

Cate C. Wells indulges herself in everything from motorcycle club to small town to mafia to paranormal romance. Whatever the subgenera, readers can expect character-driven stories that are raw, real, and emotionally satisfying. She's into messy love, flaws, long roads to redemption, grace, and happily ever after, in books and in life.

Along with stories, she's collected a husband and three children along the way. She lives in Baltimore when she's not exploring the world with the family.

I love to connect with readers! Meet me in The Cate C. Wells Reader Group on Facebook.

Facebook: @catecwells
Twitter: @CateCWells1
Bookbub: @catecwells

Printed in Great Britain
by Amazon

21532405R10142